The Pussy Trap

A Novel By
NE NE CAPRI

Wahida Clark Presents Publishing, LLC
60 Evergreen Place
Suite 904
East Orange, New Jersey 07018
973-678-9982
www.wclarkpublishing.com

ISBN 13-digit 978-0-982841488
ISBN 10-digit 0-9828414-8-5

Library of Congress Catalog Number 2011917469
1. Urban, New Jersey, New York, Bronx, Brooklyn, Orange, NJ, African-American, Street Lit – Fiction

Cover design and layout by Oddball Design
Book interior design by Nuance Art
nuanceart@wclarkpublishing.com
Contributing Editors: VIP Editing and Rosalind Hamilton

Printed in United States
Green & Company Printing, LLC
www.greenandcompany.biz

Dedication

This project is dedicated to My Princess Khairah. Everything I do is for you. Mommy loves you.

Acknowledgements

All the thanks must first go to the Most High that gives me the strength to do all things. I cannot go forward without thanking My Beloved, you made me a woman, thank you.

To my grandmother Sarah, you gave me unconditional, selfless love without judgment I miss you, R.I.P Nana. To my Uncle Nigee you are more like a dad then an uncle thanks for being there. To My dad Hasan, you are one of the strongest men I know; you taught me what a man is thank you for all your sacrifices. Mommy, your daughter is about to be a Lawyer, I could not have done it without you. To my little brother Ralphie "IRoka" you my baby I love you we will always have the wooden wall.

To Mrs. Wahida Clark, you are a strong, dedicated woman whose word is strong as oak you do what you say, thanks for being the woman you are. Nobel you have got me through so much I am blessed you are in my life. Wahida aka "Nuance" your brilliant. Hasana I admire you. To My best friend's Tiko and Tiombe we have been through the fire, thank you for all the memories and the bond that can never be broken AT&T forever. Chucky you know you my big brother. Princess you are the sister I never had love you, these chicks better be glad you hung up your gloves. Mooka can't wait for my baby Kiss the Smiling One (Boobie), Khair my son, Nagee Capricorn, Shawn, Sabrina, Qadir and Jawhar, Bruce, Kim Rashad love you. Aunt Jackie My Queen you keep us together. Love you Uncle Neval.

To the Rest of my family: Keisha Steel "my sister" you a genius girl. My little sister Angel "Cherry" my baby girl you are my motivation I pray you become the beautiful woman you are destined to be. My cousins, Nikki and Moreen love you. My big Brother Malik "Whip Wop" Williams I miss you boy. Mrs.

Wright I will never forget all that you have done for me love you R.I.P. My girls Shamell, Trice, Tanisha, Lynn, Tracey, Candy. R.I.P Bizzy, Mugsy, Tez, Red, Darell, Derik, Velour, ReRe, Anthony (lil' cousin), "Antlive", and all fallen Soldier's of 107 Wilson Pl., 108 Parrow St. and 339 Mechanic St. If I missed you charge it to the head and not the heart.

To my spiritual family: it is our trials that has made us who we are, we must be grateful for each one; the blessing we are promised are going to be so plentiful we will not be able to receive them. Street Team: Omar, Jabar, Razzaq, Shahid, and Hadiyah. WCP Authors: Ca$h, Mike Sanders, Intelligent Allah, Anthony Fields, Tash Hawthorn, Missy Jackson, Serenity Hall, Victor L. Martin, Rashawn Hughs, Mike Jerfferies. WCP "Divas" you hold us down. Davida you did your thing with this cover.

Shout out to DC Book Diva, Laquita of The Literary Joint, Horizon Books, Black and Nobel Books, T. Styles and the Cartel and all the authors, graphic artist and supports of the written word we salute you. All the authors who love this craft and make a difference "The pen is the limit."

The Beginning

Chapter 1
Greed is a Bitch

Sadeek crept in the house at 4 a.m. trying not to wake Keisha. He lay on the couch and put one of his legs on the arm rest. He had just begun to doze off when he was awakened by an ice cold shower.

"What the fuck?" Sadeek jumped up and tried to adjust his sight as water and ice cubes fell to the floor.

"Yeah, muthafucka. You think you can just walk in my fucking house at four o'clock in the gotdamn morning and just lay your head down and go to sleep?" Keisha was pissed off. She was starting to hate even the thought of Sadeek.

"I was taking care of some shit. You lucky I ain't jump up and slap the shit out of you!" he yelled, walking to the kitchen and grabbing a few paper towels. Keisha was right on his heels, her black silk nighty and robe flying in the breeze.

"Yeah right, muthafucka! You ain't that crazy. But, you got to go," she yelled, slamming the empty cup on the counter.

"Go where? Why the fuck is you trippin' at four o'clock in the fucking mornin'?" He brushed past Keisha almost knocking her into the stove. She quickly caught her balance and followed him back into the living room.

"I don't give a fuck what time it is or where you go. I can make a suggestion though. Start with the bitch whose pussy you just climbed out of. Go back and knock on her fucking door!" Kiesha stood in the middle of the room with hands on her hips. Lips twisted, eyes squinted, and breathing heavy.

2

"I wasn't with no bitch. I was taking care of business." Sadeek's voice got louder. He fidgeted with his ring, avoiding eye contact as was his habit when he was lying his ass off.

"Look, I can't take this shit no more. You got to get the fuck out. You can leave by will or by force; you draw it up," Keisha persisted.

Sadeek glanced at Keisha and bit his bottom lip while rubbing his hands together as he tried to calm down. He wanted to knock the shit out of her. His fists were balled up, but he wasn't crazy. He knew Malik would take his fucking head. More reason for him to hurry up and get rid of this nigga.

"Step lively, muthafucka. And give me my keys." Keisha held her hand out with major attitude.

Sadeek reluctantly handed her the keys and headed to the door. "I guess you can go back to playing house with Malik."

"Don't worry about what the fuck I do with Malik. You just worry about those dirty bitches you stick your dick in."

Sadeek paused then responded, "If you weren't so busy giving my pussy to the next nigga, I wouldn't be fucking other bitches." He gave Keisha a dirty look and headed out the door, he figured he'd hit his boy Tone's house.

Keisha shut the door behind him. *Sheeit . . . you damn right I'm fucking Malik and his dick is good as hell. He was all up in it the other day.* She wiped up the remaining water off the floor. Headed to her bedroom, and hopped in bed. As she drifted off, she mumbled, "Fuck that nigga!"

Later that day . . .
Sadeek walked in the Peppermint Lounge razor sharp, sporting a pair of crisp dark colored jeans laying on top of his grey Timberland boots, a charcoal grey sweater and a light weight dark blue three quarter leather jacket. His short fade and freshly shaped mustache and goatee enhanced his

smooth brown caramel skin. In Sadeek's world, nobody could tell him shit. As he made his way to the back where Raheem was sitting, niggas were shouting him out while bitches were checking him out. He nodded, shook a few hands, and grabbed a shot of Grey Goose while passing the bar and kept on moving. When he reached Raheem's table, he could see him dismissing this fine, brown-skinned honey. She saw Sadeek coming and rolled her eyes as she slid out the booth.

"Don't be salty, shorty," Sadeek said with a smile. The young woman just kept on going.

"What's up superstar nigga?" Raheem said as he extended his hand to Sadeek.

"Sheeit. I can't call it. It's your world squirrel; I'm just trying to bust a nut," he said, slapping hands with Raheem. They both busted out laughing as Sadeek slid into the booth. Raheem flagged down the waitress and ordered them some drinks.

Sadeek and Raheem downed their drinks and laughed about Keisha throwing ice-cold water on him in the middle of the night. Retelling the story caused Sadeek's whole mood to change.

"I hate that bitch sometimes," he spat as he guzzled down his shot of Hennessy then chased it down with a double deuce Heineken.

"What the fuck are you talking about 'Deek?" Raheem said in a drunken slur.

"Fuckin Keisha!" Sadeek said with a hateful tone.

"Man, get the fuck outta here. You know good and well you love that girl. That's why your ass sitting up here pouting like a fuckin' bitch."

"Fuck you, Rah. She done put me out for the last fucking time."

"That's what you said last time. This ain't the fucking Oprah sofa, nigga. You betta handle that shit," Raheem said

4

then started laughing.

"On the real, Rah, I think it's time to make that move."

"What you talking about?" Raheem asked.

"The way I see it, we been working for that nigga for over ten years and we still make just as much as the new jacks. He charges us like he don't know us. Shit, the way I figure, we cut out the middleman and we could be making all the money. Just take over this whole fucking city."

"Nigga, you trippin'."

"Shit, I ain't trippin'. What? You scared mu'fucka?"

"Scared? Hell no, I ain't scared of nothing or no one." Raheem said giving Sadeek a look that said *don't you ever question my manhood.*

"A'ight then. You ready for a fucking war?"

"Hell yeah. At any moment, but for something worth warring over. In that case, I ain't got no problem with war. I just ain't trying to go to war over no gotdamn pussy. Especially, if it ain't pussy that belongs to me."

"This shit is way past pussy. It's about principle. That nigga know he fucking owe us. And we ain't sitting on the side waiting no fucking more. We getting ready to take it. You down or what?"

The next thing that comes out his mouth better be right or he's going on the list with Malik. Sadeek thought as he stared at Raheem.

Raheem stared in space for a minute then took a pull on his blunt.

"Yeah, I'm down. But make sure it's for principle and not for greed. Because greed is a bitch," he said.

Raheem thought he and Sadeek had done some cruddy shit, but was he ready to help him take Malik out? Shit, for the last couple of weeks he was trying to come up with a plan to get the fuck out. Now this nigga was talking about going to war and taking over. This was some shit he would have to talk over with his main man, Nine.

After his talk with Raheem, Sadeek put his plan in motion, which would call for a trip to Detroit. That was how he was going to get his come up and his revenge.

***

Keisha was walking through Short Hills Mall with her aunt Pat bringing her up to speed on the other night when she had to check Sadeek's ass. Pat was only ten years older than her and had raised her due to her mom dealing with an addiction.

"Hell yeah I threw that shit on that nigga and told him to get the fuck out," Keisha bragged.

"Bitch, you lucky he ain't slap your ass down," Pat joked.

"I'll tell you like I told him, he ain't that crazy," Keisha said as they dipped into Saks Fifth Avenue and headed right for the makeup counter.

"So how many days are you going to let pass before you let him back this time?" Aunt Pat asked. She leaned in to the mirror trying on some mascara.

"Fuck him. I'm done. I hate to see that nigga coming; his very touch makes my fucking skin crawl," Keisha said with apparent anger in her voice.

"Yeah right, bitch. You say that shit all the time then that nigga be right back in there." Pat took the time to point out.

"Don't judge me. I got to do what I got to do. The only reason I still fuck's with that nigga Sadeek is because it's good for business." Keisha applied blush to her cheeks.

"How is fucking Sadeek's boss good for business? That shit is dangerous."

Keisha stopped dead in her tracks and looked at her aunt. "Look, I don't get in your business, so do both of us a favor and don't get in mine." Keisha started to walk away, but Pat

grabbed her by the arm.

"Hold up, Key. Look, I love you. That's the only reason why I'm saying something."

Keisha stopped but didn't turn around. She took a deep breath and thought about her aunt's words. "I know. I'm caught up, Auntie." She paused. "I'm in love with a man I can't have. And I hate the one that I'm with." A tear ran down her face. She turned and grabbed a tissue from the counter and patted her cheek.

"Regardless of what I say, I know that Malik loves you and he got your back. Just be careful, Key. Sadeek ain't stupid . . . and he's crazy. That is a dangerous cocktail. I don't want anything to happen to you," Pat said as she hugged her niece.

"Thanks Auntie. I'm working on it." She hugged her back.

"A'ight bitch, let's go 'cause I got to put a dent in this nigga's bank roll. Fuck what you heard, this is going to be the most expensive piece of pussy that nigga ever had," Pat said, trying to lighten the mood as she let go of Keisha.

"You so crazy." Keisha laughed. As they headed to the designer purses, her Aunt Pat's words rang out in her head "be careful." Keisha had been feeling the danger of messing with both Sadeek and Malik for the past week and praying that all the shit she had been doing didn't blow up in her face.

Chapter 2
Making a Deal

Sadeek walked out the airport with his carry-on bag, looked around, jumped on a shuttle bus and headed to Enterprise. Within twenty minutes, he arrived at the Days Inn motel at the Metro airport in Detroit; he figured he could kill two birds with one stone by making this trip for both business and pleasure so he arranged to have Kim already there when he arrived. Kim, a bitch he'd met the last time he and Malik were there was already waiting for him in his room. Since his meeting was set for 8 P.M. with the headman, who was Malik's connect, Sadeek figured until then, he could get his dick sucked and lay in some warm pussy. A few minutes after he walked into his room, Kim was riding the hell out of him. Once he busted his first nut, he turned over onto his stomach and prepared to doze off. "In an hour, order something to eat and then wake me up," Sadeek told Kim.

"No problem. Shit, you hooked me up. I'll just return the favor." She smiled. Turning on the television, she flicked the channels until she found something to watch and eventually dozed off.

By seven P.M. Sadeek had eaten the Chinese food Kim had ordered and put on his clothes, boots, and jewels. He looked in the mirror and then walked over to Kim. "Are you going to be here when I get back?"

8

"Hell yeah. I need to get thanked for that meal." She flashed a pretty smile.

Kim was definitely a dime. At 5'6", 130 pounds, legs thick, and a shapely small waist accented with a flat toned stomach. Her 36C breasts looked ever so suckable. Her toned arms led to small manicured hands that just a few hours ago were wrapped nicely around Sadeek's dick. She wore her shoulder length hair in a bun with a Chinese bang, accenting her pretty pear diamond shaped eyes that seemed to glisten with every blink. And oh yes, that smile.

Sadeek smiled, grabbed her by the waist, and kissed her lips. He patted her on the butt. "I'll see you later," he said then headed out the door.

It was a forty-five minute drive to Dread's estate. When he got there he was greeted by Scarie, the go between guy. Scarie set up all the meetings with the connects and that included more than fifteen states and two overseas spots. Of course, he was running the weed distribution in Jamaica. Dread had shit on lock and with the help of Sadeek's greed; Scarie was getting ready to loosen some of Dread's grip. Sadeek had only met both of them in person one time, but had been gaining notice by Scarie because of his heart and fearlessness, along with the rumor of his dissatisfaction with Malik. It would be just what he needed to set a plan of his own in action.

Sadeek pulled up to the gate and he could not believe his eyes. The house looked like the fucking president lived there. Big willow trees and manicured lawns with ground keepers scurrying around to keep shit in order. The house had a modern castle look to it.

Scarie waved him through the gate then it slammed closed behind him. He followed him to the house then was appointed a parking spot. Sadeek parked, got out, and shook hands with his soon to be partner. They stood trying to have a conversation when three Cadillac golf carts drove toward them. One was driven by Dread, and the other two by his bodyguards carrying AK47s. Dread was an older Jamaican dude who grew up in London then settled in Toronto, Canada. Lots of those Jamaican cats would come and run shit in Detroit. Dread stepped out of the cart and looked Sadeek up and down like: What the fuck is he doing here? He walked right past him and his bodyguards followed suit.

Sadeek looked at Scarie then whispered, "What's up with that?"

"Don't worry, it's all good. Did you bring the money?" Scarie tried to comfort him.

"Yeah. It's all here," Sadeek said, still leery of the interaction he had just had with the top man.

"Come on," Scarie said, walking toward the steps. Sadeek reluctantly followed.

They entered the house and the shiny floors and huge statues of half and fully naked women amazed Sadeek. Exotic plants and paintings adorned the wall. They walked down a long hallway and entered an office on the first floor. Dread was seated comfortably behind his huge mahogany desk. He reached inside a small wooden box, took a fat spliff, and lit it up. Then he inhaled and blew a big cloud of smoke toward Sadeek. Scarie whispered in Dread's ear. Dread broke the silence with his thick Jamaican accent.

"What the fuck you come by me, pussy boi. Me nah know you?" The statement threw Sadeek totally off.

Sadeek squinted, and his eyebrows wrinkled. "I met you one time. I came to Detroit with Malik before," Sadeek managed to get out in a low voice.

"What's dat you carry der, boi?"

"It's the money I am offering you to start our new business venture." Small beads of sweat formed on Sadeek's brow. Dread looked as if his next move was going to be giving the order to rob and kill this nigga. One eyebrow was raised and the other rested over a squinted eye.

"You got balls bona coming wit' dis amount of money. You trying to bring trouble 'pon me?"

"Nah. I'm just ready to come up. I figure I can help you and you can help me," Sadeek said, obviously getting upset at how the whole thing was going down. He bit his bottom lip and tapped the side of his leg.

"You have no seniority to come here. Take this bumbaras from fronta me!" Dread slammed his hand on the desk, staring Sadeek dead in his eyes.

"Look Dread, I'm hungry. I'm ready to take this shit to the next level!" Sadeek made one last plea.

"How you gon' come to me house speakin' all freestyle? Me nah know you, pussy clot. Get the fuck outta here for me dead you!" With that statement, Dread's bodyguards moved toward him.

Sadeek backed up. Scarie quickly grabbed Sadeek by the arm. "I'll see him out."

When they got to the car, he said to Sadeek, "Look, go to the hotel. I will be there in about an hour."

"What the fuck is going on? I thought you said he would be ready to do business?" Sadeek asked.

"Look, go to the room. It's a change of plans. I'll talk to you when I get there," Scarie reassured him.

Sadeek turned his head, looking down and rubbing his hands together. He looked up at Scarie as his nostrils flared. *No the fuck you didn't get me all the way out here for this shit.*

Scarie picked right up on the thought and said, "Trust me. Let me defuse this shit and I'll meet you in an hour."

Sadeek jumped in his ride and headed back to the hotel. *Who the fuck do that Dread nigga think he fucking with? Yeah, I got his pussy clot all right.*

When Scarie returned to Dread's office, all he got was dirty looks. "What the *fuck*, boi? You getting weak? Must be all that coke you put up your nose," Dread growled.

With hatred in his eyes, Scarie glared at him. "He is Malik's boi. He is just trying to do a little something on the side so I thought . . ."

Dread cut him off. "You thought. You thought what? That I would want a stranger standing in mi fuckin' house. Oh, then you thought that I would do business with a nigga mi don't know? The main ting I have always taught you, boi, is loyalty. Mi about loyalty. Mi a deal with Malik. Mi don't know that other muthafucka. Don't bring him near me again. Him have a look of a vampire, and him won't quench his thirst here."

Dread sucked his teeth. "You're dismissed."

Scarie left the office feeling like a five-year-old. But he would be feeling like a grown ass man by the end of the night.

Back at the hotel...

Sadeek pulled into the hotel parking lot still mad as hell. He had a taste for blood and didn't give a fuck whose blood it was. When he got to the room, he was greeted by the lovely he had left there, butt-naked and horny. As soon as he closed the door, she went to her knees, pulled out his dick and looked at him with a sneaky grin.

"I was waiting for him." She said referring to his dick.

"Damn shorty, you going to make me take you home with me," he said, rubbing the top of her head. Stopping to get a handful of hair to hold his balance.

"Don't talk, just listen," she said, taking him into her mouth. Kim began licking and sucking all over the head and then forced him to the back of her throat. Slurping and slobbing all over his dick. Sadeek's knees buckled.

"Oh shit . . . hold up, baby . . ."

"Mmmmm . . ." She continued to bring on his intense orgasm.

After ten more minutes, all she heard was "Aaaahhhh . . . Oh my god!" He pulled her hair tighter and released in her mouth. She sucked him until the last drop was gone. Easing him out her mouth, she ran her tongue down his shaft and sucked lightly on his balls. Electrical shocks shot up and down his spine.

"Shit . . . you trying to fuck with a nigga's emotions."

As she rose to her feet, she gave him a look that said it all. Walking over to the dresser, she took a shot of gin and lit a blunt. Sadeek fell back on the bed in an attempt to pull himself together, then took off his pants and boxers. Turning around to see he was still at attention excited her. She walked over to the bed while taking long drags on the blunt.

"He needs you to—"

"No problem." She climbed on top of him and eased down slowly on his dick, giving him the ride of a lifetime. Forty-five minutes later, he was laid the fuck out.

His cell rang and Sadeek answered, "Hello."

"I'll be there in about fifteen minutes," Scarie said, his strong accent came blaring through the phone.

"A'ight," he said then disconnected the call.

Sadeek headed to the shower. "I got somebody coming by here in about fifteen minutes. Can you straighten up for me?" he asked.

"I got you, baby," Kim replied.

When he came out, Kim had straightened up and dipped off so he called her phone. "What's up? Why you dip?"

"I'll be back in an hour. I need to get some clothes."

"Okay, I'll see you later."

Just then, he heard a knock at the door and went to open it. "What's up, my dude?" Sadeek said, shaking Scarie's hand. Scarie came in and sat at the table.

"Can I light up one of these blunts?" Scarie needed to get his head tight for what he was getting ready to say. Once he lit up, he took a deep breath and began his proposition.

"You kill my boss. I'll kill yours."

Sadeek seized the blunt from Scarie, took a big hit, and immediately began to cough. Sixty seconds passed as he sat there staring at him processing the information. "Let's do it," Sadeek finally said.

Scarie began rubbing his hands together. "Dread has one love—the strip club. He goes every Thursday night, which is a day away so we have to move on this shit." Scarie was running the plan as if he had had it down for months. Sadeek just sat there taking it all in and nodding his head.

"Dread always gets a private lap dance, some head, and maybe even some pussy depending on the mood. I'm planning to put him in the room with the hidden door, that way you can slip in and out undetected. The bodyguards will be posted outside the door unaware of the execution-taking place on the other side. Club 4 Play has some of the baddest bitches in attendance so a distraction is not impossible but, be quick and have as less a struggle as possible." When Scarie finished laying the framework for his plan, he shook hands with Sadeek and headed to the door. He turned and said, "Meet me at the downtown spot at nine o'clock p.m. Don't be late." Then he was gone just as quick as he came.

After Scarie left, Sadeek drank half a bottle of gin trying to wrap his head around the fact that he had come out here to make a deal with the headman and ended up in cahoots with the man's very partner. What the fuck had the universe just put in his lap? Just when he got ready to second-guess the situation, he heard a knock at the door. He checked the peephole before opening it. Kim stood there in a Versace black strapless body dress and a pair of stilettos.

"Hey, Mr. Sexy. Did you miss me?" she asked once he let her inside.

"Hell yeah, but I think he missed you more." He grabbed his dick and began stroking it. She smiled, already well aware of what he was capable of doing with it. For the rest of the night, they sucked and fucked each other into a stupor. Sadeek forgot all about what lay ahead; he was in heaven and didn't want to leave.

****

Thursday night came and everything went just as planned. Scarie put a girl on Dread that he knew he could not resist, and as usual, he went in the room all alone. She danced sensually, grinding on him as Sadeek waited in the cut. As soon as the woman pulled Dread's dick out and started to suck, he lay back on the large couch and closed his eyes. While Sadeek was squatting down waiting for his attack, sweat was running down his back and face as he tried to control his breathing. He began to slide along the wall getting closer to the trap door. He reached out, cracked it, and saw Dreads contorted face as the woman worked his steel. Sadeek took a deep breath, jumped out from the side of him, and cut Dread's throat from ear to ear. The woman fell back with fear in her eyes as blood ran from Sadeek's blade. Dread struggled for a few seconds then lumped over to the side. Sadeek grabbed the woman by the arm and forced her into the small opening, then he climbed in right behind her. Just like that, he and the woman smoothed out the secret door without a trace.

When they got to the alley, Sadeek's adrenalin was working over time. He ran one way and the girl ran the other.

He looked back and saw her being snatched into a black van. Sadeek turned and kept running until he neared the block where he was to be picked up. The headlights of a vehicle flashed twice and he sprinted to the vehicle. The door popped open and he dove in. All he heard was the doors lock and tires screech. He lay on his back, head up against the door and breathing heavy. Once they arrived a few blocks from the motel, he jumped out, pulled his hat down, and then shoved his hands in his hoodie pocket. Looking in all directions, Sadeek began double-timing his pace.

Back at the motel room, Sadeek was all charged up, looking at the blood staining his hands and shoes. He walked in the room.

"What the fuck happened to you?" Kim ran over to him.

"Nothing. Watch out." He pushed past her and went to the bathroom. Clearly, she was not trying to hear that.

"Are you okay? Let me help you." She knocked on the bathroom door.

The door flew open. Sadeek stormed out and pushed her back toward the wall.

"Didn't I fucking tell you to get the fuck back? Don't make me slap the shit out of you."

She looked at him like an arm was growing out of his head. Her eyes narrowed and her breathing increased. She balled up her fist tight. As he turned to walk away, Kim tapped him on the shoulder. He turned and she punched him dead in the nose. He fell back on the bed as she followed up with three more blows, cursing and yelling in now what sounded like a Jamaican accent.

"You don't know who you mess wit', boi."

Sadeek managed to get her off him and the tables had quickly turned; he was now choking the shit out of her. He blacked out for about forty seconds and when he came to he had choked the very life out of her.

"Oh shit . . . what the fuck?" he said, jumping up and walking around the room holding his hands up to his head. "What the fuck did I just do? Shit! I got to get the fuck out of here." Grabbing everything that could link him to the room, he wiped shit down as Kim's lifeless body lay on the edge of the bed. Picking her up, he placed her in the middle of the bed. *Her body is still so warm*, he thought as he looked her over. Her breasts sat up firm and perky. He slid his hand between her legs and felt her moistness. "Shit, I was planning on getting some more of this. Why didn't you just shut the fuck up like I told you?" With that thought, he put on a condom, got on top of her, and pumped until he came. Snatching off the condom, he put it in a napkin on the edge of the nightstand and then pulled up his pants. Careful to leave no evidence behind, he put the napkin in his pocket, grabbed his stuff and rolled out.

When he was good and on his way home, he called Scarie to let him know he was leaving town. He drove back to Jersey with haunting thoughts of killing Dread and the girl. Then came the demented thought of how good she felt even after she was dead.

Sadeek arrived in Newark the next afternoon and checked into the Robert Treat Hotel downtown. Then he placed a call to Raheem and asked him to meet him there.

When they met up, Sadeek revealed everything except that he'd killed a woman and then fucked her corpse. Sadeek then laid out the plan to kill Malik and informed him that it was already in progress.

Raheem was starting to feel uneasy. He walked over to the window and stared at the New York skyline, tossing the information around in his head for a few minutes. Walking over to the table he sat in silence, and for the first time, he had absolutely nothing to say. Raheem watched Sadeek stare off into space with coldness to his eyes. He could see that

Sadeek had gone to the extreme and there was no coming back. Raheem didn't have a problem with a come up, but to the demise of Malik, was it worth it? Even though Malik was charging them a grip, they were making a grip and he had never disrespected them. In fact, it was the total opposite. That nigga would give you the shirt off his back then ask you if you needed his pants. Raheem looked at Sadeek with a blank expression. It was like he didn't know him. The stench of greed and pride oozed from his pores; his very soul was on fire. And Raheem couldn't just see it; it was more like he smelled it and he knew the scent of death would follow. He decided to just go along for now until he could figure out the next move.

Chapter 3
The Twins

W hat's up, my nigga?" Sadeek said to Tah'leek letting himself into his apartment.

"Ain't nothing, nigga," Tah'leek said, leaning up from the couch to shake hands with his twin brother. Since birth the two were inseparable. Only a few could tell them apart only added to their closeness. However, lately Tah'leek was having a huge disconnect with his brother. Tah'leek was ready to leave the streets while his twin was diving head first into very deep and dangerous waters.

Sadeek sat on the love seat across from his brother and wasted no time giving him the update on their next move. "So everything is in motion. I went to Detroit and met with the headman. He will be here in about a week to meet with all of us. I want you to be my right hand."

Tah'leek processed the information.

"So what about Malik?"

"He's a dead man and don't even know it," Sadeek answered real smooth like it was nothing. Tah'leek sat up, grabbed the bottle of Jack and took it to the head. Sadeek watched his brother kill the liquor and not respond as if he wasn't down.

"So what the fuck? You ain't ready for this change of hands." Sadeek looked disappointed.

"This ain't no change of hands. Your ass went out there

19

and got in bed with some fucking strangers. How the fuck you know these muthafucka's are going to honor their word? You went out there, killed their boss, and then they gave you some see-thru ass promise. What guarantee do you have?"

"What the fuck are you talking about?" Sadeek rose from his seat "You act like you ain't trying to have my back."

Tah'leek stood. "Muthafucka, I have had your back from day one. Your greed got you making dumb ass moves."

"Man, fuck this. I'm giving you, my blood, an opportunity to be at the head of the table with me and you acting like I done signed our souls over to the devil," he yelled.

"That's what the fuck I'm talking about. It's all about you wanting something. Every time you want something my shit gets fucked up."

Sadeek stood eye to eye with his twin brother. It was like looking at his own face, but instead of seeing happiness, all he saw was disappointment. He stepped back nodding his head up and down.

"You know what? You right. It is about what I want. And I'm going to kill anybody that stands in the way of that."

"You threatening me, 'Deek?" Tah'leek asked with a bit of pain in his voice.

"Nah playboy. No threat necessary. The shit has been put on the table, you draw up." Sadeek, for the first time, turned his back on his brother. Headed to the door with hate in his heart and power on his mind, he didn't give a fuck who he would have to step on to get it.

Chapter 4
Keisha

"Oh my god . . . Mmmm. Malik."

"Does it feel good to you, baby?"

"Oooohhh . . . yeeeessss . . . I'm about to cum."

Malik had Keisha bent over the dresser long stroking her. She was on her fourth orgasm and loved every minute and every inch of Malik's sweet chocolate dick.

"Damn girl, you fucking me like you miss me."

"You know I always miss you, boy," she said in a seductive tone. Malik picked up the pace, bringing on her orgasm in magnetic wave after wave.

"Oh my god, Malik . . . aaaaahhhh . . ."

They were both sweating and breathing hard, and instead of holding back, he came with her. They fell forward onto the dresser. Once they caught their breath, Malik pulled out slow sending chills up and down Keisha's spine.

"Sssssss . . ." was all he heard from her. He pulled her up and turned her to face him.

"Thank you for being the woman that you are."

"You make it easy to love you, baby," Keisha said.

Malik hugged her tight, enjoying every curve of her body. They kissed and enjoyed the nut they both busted and then Malik headed for the shower.

Keisha was Malik's bottom bitch, down for whatever. No matter what he needed or when he needed it, she was always there. Keisha was the type of woman that every man needed

21

on his team. If you looked up 'ride or die chick' her face would be right next to the definition. Keisha had been attracted to Malik from the first day she saw him. Malik, a sexy ass chocolate brother stood only 5'7", 150-pounds, but what he missed in height he made up for in attitude. Cocky as hell. No matter where he went he was respected and not just because he was a killer, but inside that killer was a heart of gold. If he got it, you got it, but don't cross him because you will find yourself leaking. Even though Keisha was Malik's sidepiece, he never made her feel like she was second; in her world, she was number one.

Malik's wife, Sabrina is what you call a good girl. Educated with a Master's degree in finance and employed in a high-powered job in Corporate America. They shared a house in the Seven Oaks section of Orange, New Jersey. She was Malik's high school sweetheart and had loved Malik since she was fifteen-years-old. Instead of following Sabrina to college after high school, Malik took to the streets to get an education that you couldn't learn in a classroom. When he got on top of his paper, he ran into Keisha at Club Sensations in Newark, New Jersey. That night he was being introduced to this guy from the Colonnades to get introduced to a new coke connection. Keisha happened to be in the men's room copping some pills when she overheard the guy planning to rob Malik. She slipped out, made her way to where Malik was sitting, and gave him the low. Keisha had been hearing Malik's name ringing in her circle and wanted to get at him for a while, however the opportunity had not presented itself until now and she decided to take full advantage.

"Look, you don't know me but I know you, and I believe them niggas from Branch Brook are going to try some shit tonight. Watch your back," Keisha said in his ear, slipped her number in his hand and was gone. Malik was able to avoid a major fuck up. He hooked up with Keisha, hit her off with a few stacks for looking out, and shortly after that she became his street Intel. If Malik needed a bitch checked, Keisha would bite a bitch. If he needed a hide out or a mule, she was right there, and because of her loyalty Malik made sure she had whatever she needed.

Even though Keisha was firm in Malik's heart, he married Sabrina after she graduated from Rutgers, but that did not change anything between him and Keisha. Keisha always made sure she was respectful of his life outside of her and valued any time she got to spend with him. Keisha was the type of bitch that knew how to play her role and because of that, he always made sure to break her off proper.

Malik came out of the bathroom wrapped in a towel. Keisha stared at him like she could have gone for round five, but he knew he had to save some of that good dick to take care of home. He applied lotion to his body then got dressed. He heard his little princess cooing over the baby monitor. Keisha went to retrieve the baby. When she returned, all he could do was smile from ear-to-ear at the sight of the two beautiful ladies.

"Da . . . Da . . ." the baby said, reaching her arms out for Malik. He took her into his arms, hugged, and kissed her. Taking a seat on the bed, he stared at his little precious.

"It's not going to be like this forever," Malik said.

"What do you mean?" Keisha asked in a curious voice.

"I plan on telling her about the baby. I want them to have a relationship with each other regardless of what our status is."

"Malik, you know that I am not concerned with that. I love you. Our daughter was made in love and the only person I am concerned with loving and knowing her is you."

"I know that. And that's why I love you. Just hang in there. As soon as I finish this business, things are going to be different."

With that, Malik spent another half hour holding and kissing his little princess until she fell back to sleep. Keisha picked her up from his chest so he could leave. Malik hugged and kissed Keisha then planted one on the baby's head. Putting on his coat, he headed to the door. She was right on his heels as he stood in the doorway. Malik turned to look at her.

"What? What's the matter?" she asked.

"Nothing. You are so beautiful. Ride with me for a little longer and you will have everything."

"All I ever need is for you to love and respect me. I have all of that, everything else is a bonus." She smiled that pretty smile and he smiled back.

"Why you always make it hard for a brother to leave?"

She grabbed his dick and said, "I'll make it hard all right." Then kissed him one more time.

"See, there you go starting up. Go lay my little princess down before you get us in trouble." He patted her on the butt then walked outside. She closed the door, went to lay the baby down, patting her back, and stared at her for about ten minutes thinking how precious she was. Once she walked out the baby's room, she heard the bell ring. Keisha tightened up her robe.

"Oh Lord, he must have forgotten his keys." She looked in her bedroom on the nightstand before heading to the door but didn't see them. "You're always forgetting something," she said in a loud voice as she rushed to the door. She grabbed the door handle, unlocked the door, and cracked it to peek out.

BOOM!

The door flew open and busted Keisha in the head. She flew back on the floor. Dizzy and disoriented, all she could see was a man in a black mask. He leaned over her and whacked her in the head with the end of his gun. She passed completely out.

Reminiscing

Malik was almost home. He grabbed a blunt out of the ashtray and lit it up. Inhaling deeply, he reminisced about Keisha. He had always admired her loyalty to him and the organization they built, but she had gained all his respect that night they were heading back from a mission with cocaine and a gun in the car. They were pulled over. She turned to Malik and said, "Baby, I got this." She took all the weight, went to trial, and got fifteen years. Because of Malik's connections on the inside, her sentence was reduced to eighteen months. Keisha served every day without regret. The part that tugged most at his heartstring was her serving her sentence while being pregnant with his daughter.

When Keisha stepped out of Clinton, Malik had a condo, bank account, a car, and some good dick set up for her whenever she wanted it. She never complained and came out with a stronger attitude than she went in with.

The only problem they ever had was that nigga, Sadeek. He was Keisha's boyfriend and one of Malik's workers. Being as though Malik had his main girl, he gave the okay for Keisha to be with Sadeek but as time went on, it became harder for him to see her with Sadeek and Sadeek could tell that it was more than business between Malik and Keisha, which always created tension between them. After a while, both of their hearts were filled with hatred for each other. Sadeek would send hate mail to her in jail and threaten to take the baby and leave. Sadeek was under the impression that the baby was his, and Malik and Keisha let him think that for the betterment of business. This nigga could cause a hell of a war if he wanted to. So they kept it a secret, but Malik was getting tired of enduring Sadeek's mistreatment of Keisha. He was getting ready to put an end to it all.

****

Malik pulled into the driveway and pressed the automatic garage opener. Once parked, he got out and walked through the door that led to the kitchen. He opened the door and he saw his reason for living. Sabrina turned her beautiful face around and smiled those thirty-twos at him.

"Hey, baby."

Malik grabbed her around the waist and planted a big kiss on her cheek.

"I missed you today," Sabrina said in her naughty voice.

"Yeah. Are you going to show me how much you missed me?"

"You know I am. I hope you got some sort of rest today because I want the royal treatment tonight," Sabrina shot back.

"You know you can't handle the royal treatment. You always be trying to get away from a brother."

"Well, tonight it's on."

"Yeah, we'll see." He kissed her lips and was interrupted by the sound of his little princess giggling from the high chair.

"Hey daddy's girl." He went to pick her up. She reached out and was swinging her legs getting all excited.

"Look at you, all happy to see daddy."

As he pulled his little angel into his arms, all he could think was that he had two beautiful daughters. Even though they were conceived under two different circumstances, he wanted them to be close and love each other the way he loved them.

"Has she had her bath yet?" Malik asked Sabrina.

"No. I was getting ready to take her upstairs."

"I got it. I want to spend some time with her before she

goes to sleep," Malik said, staring into his daughter's eyes.

"You're not hungry?"

"Yup. But for pussy." Get it ready, I'll meet you in the room." He gave her that look like he was going to tear it up. Malik went upstairs, gave the baby a bath, and then dressed her in her pajamas. Then he sat in the rocking chair in her room, sang, and hummed her to sleep.

Sabrina went upstairs, lit some candles, turned on some slow music, and hopped in the shower. She wanted to make sure she was fresh for the evening's events. As the warm water beat on her back, she glided the loofa over her breasts and stomach; eyes closed picturing her husband tasting her. She slid her hand down between her legs and circled slowly on her clit. Soft moans came from her lips. She leaned her head back, allowing water to run over her hair and face then down her lips. She felt the contractions of the orgasm coming on strong, her moans got louder. Malik entered the bathroom just in time to experience the sweet sounds of ecstasy.

"I'll finish that for you."

Sabrina opened her eyes as Malik stepped into the shower, he went to his knees and placed one of her legs over his shoulder and began to suck on her already erect clit. She was unable to hold out another second and her moans became louder.

"Malik, take me there." He grabbed her butt with both hands and sucked a little harder

"Ahhhhhhh . . . aaahhhh . . ."

"Yessss . . . baby . . . Yessss . . ."

She was coming and coming hard. Then she came all over his face. Malik slowly tickled her clit with the tip of his tongue, bringing on aftershocks that had her body jerking and her legs weak. He stood up, got a handful of water, and ran it over his face.

"Damn girl, you be getting yours."

"Don't hate."

"Oh, I ain't hating because I know you're going to hook a brother up."

"Sure am, let's get out, I want to give you something special."

Malik was excited like it was Christmas Eve and his mom said he could open one present. They exited the bathroom and went to their bedroom. Sabrina told him to stand with his hands straight out and she proceeded to rub coconut-warming oil all over his naked chocolate body. After the first two minutes, it heated up making him feel horny. She gently rubbed her hand along the length of his dick then slid her hands between his legs caressing his balls.

"Damn baby, that shit feels good."

His dick was hard as hell; all the veins were at full alert mode. She began gently kissing the head and licking all around the rim. Malik was on fire. In one swift move, she grabbed his ass and deep throated his whole dick and slid back, tightening her jaws along the way caressing every inch.

"Ooooooh . . . baby."

He wanted to grab her by the hair and force himself deeper every time she pulled back, but she was in control and he wanted to benefit from whatever she had planned. Sabrina could see she was driving Malik crazy, so she picked up the pace moving her head from side to side and sucking hard. He could no longer resist. Malik put his hands on each side of her head, but she moved them. Sabrina continued to take him in her mouth deep and fast, sending chills up and down Malik's whole body.

"Oh shit . . . I'm about to come." His breathing picked up.

She let go of his ass and grabbed his hands, locking her fingers in his. He squeezed tight as he released what felt like buckets. He shook three times as she released him from her mouth, licking and sucking on the head to swallow the last drops of life from his powerful orgasm. Malik stood there unable to move or think. Sabrina smiled from ear-to-ear.

As he tried to compose himself, Sabrina stood and sashayed off to the bathroom and rinsed her mouth out. Upon her return, she saw Malik still standing there.

"Fucked your head up, didn't I?"

"Hell yeah. Where you been hiding all that good head?"

"Well, I have to save something or you will get bored."

"Can we put that on the schedule for at least once a month?"

Sabrina covered her mouth and laughed. "You are so crazy. Now come hook mama up."

Malik walked over to her and said, "Touch those toes for daddy."

She spread her legs and placed both palms on the floor. Malik slid up in that hot, wet pussy and went to work. He pulled her up slightly so he could lean over and gave her long hot kisses up and down her back. He stood and went back to grinding deep and close, making sure to pay attention to her every moan and would match it with one of his own. No matter what he shared with Keisha, he always made sure he was making love to his wife. Once she came, he led her to the bed so he could lay her down, get those legs on his shoulders, and give her what she called the royal treatment. After a few hours, they were knocked out.

When Malik woke up he watched his wife get ready for work. She was rushing all around the room because their last night activity threw her schedule off and she was now running late.

"You can stay home today. I'll pay you to do some work right here," he said, patting the empty spot next to him where she once lay.

"You know we are being audited this week, I have to be

there," she said not even stopping to entertain his advances.

Malik got out the bed, grabbed her around the waist, and planted a kiss on her lips and then her collarbone.

"Damn, you smell good. I want to eat you up."

"Well, that is going to have to wait until later. Because I have to gooooo," she said as she melted in his arms.

Malik continued to rub up and down her back in an attempt to get her to stay home, but he was given pause by the sound of their daughter calling out for mommy.

"See, she even knows that her daddy is in here being bad." She pushed him back a little and headed to the baby's room. When she came back, she had a diaper and washcloth in her hand. "I am going to change her and get her ready for Dawn. She should be here in an hour," Sabrina said.

"You can tell her not to come today. I had plans to take her out with me today."

"Where are you going? Are you still going to be able to take my car to the shop for a tune up?"

"Yeah. Put the keys on the dresser. Drive my car. I'm going to get Raheem to pick me up. Pass her to me. Hey daddy's girl." She fell into his arms giggling and touching all over his face.

"Baby, please don't give her things she shouldn't have. It makes it hard for Dawn to deal with her when you are not home."

Sabrina leaned in and kissed him then headed downstairs. Malik went downstairs to see Sabrina off. She had just prepared her lunch and was gathering her briefcase and jacket. They walked to the garage. Malik looked Sabrina in the eyes and said, "I love you, baby. You and baby girl are my world."

"I love you, too, Malik." She got a little misty eyed then wrapped her arms around his neck and hugged him tight. She kissed the baby then got into the car.

"Are you going to be home when I get in?"

"If I am, can I get some more of what you gave me last night?"

"You are so bad."

"If you stop holding out, I wouldn't be acting up."

With that, she started up the car and turned to her favorite morning talk show. Her song was on so she did a little dance in her seat and hit the garage door button and watched it rise from the rearview mirror. As she backed out the driveway, Malik took the baby's arm and began to wave at Sabrina.

"Say bye-bye to Mommie."

When she got to the end of the driveway, she stopped and waved back. They blew kisses to each other. "I love you," she mouthed and proceeded to back out.

BOOOOOOM!

The car blew up, blasting Malik and the baby farther back into the garage. As Malik lay there on the floor unable to hear or move, tears ran out the corner of his eyes as the feeling of helplessness came over him. He couldn't tell where his daughter was or if his wife was alive or dead.

A few hours later...

Tah'leek and Raheem had not yet heard about what happened at Malik's house. They sat in a local bar talking; trying to figure out what it was that Sadeek was getting them into. Tah'leek was feeling like he wanted to get the fuck out, take the shit he had acquired, and just be a father to his son and a husband to Trina. Then on the other side was his twin brother, who had come up with a plan to keep him in the business and maybe a way of getting rid of him, too. Why the fuck did he trust this nigga, Scarie? The more he sat on it, the more suspicious he became. Tah'leek sat there getting all fucked up with all these contradictions in his head.

"Man, I don't know what the fuck has gotten into Sadeek," Raheem said.

"Man, it's that bitch, Keisha, that got him all fucked up."

"All I know is a nigga got to sit on this Malik shit he got planned for a couple days. Look, I'll hit you later. I gotta go uptown to take care of some shit." Raheem got up and set his glass down.

"A'ight, I'm headed across town. Hit me up when you get back." Tah'leek gave Raheem some dap and they headed to the door.

Tah'leek headed over to Wilson Place Projects to get with his partner, Moon. It's funny because even though Raheem, Tah'leek, and Sadeek were as thick as thieves were, they never really trusted one another.

Tah'leek jumped in his car, hit the CD, and bumped "Cell Therapy" by Goodie Mob. As he drove, he thought back to a little over a year ago when he met Trina. All he could do was smile. Regardless of all his faults, he knew how much she loved him. She had changed his whole way of thinking. He was ready to get out and settle down. He damn sure wasn't trying to lose his life and his wife over some bullshit.

Chapter 5
Catastrophe

Damn, what did they do to this young lady?" one doctor asked another. Keisha had been found in a vacant lot by a woman walking her dog.

"I don't know, but she is going to need a lot of help if she pulls through." The other doctor responded.

"Just keep her sedated and get her prepped for surgery."

"She is going to need extensive repair to her rectum and her vaginal area not to mention all the other lacerations. See who's on call from plastic surgery."

"What the fuck were they trying to do to this girl?"

"Order a battery of tests from toxicology."

"We also need to get a social worker up here to see if they can help her through the psychological damage when she finally wakes up from surgery."

The doctors were talking about Keisha as if she wasn't even there. But in the state she was in, well, what was left of her resembled an empty shell.

What did I do to deserve all of this? She wondered.

Then she heard Sadeek's voice, Sadeek asking questions and wanting to see her. The feelings of abandonment and fear turned into relief. If nothing else, she knew he would make sure she was all right. The doctor told him that she was in and out and he could only stay for a minute since she had been sedated and prepped for surgery.

Sadeek entered the room and she could hear him

breathing, but she could barely see him through the slits in her eyes. He walked over to her bed and whispered in her ear.

"Baby, I'm here," he said with a smirk on his face.

For a moment she was relieved, but that all quickly changed to fear and despair when he said, "And I only came to tell you that if it was up to me, you would be dead already. Dirty bitch. I guess all that fucking around finally caught up with you. All I wanted was to love you and our daughter and keep you safe, but no, you wanted to trick around with nigga after nigga. Yeah, I know about you and Malik, and Tom, Dick and fucking Harry. Well, the jokes on you. I hope you lay here and rot. Then join his wife. Maybe y'all can take turns fucking the devil. Bye bitch, I'm going to make a better life for my daughter and me. The only regret I have is that I found you alive." He pulled out a needle and stuck it in her vein. He backed up and walked away.

Tears fell down her face. *My daughter. Not my daughter. I need her.* Keisha's heart started to race. *I can't breathe.* Feeling herself drifting off, the last thing she heard was the heart monitor. *Beeeeeeeep . . .*

The Aftermath

Once news hit the streets about Keisha's death, it put the police and FBI on high sensitivity, being that she was the main piece of bait they were going to use for their investigation. And what made matters worse was to find out that not only was she dead, but her boyfriend's wife. What the fuck was going on?

Rajon, Keisha's cousin, arrived at his mom's house and when he saw his aunt crying hysterically, he knew that shit was real bad and only going to get worse. The police were trying to calm her down and Rajon was hoping that Keisha wasn't hurt too bad, but no such luck. The drugs in her system along with the trauma she experienced never allowed her to make it out of the operating room.

When Keisha's mom, Brenda was told of the news she dropped to her knees and every feeling of regret, hate, and disappointment went through her body all at once. Why did God have to let this be the icing on her punishment cake? Brenda ran the streets and had the same type of lifestyle that had just taken her daughter's life. She had only been clean for a few years and was trying to make it up to her by spending plenty of time with her granddaughter. But as they say, what goes around comes around. Karma had made its way back and was ass fucking her with no Vaseline.

Keisha's aunt, Pat was the only calm one because she was the only one with all the pieces to the puzzle. She had been warning Keisha to get the fuck away from Sadeek and that fucking his boss was only going to come back and bite her in the ass. But true to form and being her mother's daughter, she was street smart and dick dumb. *What the fuck was wrong with these young girls? Damn! Get a good piece of dick and lose they muthafuckin' mind. Don't make no sense. Why a bitch can't ride a dick till the wheels fall off and call it what it is, a good fuck and then go handle their business? Damn.*

Pat's next thought was the baby. She needed to get her as far away as possible. She knew her sister; Brenda would not be in any state to take care of a baby. Plus, with Keisha's death, her next five dollars was going to the dope man. *That raising kids shit ain't my style*, Pat thought. All she would do was raise another hustler because that's all she knew. However, Pat knew one thing for sure. The streets had codes. And at the top of the list was *Kill everyone involved, even the seed or it will rise up and take revenge.*

Ne Ne Capri

The Takeover

Malik was all fucked up over the catastrophe that had just fallen into his lap. He was sitting in the house having one too many when he got a call from Sadeek. He almost didn't answer it, but instead he did.

"What's up, Malik?"

"Man, I can't call it. I think God hates my fucking guts. We been combing these streets for days and we ain't got shit to show for it."

"Well, I have some information that may help you get back on speaking terms with him," Sadeek stated.

"Yeah? What's up?" Sadeek had Malik's full attention. Although he was suspicious, he had to hear him out.

"I know who put that hit on our people and it just so happens that I have a meeting with them tonight."

"Don't fuck with me, 'Deek." Malik stood and the look on his face could have leveled a city block. He thought that he might have had something to do with it, but he never suspected him to be bold enough to call and show it.

"Nah, partner, I set everything up and we're getting ready to fuck these niggas."

"Round up whomever you can and come and get me." He hung up and got strapped. He took a few more drinks and waited on Sadeek.

Thirty minutes later, Sadeek pulled up and they were off to the meeting spot.

Malik sat back in the seat thinking about his wife and daughter and now Keisha. Tears started to form in his eyes, but he didn't allow them to fall. "So how'd you find these niggas?" he turned and questioned Sadeek.

"It was more like they found me." He glared at Malik.

"What a fucking coincidence." Malik didn't believe Sadeek for one minute. He smelled a rat and that stench was

36

coming right out of Sadeek's mouth. But with his family gone, he really didn't give a fuck if it was his end. He felt like at least he could meet back up with them. "Well, the way I feel, somebody is going to die tonight."

Sadeek looked over at him again and said, "Don't worry. We settling all scores tonight." He turned his eyes back to the road. Malik got quiet and just stared out the window.

They pulled up to a set of warehouses in the iron bound section of Newark. Just as they proceeded to get out the car Raheem and Tah'leek pulled up behind them. Malik stepped out the car slammed the door behind him, Raheem and Tah'leek came and stood beside him.

"What's good niggas?" Tah'leek said fixing the zipper on his coat.

"Ain't nothing lets go straighten this shit out." Malik replied.

Malik looked around and saw a few cars, but he didn't recognize them. He was trying to put together who could be inside, but came up with nothing. They walked inside and into the darkness of the empty warehouse filled with the sound of broken glass crunching under their feet and the faint sound of dripping water in the distance. They moved through the open doorways until they came to some steps. There, they stood at the bottom of a staircase welcoming their soon to be victim.

Malik looked up and saw three silhouettes approaching him. He immediately drew his gun. It was Scarie and his bodyguards coming down the steps. "What the fuck is going on?" he asked. Malik was ready to blast until he realized it was his boy. Then he lowered it.

"What the fuck are you doing here?" Malik asked Scarie.

"Dat's a question for your boi," Scarie said in his thick accent.

Malik turned and looked at Sadeek. "What the fuck is

going on?"

"Restructure," Sadeek said with a nasty look in his eyes.

Then Malik looked at Raheem and Tah'leek. "What the fuck is going on?" Raheem shook his head from side-to-side. Tah'leek didn't even respond.

Malik turned back toward Sadeek.

"Oh, so you want to be me? Well, I'll tell you like this: It don't matter how hard you try, you ain't going to be nothing more than a greasy ass nigga. And when you come up off of greed, it always bites you in the ass." Malik turned his back on Sadeek. "Well, go ahead and do what you came to do, but you got to kill a nigga the way you came at him, so excuse my back." Malik spit on the floor and braced himself for his fate with his family, all dismantled he had no desire to live.

With that, Sadeek shot Malik five times in the back and then spit on him. "Wrong answer, muthafucka," Sadeek said.

Raheem put his head in his hands and immediately felt fucked up. Tah'leek stood there staring at Scarie and his crew with an evil coldness to his eyes debating whether he should pull out and blast Scarie and his whole crew or put one in his dumb ass brother.

"You want what I gave this nigga, or are you ready to go forward and do what we got to do?" Sadeek yelled at Raheem.

"Nigga, fuck you. I ain't trying to hear all that shit you talking. If we go forward, then we do this shit together. You ain't my gotdamn boss, nigga."

"Shit, I can't tell. I'm the one with the connect. I'm the one that made the sacrifice, so as I see it, nigga, you work for me. Or hit the muthafuckin' unemployment line because I'm running this shit."

Raheem looked at him like he was crazy. Then Tah'leek yelled at Sadeek "What the fuck is wrong with you? You letting these niggas come between us?" he got louder with each word.

"Well, I can settle who is in charge. Neither one of you niggas," Scarie spoke then he shot Sadeek in the stomach.

"What the fuck are you doing? We had a deal," Sadeek yelled out in agonizing pain as he placed his hand on his wound. He fumbled with his gun causing it to fall to the floor. Tah'leek and Raheem was in a standoff with Scarie and his boys.

"The key word is *had*. Do ya remember the girl you fucked at the hotel and killed?" Sadeek's eyes got big as hell; shit got so quiet you could have heard a rat piss on cotton.

"Yeah, nigga, dat one. Well, dat was me cousin." Scarie shot him again. Sadeek fell back into Raheem then a rain of bullets fell over both of them. Tah'leek turned to run with his arm turned back at his enemies. He let off shots but his gun was unlucky that night. He was shot several times in his back, fell into a pile of iron rods, and fell on his stomach dying instantly.

As Raheem lay there dying, all he could think was why did he agree to fuck with Sadeek on this shit. All of his fears were confirmed. Sadeek had made a deal with the devil.

Ne Ne Capri

Fifteen years later

40

Chapter 6
KoKo

ey Family, this is KoKo. I know y'all had to sit through a few stories before y'all got to meet the baddest bitch you will ever read about, but it's all good. The shit was necessary. But check it, shit is getting ready to move real fast so pay attention and get at a bitch at the end.

It was a Friday night and KoKo was chilling in the bar with Scales, Wise, and Baseem from Yonkers.

Aldeen was the man next to the man. He was humble but deadly. He was responsible for bringing KoKo her orders and because of that fact; she only gave him the money and reports.

Scales was this tall, lanky nigga with a slick ass tongue and an insatiable taste for cards and dice. Night after night, he would get all the little niggas in the back of the bar, school them, and talk shit about his winnings. "Let your next move be your best move, little youngin," is all you would hear echoing from the back of the bar.

Scales had mad love for KoKo and because of his loyalty; he didn't have to move shit but his mouth. He was the only one on her team paid to just be there and keep her informed.

Then there was Wise, one of KoKo's appointed henchmen. 6'1", 200 pounds, light skinned with wavy black hair and a body built like a god. He had a no nonsense attitude; if a nigga got out of line; he checked them on the spot. He lived by the philosophy that *if you play with a dog, he will lick you.* So he made sure never to play with a nigga. He would always say, "I laugh and I joke, but I don't play." Proverbs were another one of his attributes, which got him the name, Wise.

Wise and KoKo were like brother and sister ever since the day she had cut this bitch seven times for burning him. They were in the pizza shop ordering a few slices and the bitch walked in acting like America's Next Top Model, flaunting around like she was the shit with her drippy pussy.

"Get the fuck off the block. Don't nobody want none of your funky ass," KoKo yelled.

She shot back, "Bitch, you just mad because they ain't trying to fuck you, fucking dyke."

And as if KoKo had wings, she jumped on her and sliced her face seven times with a straight razor before they could get KoKo off her. She stood up and smirked. "Now your face will be barking just like your pussy." Koko spit on her then walked to the counter, paid for her pizza, and bounced. Everybody stood around looking shocked. When Wise saw that she was the type of bitch that didn't give a fuck, he knew she was team material and had been teaching, training, and watching her back ever since.

KoKo had come up hard. She grew up in the Wilson Place projects in Orange, New Jersey. Her mom had passed away when she was small, so her grandmother raised her. They moved to the projects in 1980 after her mom died. Her grandmother sold the house and moved into a two-bedroom apartment to save money. When she started elementary at Oakwood Avenue School, she met her two best friends, Tionne and Tabatha. They hit it off as soon as they met and were inseparable. They had formed a bond that no one could break or so they thought.

By the time KoKo turned nine years old, the 'jets were changing; crack had taken over the streets and she saw more niggas killed than a little. The straw that broke the camel's back for her grandmother was one summer night. Gunshots rang out in the hallway and her grandmother came running into her room scared as hell, crying and saying somebody got shot in front of their door. KoKo jumped out the bed and looked out the peek hole. She could see ReRe and Cordy standing over somebody crying and yelling for help.

Even though she was scared, curiosity took over and she cracked the door. What she saw would change her life forever. There he laid, one of the kingpins of Orange spread out with blood and white shit coming out of his nose and mouth and his body full of gun holes. KoKo stood there staring. Her grandmother was pulling her arms and trying to get her to come back in the house, but she couldn't move. Bizzy was one of the project's role models. Although he sold drugs, he wasn't like the typical dealer. He was about 5' 6", chocolate brown, and a sweetheart. He would pass money out to the kids and help out with the local ball teams so that the kids who didn't have sneakers and stuff could play. In the summer, he would help organize trips so the kids could get out of the projects and have fun. He had just bought his mom a condo and always kept a good rapport with all the people who lived around there even though he didn't. Seeing him laid out crushed KoKo to her very soul. Then to see his boys crying and yelling—all the people that she looked up to, was devastating.

Her grandmother finally pulled her inside then locked and chained the door. She tried to get her to go back to bed, but who could sleep after that? KoKo lay there looking at the ceiling for at least two and a half hours before drifting off.

When she got up to go to school the next morning, she

was haunted by the thoughts of what she saw. The reality of it all hit her hard when she stepped out her door. There were gunshot holes in the floor, wall, and her door, along with smears of blood. Her heart raced and tears came to her eyes. She jumped on the elevator and headed to the fifth floor to Tionne's house. The same spirit Koko was experiencing at home was also at Tionne's house. Her cousin, who was one of the top dealers, lived there and was very close to Bizzy. No one was really talking and the usual laughter that she would have heard every morning before school was nonexistent. It was just a somber feeling as everyone got ready for school.

The next couple of events didn't help much; the killings kept coming. It was something unnatural about seeing a dude's head blown up so big from a gunshot that it barely fit in the casket. Everyone was sent to Woody's funeral parlor, which sat on the corner of the projects. How ironic for it to be positioned at the base of a killing zone and they was getting rich on mass murder? You would have thought a situation like that would turn any kid into an A student with the hunger to get out. But for KoKo it was the total opposite: She loved the feeling of the streets, and as for death, she felt it was a part of life. And if a muthafucka got to go, he got to go. She dove head first into the streets, muling drugs from one side of town to the other and holding guns for several local dealers. By the age of twelve, she was making more money than most of her friends' parents. KoKo's grandmother's heart was breaking; she could see if she didn't do something fast, she would lose her.

At thirteen, KoKo hung out with her girls on a hot summer night. A stick up kid came to Parrow Street and tried to violate the 108, asking who he could rob. He was told to get the fuck outta there because everybody out there was family. As he turned to walk away, someone put a bullet in his head. The scary part was that he was walking right past KoKo and her friends. Everyone thought they were shot too, but they had ducked behind a mailbox. The worst part was the FED's thought they had a witness in KoKo, but true to form, she didn't see shit and didn't say shit. However, their visit to her house and questioning tactics was what signed the deal for her grandmother. She moved out by the winter. That landed KoKo in a brownstone in Brooklyn, Prospect Park section to be exact. That would be the turning point of KoKo's development, sending her further into the drug game instead of pulling her out. She met Wise when she was fifteen and had become one of the strongest forces on the streets.

Chapter 7
Kayson

"Give me the numbers," Kayson spoke in a monotone voice as was his practice. He was the type of nigga you didn't want to see mad because if you did, somebody had to die. Aldeen watched Kayson move slowly toward his big leather chair that sat behind a huge, dark wooden desk.

"We brought in about $500,000 from that event. That nigga, Raul is still acting the fuck up." Aldeen was obviously becoming frustrated dealing with this nigga.

Kayson took in the information and then spun his chair around toward the picture window right behind his desk. He took a deep breath then turned back to Aldeen and said, "Never hate your enemies. It fucks with your judgment. Remember what Robert Greene said in 48 Laws of Power, "When you force the other person to act, you are the one in control." He went on to say, "We must remain in control. We have to move these pieces strategically across the board until we checkmate these muthafuckas."

With that, Aldeen nodded his head in agreement. Kayson always came with some shit that all you could do was agree with him. "What else is going on?" Kayson wanted the rest of the Intel.

"We got KoKo rising up with street credit and handling her business; the bitch is bad. She moves like you move. No phones, only talks to a few, and has eyes and ears everywhere.

Shit, she tied to people I don't know. Then she had the nerve to tell me that it's best that way so when they take a vice grip to my nuts and I say I don't know, I really won't know shit." Aldeen laughed.

Kayson brought a half smile to his face. "She get down like that?"

"Hell yeah. She's gonna be perfect for this next move. She is crazy as hell, but if you can calm her down she will be untouchable," Aldeen said with confidence.

"We will see. Go ahead and take care of the first steps, let me worry about Miss KoKo."

Aldeen got up and shook Kayson's hand. "A'ight I'll catch up with you later. Same time, same place?"

Kayson nodded and turned to look out the window as Aldeen exited his office. Kayson took a minute to look back on how he used to be and how it paralleled what he was hearing about KoKo.

Kayson grew up in the Bronx; he was always a very intellectual child. His mother was raising him by herself and because she worked a lot, she had him into all kinds of activities; the chess club was one of his favorite. He also had computer classes, piano lessons, and was on the debate team. Besides all his activities inside and outside of school, she kept his head in books. When Kayson turned thirteen, his uncle got him a membership to the gym and put him on the boxing team. His mother was opposed to such a barbaric sport, but her brother Rabb kept saying, "My nephew ain't going to be no punk." She finally gave in, but on the condition that her brother made sure to encourage him to not be sidetracked from his academics.

Because Kayson was smart as hell, he looked at everything as a chess board and at every one like the pieces. Kayson was always on a mission. He thought that if you moved your pieces wisely and never without protection, seeking to take out any opposition, then and only then could you wear the crown. He had a natural talent in boxing. His discipline to train had his body and mind in superior shape. No one could touch him in the ring. His uncle was so proud of him; he immediately set up fights all over the city, both professional and street fights. Kayson would size up his opponent and knock them the fuck out.

Kayson's uncle kept him with him all the time, another idea his mother was opposed to because he had some suspect activities and as she saw it, he was definitely grave bound. However, Kayson enjoyed every minute he spent with his uncle. It wasn't the money that attracted Kayson; it was the power. He loved the idea of getting people to do what you wanted them to do while making them think they came up with the idea.

Kayson would advise his uncle, teaching him all the things he learned in books such as *The Art of War* by Sun Zu and *48 Laws of Power* by Robert Greene and *Uncle Yah Yah* by Al Dickens. These books specialized in how to deal with your enemies and how to move people around to serve your purpose. Because Kayson was dangerous with his hands and a nigga might try to test him, his uncle began teaching him to use different types of guns so he would be a full package.

When Kayson turned sixteen, his uncle gave him a pack of magnums and took him to the hotel to meet up with this twenty-two-year-old woman named Dominique. When they pulled up to the hotel, his uncle Rabb turned and strongly stated to his nephew, "Look, little nigga, you can't be no fucking virgin."

Kayson looked at him then said, "How the fuck you know I ain't get no pussy yet?"

"Nigga please, I can tell you ain't got that shit wet yet." Then he did his signature laugh, throwing his head back. "Look, I got some shit hooked up for you. Don't worry; she's going to take care of you. Remember, get pussy . . . never let pussy get you."

Kayson nodded in agreement. "I got it."

"Don't get fucked up, up there," his uncle said before letting him out the car. He was impressed with his amount of reserve. He handed him the key card and smiled.

"I'll pick you up in the morning." Then he watched Kayson as he bopped into the lobby. All he could think was, *that nigga is going to be dangerous.* Then he pulled off.

What his uncle didn't know was that he had already had sex, when he was twelve. He and Lisa, his mom best friend's daughter had been practicing oral sex every weekend. He had gotten eating pussy down to a science. He had been giving Lisa multiple orgasms since they were thirteen and his confidence was up.

Kayson walked in the lobby, looked around and then found the elevator and got on. He got off on the sixth floor, strolling his cool ass down the hall and sticking the key card in the slot and came into the room. When he looked up, Dominique stood in the middle of the room. She was 5'5" and 120 pounds, beautiful brown skin with dark brown eyes and a short Halle Berry haircut. All breasts and ass with perfect little manicured hands and feet. Her body was oiled up from head to toe and she wore a white lace see-thru bodysuit showing her nipples and pussy print. His dick jumped.

Dominique broke the silence with, "What do you want t—"

"Shhhhhh . . ." Kayson put his finger up to his mouth. She was thrown off and just stood there. Then Kayson walked toward her looking right in her eyes. Slowly, he circled her, sizing her up trying to see what he was working with. She felt nervous like it was her first time. She was expecting to just have her way with this young fifteen year old, but what stood before her was a 6'1", 160-pound muscular body with the presence of a man. When Kayson stood in front of her, he again stared in her eyes.

"Do you like what you see?" Dominique tried to gain control of the situation.

"I don't know yet. Take all that off and meet me in the shower." Then he turned and headed toward the bathroom. He stripped and hopped in the shower. Dominique was right on his heels, unsure of what was going to happen next. All she could think was, what did I get myself into? Shit, she was told he was a young boy that needed his cherry popped, and that she should be able to stun him with her body. Then fuck the shit out of him, make him cum quick, then sneak out when he was passed out with his thumb in his mouth. But the way it appeared, he was getting ready to have her sucking her thumb.

When she entered the shower, his back was turned and she was pleasantly surprised. His back was well-defined, shoulders tight, muscular ass. "Damn, this little nigga is sexy as hell," she mumbled under her breath.

Quickly moving close to him, she put her hands on his back and began to kiss the middle of his spine. Grabbing the cloth, she put some Dove body wash on it and began to wash his back. Watching the bubbles slowly slide down his butt, she bit her bottom lip anticipating his touch.

Kayson turned around giving her that same intense stare. Dominique looked down, circling the cloth on his chest and abs. The V shape at the end of his six-pack led to a dick that she could only describe as beautiful. Long and thick with a pretty mole right on the tip. She admired it as she watched the soap slowly glide down his shaft.

"Do you like what you see?" Kayson said with a smirk on his face.

"I sure do." His cocky attitude turned her on.

"Tell him," he said. Squatting, she opened her mouth to receive him and was greeted first with the water running off his dick. She swallowed it, then him.

Kayson enjoyed the feeling she was giving him. He towered over her, watching her every move with seriousness on his face while never taking his eyes off her. Excited, Dominique used every trick she knew. The sound of slurping and moaning turned Kayson on. He let out a small hiss from his lips. Dominique took advantage of that moment, sucking harder and faster. Kayson placed his hand on the back of her head, feeling the strong urge to cum. He released into her mouth and she swallowed every drop then smiled at him. But his facial expression never changed.

"Stand up," Kayson commanded in a deep relaxed voice. Taking her by the hand, he turned her face toward the water. "Rinse your mouth out," he said. As she complied, he soaped up the sponge and began washing her back and butt then turned her around and lightly brushed it across her breasts. With the other hand, he circled the suds around her nipples and ran his finger between her breasts, down her stomach, then slowly between her legs. Closing her eyes, she softly moaned in pleasure. Once satisfied, he turned her again and said, "Rinse off so I can taste you."

When all the soap was off her body, he went down to one knee and gave her some of that diesel tongue. Kayson was doing what he did best and she was climbing the walls. He grabbed her tight, giving her clit a fit. Dominique felt an orgasm coming on strong.

"Oh my god. . . ahhhhhh . . . oh shit . . ." She came so hard, she thought she was going to fall out. Kayson stood and ran water over his face and rinsed his mouth out. Then he faced her, grabbing a hand full of her hair and pulling her head back, kissing and nibbling on her neck. His hand slid between her legs massaging her clit. Once he had her full attention, he inserted his finger deep inside her—another thing he had gotten good at. Enjoying every minute, she was on the verge of cumming again.

"Oh my god, I'm cumming again."

"Let that shit go," Kayson said in an aggressive tone.

"Oooohhhhh . . . sssssss," she hissed and fell forward on his chest.

"Let's go to the bed so I can get me some of this sweet pussy."

Dominique couldn't even speak; she followed his orders. He lay her on the bed and began kissing her legs and sucking her inner thighs. He was driving her crazy. Squirming all around in anticipation, she sank her head into the pillow and bit down on her bottom lip as she began rubbing the top of his head with both hands.

Just as Kayson was about to continue his attack, the hotel phone rang. He reached over and grabbed it "Hello. I'll be right there." He hung up and climbed off the bed, grabbing his sweat pants and hoodie. Dominique watched as he dressed then said in disappointment,

"Where you going?"

"Keep it wet for me, I'll be right back." He grabbed his nine, placed it in a small black bag, and headed for the door. Dominique was confused. As she started to get off the bed, he turned and said, "Don't leave the room and don't use the phone." He opened the door and with the look of death in his eyes, he headed for the stairs to carry out his mission. When Kayson got to the twelfth floor, he opened the bag and tucked the gun safely in his waist. He pulled his hoodie down, opened the exit door, and moved swiftly down the hallway. When he got to room 1215, he knocked three times. When the door opened, a tall brown-skinned woman wearing nothing but some stilettos greeted him. She pulled the door back allowing him to enter. "Did you put that nigga on doze?" Kayson said in a whisper.

"That nigga is almost comatose."

"Get dressed and wait for me by the door." He pulled out his gun and handed her the black bag. As he crept to the bathroom door, he heard the nigga yell out, "Who is that at the door?" Mano sat in the tub stroking his dick anticipating her return.

"It was housekeeping dropping off the extra towels," Tomeka yelled back.

"Hurry up so I can make you earn your paycheck," Mano said. He closed his eyes, slid down in the tub and continued to stroke his dick.

Kayson entered the bathroom and was immediately appalled by the sight of this nigga laid up in the tub butt ass naked. *This nigga got pussy on deck and fucking himself.* Kayson leaned up against the sink and began tapping his gun on the edge of the counter. Mano opened his eyes. Taken totally by surprise, he jumped and grabbed the edge of the tub in an effort to get out. Kayson pointed the gun at him and said very casual, "Don't get up on my account." He pulled his hoodie back exposing his face. It was then that Mano realized who the young gunman was and the flash of events played in his mind like an on screen movie.

Earlier that night, Rabb and his crew had taken Kayson to a strip club to celebrate his birthday. Rabb had done it big. He rented out three VIP booths and had the baddest bitches working the rooms. All night, bottles of expensive champagne and dark liquor were there for the taking, and they were drinking that shit like it was water. Rabb had Kayson sat in a chair in the middle of the room while several dancers were all over him. Kayson wasn't even fazed. He kept a half-smile and even less participation.

"Go ahead little nigga. It's your party, grab some of that ass." His uncle's boy, J-Bone yelled. out.

"Little nigga you act like pussy don't excite you." His uncle's boy, Kev yelled out then rained dollar bills all over the strippers. Kayson thought, *y'all niggas is silly as hell letting bitches take your money and you ain't get shit but a fucking lap dance.* Kayson had been sitting there watching all the niggas go wild over these bitches. All he could do was take note seeing the power these bitches had, thinking pussy brings a nigga into the world and then can take a muthafucka out.

He gazed over the crowd and spotted some of his competition. While everybody else was there to play, he was there to work; taking note of all their weaknesses. As Nikki danced in front of him, he used her body as a shield to look over at Mano's table. This nigga ran Crown Heights and he wanted it. He watched as Mano's crew was fucked up and threw money around like they had a fucking printing press in the back. Kayson realized that pussy had power and if the pussy was powerful enough, he could use it to bring these muthafuckas to their knees.

"Go dance for him, I have to do something," Kayson told Nikki as he got up from his seat and led her toward J-bone. Nikki reluctantly went; she had her orders to turn him out and wanted to make that money. Kayson got up and went to sit in the booth next to Rabb.

"You having fun, nephew," he said in a drunken slur trying to shout over the music.

"I'm good," Kayson said, nodding his head. Kayson wasn't concerned with these bitches shaking their ass. He was on a mission and with Mano in his crosshairs; he was getting ready to make his next move. Within minutes, he got up to go to the bathroom. "I'll be right back," he said and moved through the crowd. As he got closer to the bathroom, he noticed Mano coming his way. He had his arms around two females, laughing and talking loud. He met eyes with Kayson and his smile dropped.

"What's up, little nigga? You been watching me all night."

Kayson didn't respond. He kept his eyes locked on Mano. They were now in a stare off. Mano was getting frustrated that he wasn't even fazing this young boy. Taking his arms from around the two women, Mano got closer to Kayson. "Damn nigga, you act like you wanna give me some pussy." Kayson didn't blink. Mano's boys were moving toward him and Kayson. At the same time, Rabb looked up and noticed the exchange.

"Oh shit. Move!" he yelled at Nikki, pushing her aside. Rabb moved swiftly through the crowd with his boys on his heels. When he got to where they were standing, he quickly threw his arm around Kayson's neck. "Ho, ho, ho. What's going on?" he asked, trying to bring some calm to the situation.

"Ain't nothin. Just trying to pay tribute to a fan," he said, still not breaking eye contact.

"This is my nephew, Kayson, it's his birthday. We just gettin' a little celebration in. He was probably just checking out all those fine ass females in your corner," he said, tugging at Kayson's neck in an effort to get him to calm down. All that went up in smoke when Mano pulled a move that was disrespectful to the highest order.

"You better be lucky you're my man's nephew. Go buy yourself some ass or something." He reached in his pocket, pulled out a wad of twenties, and smacked Kayson in the face with them. The money flew all over him and rained to the floor at the same time. Heated, Kayson reached for his gat, ready to blow the whole fucking building up. Niggas from both sides moved in.

"It's all good; we came here to have a good time," Rabb said as he grabbed Kayson and pulled him toward the bathroom. He gave Jay the eye to dead that shit.

"Chill, Kayson, he's just drunk. Let that shit go. Let's go back out there and enjoy the rest of the night." He patted him on the chest. "It's all about you tonight." It damn sure was and Mano had just paid for it with his life.

So there they were, face to face again and this time, Mano was ready to shit himself. "What the fuck you want?"

"I thought I would take your advice."

"What's that?"

"I bought some ass. Was it good?" Kayson asked with a smirk on his face. He had paid his girl, Tomeka to keep that nigga on ice.

Mano sat thinking of his next move, but the shit was looking grim. "This is what is going to happen. I want the Heights. And I need you to make it happen." Kayson reached into his pocket, pulled out a burner, and dialed his boy, Aldeen.

"What the fuck you talking about?" Mano asked as fear set into his soul. He was sweating and breathing heavy.

Kayson locked one in the chamber, pointed the gun at Mano's now shriveled dick and said, "Your brother is Steve, right?" Fear came over Mano's face. "Yo, put that nigga on the phone." Kayson hit the speaker button as Steve yelled out in excruciating pain,

"Ahhhhh. Okay. Okay." Aldeen had him hog-tied and was beating him in the head with the butt of a gun.

"Nigga, you better not hurt my brother." Mano tried to assert himself.

"Hit that nigga again," Kayson ordered into the phone.

Mano could hear his brother yelling in agony. "All right, little nigga. I'll give you what you want. Just spare my brother," he pleaded.

"I'm going to hang up and I want you to call your supplier and let him know you have a new man in charge. Then set up a meeting. Then all of this will be over in a matter of minutes." Kayson looked at his watch.

Mano took a deep breath. "A'ight. When will my brother be let go."

"As soon as you handle your business. But if we don't call that crazy nigga back in five minutes, your brother is a dead man," Kayson responded. He threw the phone at Mano and he caught it in his hands barely missing the water. Mano made the phone call, set up the meeting, and then threw the phone back at Kayson.

"Make your call," he said.

As Kayson caught the phone, he chuckled then got serious. "Nigga, you ain't in no position to make no fucking demands." He dialed Aldeen and said, "Finish him." Then pulled his gun up and prepared to take Mano's life.

Mano held his arms out in front of him. "Man, don't shoot!" he begged. "I ain't going to be a problem. You can walk out of here with everything you want. Please man, don't do it." He was almost in tears.

Kayson stood without taking his gun off of Mano, and then he squeezed letting off three shots; one to the stomach, chest, and head. "Punk muthafucka," he spat, turning to walk out of the bathroom.

He and Tomeka quickly opened and spread an ounce of coke on the table and floor along with the money he threw at Kayson earlier. Tomeka was dressed in the bulky clothes that Mano wore. She pulled the baseball cap down over her short haircut and threw on some shades. They walked out the room and she jumped on the elevator while Kayson took the stairs. Kayson smiled, knowing he was about to become the king of the Heights.

Chapter 8
Back to Business

Kayson came back to the room pulling his hoodie over his head. Dominique rose from her pillow and immediately spotted the gun tucked in his waist. He placed it on the dresser and threw the bag on the chair in the corner. As he stepped out his sweat pants, he said, "Did you keep it wet for me?"

Dominique smiled and said with a little hesitation in her voice, "I didn't think you wanted it. You left me here all alone."

"I had some business to take care of. But don't worry I'll make it up to you," he said, standing next to the bed—dick about to bust out of his boxers.

"You better," she said, sitting up and pulling at the sides of his boxers until they were around his ankles.

He stepped out of them, grabbed a magnum, and handed it to her. "Put this on the enforcer," he said in a sexy voice. She slid the condom down slowly and he watched her little hands handle his big dick.

"I hope you ain't got shit to do because I'm getting ready to get up in this pussy and act a fool."

Dominique looked at him. "Treat it like it's yours."

"Oh, don't worry, after tonight it will be." He leaned in and kissed her lips, sucking on her tongue and making the pussy soaking wet. He then slid in with ease.

"Ooohhh . . . ahhhhhh . . ." Dominique was trying to adjust to his size. Kayson picked up speed and was hitting every wall she had.

"Kaaaayyyy."

He didn't respond, he kept on hitting it good and steady. When he felt the urge to cum, he pulled out and went back to sucking on her clit. Once she came, he slid back in and rode her orgasm. Dominique was on fire. Gripping her legs, he placed them on his shoulders and went in deeper.

"Yeessss . . . yeessss . . . aaaahhhhh."

She felt another one coming on and so did he, but he wasn't ready to cum yet, so again he pulled out and placed his face between her legs. Nibbling on her inner thighs, he went back to sucking her clit aggressively and then gently while running his tongue up and down her lips, then back to attacking her clit.

"I'm cuuuummming . . . ooohhhh . . ." She skeeted all over his face. As her hand grabbed at the sheets, her heart raced. He had just taken her breath away. Then he climbed back in, sucking and licking her neck. "Can I have some more?" he whispered.

"You can have whatever you want." She wrapped her arms around the back of his neck and began tasting his lips then biting into his flesh. Dominique was sucking that spot under his chin and it was turning him on. He moaned out, "Ssssssss . . . Mmmm."

He sped up, placing his mouth over one of her nipples, like he was drinking from it. She held on to him, loving how good he was making her feel. Again, a huge orgasm was approaching. He pulled out and said, "Turn around, let me get some from the back." She turned around on all fours, looking back at him over her shoulder. "Handle it," she said. He did just that. Gripping her hips, he went in hard stroking long and fast. Dominique bit into the pillow as a combination of pleasure and pain overtook her body. "What did you want me to do to it?" Kayson was talking shit with confidence.

"Handle . . . ittt . . ." she responded and then looked back again. "Damn boy . . . you a beast . . ." She moaned loudly.

"That's all I needed to know." Pulling her to the edge of the bed, he stood behind her for leverage. Then he tore that ass up for almost an hour. He was riding and popping her on her ass. She yelled, "Yessss . . . fuck me . . . fuck me."

Kayson rode her for a few more minutes until she came again and so did he. He pulled out, snatched off the magnum, and busted all over her ass. She quickly turned around and sucked on the head of his dick, drinking the rest of his seed. Finally, she fell back on the bed, legs shaking and pussy throbbing.

Kayson lay next to her. "You good, ma?"

"Uuuummmm . . . yeeesss," she said, not believing that a sixteen-year-old boy had just fucked the shit out of her.

As if he could read her mind he said, "Yeah, you thought you were messing with a lamb; you fucked around and ran up in the lion's den."

A smile formed on Dominique's mouth. "Yes I did, and you ate my ass up," she said in a drowsy voice.

"I aim to please," Kayson said full of pride.

A long silence ended their conversation. Kayson glanced at Dominique as she dozed off. *Damn shame, can't even hang with a young boy,* he thought.

He called room service and ordered some wings and two orders of pasta alfredo with shrimp. Then he showered and re-entered the room, admiring his handiwork as he looked her over. Laughing and shaking his head, he poured himself a glass of champagne and two shots of Jack Daniels. He rubbed the small sample of lotion on his body as he stared in the mirror.

"You heard what she said. Boy, you a beast," he said, grabbing his dick. He put on the hotel robe, swallowed the shots of Jack, and prepared to settle down. Then a knock came at the door. He grabbed his nine and moved to the door.

"Who is it?"

"Room service." The voice came from the other side of the door.

He looked out the peek hole to confirm. "Hold on." Kayson grabbed a hundred dollar bill, slipped the gun in his pocket, and opened the door.

The young white boy pushed in the cart and looked over at Dominique who was passed out. Kayson looked at the young boy turn red and a smile came across his face.

"That will be $42.50," his little squeaky voice bellowed out.

Kayson handed him the hundred-dollar bill and said, "Keep the change."

"Thank you, sir. Enjoy the rest of your evening." He smiled from ear to ear. With that, he was out the door.

Kayson looked under the top of each dish. It smelled so good. On the bottom was an extra tray. He opened it and saw a little cake that read: Happy Birthday Nephew. Love Unc. He smiled, closed the lid then walked over to the bed and woke Dominique up so she could eat with him. He sat next to her and patted her arm. She opened her eyes. "Wake up so we can eat this food," he said. She rolled over, still groggy.

"I am so sleepy, Kayson," she said, flashing him a sexy smile.

"Don't worry; daddy will rock you back to sleep."

All she could do was shake her head. She had not been that sexually satisfied in years and by a young nigga. She got up and joined him. They ate and laughed and then true to his word, he fucked her right back into a coma. They both slept until check out. From that day on, Dominique was hooked on that young dick and willing to do whatever she had to do to get it.

By the time Kayson was seventeen, he was no longer his uncle's shadow; he was more like his oracle. Kayson would show on the scene, sit in a corner, and listen to them plan. Once they were done, they would turn to Kayson and ask him what he thought. Then follow it to the letter.

****

Kayson was in the local bar sitting in the back with a hoodie on his head and reading a book called *As a Man Thinketh*. Three dudes came walking in the bar, but Kayson never looked up. Instead, he became a chameleon so he could listen and observe. They sat down at the bar, ordered a few drinks, and started to run their mouths. The subject at hand was his uncle. All Kayson could think was how bad it was to sit in public and discuss business; especially the demise of a nigga, while totally oblivious of the surroundings.

Kayson was able to get every one of their names and peg where they were from. They finished their drinks, and then another man came walking in. He spoke, gave them an envelope of money, and said, "It's all there, handle it and make it quick." Then he headed back to the door.

Kayson let thirty seconds pass, then he smoothed passed them and posted himself outside. He watched the man get into his car and mentally noted the license plate and watched him pull off. Once he was gone, he quickly wrote it down. He posted himself across the street on the bus stop like he was waiting on the bus.

When the other three men came out the bar, he watched each one get into their cars and wrote down each of their plate numbers. He went to work on finding out who they were. Kayson didn't tell his uncle what had went down; he wanted to make sure he had something first. From the pay phone, he called Dominique who had a friend who worked at the department of motor vehicles and gave her the numbers.

Within the hour, Dominique gave Kayson the information he needed. Out of the four, only one of their cars was registered to a female. The dude that came out the bar first who had paid the other three lames to put the hit out. That must have been his woman whose name was on the car. That night, Kayson suited up, got his two forty-fives, and he went to the block where his informant told him they hung out. There they were, all three, sitting in front of the corner store engrossed in conversation oblivious to the danger that lay ahead. He slid along the shadow and crept up on them and started blasting, laying them down one by one. The first two died instantly and when he got to the last one, the nigga was pleading for his life. Kayson said in a calm voice, "Where is the money he paid you to kill Rabb?"

"I don't know what you talking about, man."

Kayson shot him in the kneecap and the lame screamed like a bitch. "I'm going to ask you one more time, where is the money?"

"In that green Range Rover, man. Just stop shooting me. Shit, I don't even know why the fat man wants Rabb dead."

Kayson walked over to the Rover, busted the window, and grabbed the envelope between the seats. He walked back over to guy who had just given him the information and blew his brains out. Then he walked over to where the other two lay and put three more bullets in each of them to make a point. Pulling his hood over his head, he walked off like nothing happened. People looked on in horror.

Kayson's next move was to get to the head nigga's house, Fat Sam. He pulled up to the address registered to the woman whose name was on the tags. The same car he saw him get into earlier was parked in the driveway. All the lights were out, so he crept around the back of the house and found a window open on the first floor. He climbed in nice and easy. When he approached the room, he heard what sounded like a woman moaning.

Kayson eased to the door and peeked through the crack and just as he thought, Fat Sam was deep in some pussy. He pulled out his gun, busted in the door, and shot him two times in the back. Sam had fallen to the floor crying like a bitch. The woman screamed.

"Shut the fuck up!" Kayson yelled as he smacked her in the head with the gun.

"What's your beef with Rabb?" Kayson asked with his teeth gritted.

"I don't know what you're talking about," Fats said, laying there in agonizing pain.

"Do I look like a muthafucka that would have the wrong address?" He shot him in the kneecap. "I got shit to do. I don't have time to play one hundred fucking questions with you."

"Damn! Aaahhh . . ." Sam cried. The woman was scared as hell, up against the headboard crying hysterically and holding onto the sheets for dear life.

"Tell him what he wants to know," she yelled.

"Shut the fuck up, Carmen!" Sam managed to yell while in excruciating pain.

Carmen yelled, "It was J-Bone."

Kayson's eyebrows tightened and his nostrils flared. J-Bone was his uncle's right arm. With that, he took one last shot at Sam shooting him right between the eyes. Carmen pissed herself. When Kayson turned his attention back to her she said, "Wait. Please, don't kill me. I told you what you needed to know."

"Bitch, we at war and you know what you are?"

64

"What?" she asked crying and shaking.

"A casualty." Kayson spat then put one bullet in each one of her eyes. "Next time see no evil, bitch." He put his hood over his head and left out the same window he came through. Reaching the nearest pay phone, he called his uncle at the spot.

"What's up, Unc?"

"Nothing nephew. What's up with you?"

"Ain't nothin'. Headed your way. Is everybody there?"

"Yeah."

"Hold them until I get there. I got something to tell y'all."

"A'ight. Yo. Jay, make sure everybody stays put. Nephew got something for us," he heard him yell out.

Kayson hung up and headed to the spot. When he arrived, he gave the secret knock and was let in by Butchie, the doorman. He gave him some dap and headed upstairs. Walking through the door with a serious look on his face, one his uncle had never seen on him before made him a little concerned.

Rabb was seated to the right of the table. Everyone else was seated to his left. Kayson moved his eyes across the room and when he got to J-Bone, he pulled out his gun and shot him in the middle of his forehead. Everybody jumped up and ran toward J-Bone. "What the fuck is wrong with you?" his uncle yelled out.

Kayson looked at him then pulled out the envelope of money and threw it on the table.

"What the fuck is this?" Rabb yelled as everyone else was stunned at what had just happened.

"Bounty," Kayson spat.

"What the fuck are you talking about? How the fuck do you know that?"

"I just so happened to overhear the plan and watched the exchange. But don't worry; I took care of all that."

"Why didn't you call me or let me in on what the fuck was going on?" Rabb was getting agitated because, his best friend was over there leaking.

"Look, we can exchange why's all night. However, if I didn't put a hole in those niggas, I'd be digging one for you. Send somebody over to Rosedale Projects to take over their block. Them niggas is shell shocked right now. We need to move on this shit quick." He turned to walk away, pausing to say, "Unc, meet me at our spot in three hours. We need to restructure."

"Where the fuck are you going?"

Kayson turned around and smiled. "To get some pussy. Killing them muthafuckas made my dick hard." Then he went down the stairs and out the door.

Kareem went over to Rabb and asked, "Who the fuck do he think he is?"

"The boss," his uncle said with pride all over his face. "Take a couple of dudes and head out to Rosedale Projects. The rest of y'all get rid of this nigga. Watch y'all back. I'll get at y'all later."

That day defined who Kayson is and was going to be, "The Boss".

Chapter 9
The Meeting

It was the middle of summer and the block was bumping with cars playing the latest hot shit. The corners were full of runners hustling around trying to make their daily quota. In the front of the local corner store, several niggas were hitting some dice and others were smoking blunts and talking shit. Coming down the street was an all white on white Navigator. When it pulled up, one would have thought Moses had parted the Red Sea. Niggas started getting on point like their life depended on it. It was Kayson, 'The Boss' as they called him.

Wise kicked Aldeen. "What the fuck, man?" Aldeen turned and saw Kayson parking and stood up and made everybody get back to work. Kayson didn't come down unless it was all business. He had put in enough work that his presence wasn't needed, and if he had to come out, a muthafucka was definitely in trouble. He didn't use any phone for anything; he just showed the fuck up whenever necessary.

This day, he was trying to find out why the name KoKo was ringing in the streets like she was the next big thing. Kayson stepped out of the car looking like GQ was doing a photo shoot on Lenox Avenue. He had on a white linen Armani Exchange suit, with a three quarter sleeve shirt. The length allowed him to show off his platinum watch on one arm and a platinum and diamond barrel bracelet on the other. The one ring he wore on his pinky was platinum with black diamonds. On his feet, he wore Mauri gators. When he stepped out of the car, his 6'3" frame moved like he came with theme music. That muthafucka was suave as hell and now being twenty-four, he had really grown into his manhood. His mocha skin was smooth and even. He didn't have to speak much because those hazel eyes would stare fire into a man's soul. As he approached the corner, he was checking out the surroundings making sure shit was running like it was supposed to. He walked right up on Aldeen.

"Muthafuckas must be rich already, huh?" He was referring to the dice game he saw going on.

"Nah, Boss, just trying to pass a little time," Aldeen answered in his lazy 'I'm high as hell voice.'

"That wasn't a fucking question," Kayson spat back, giving him that death stare. Aldeen was crazy as hell, but he didn't fuck with Kayson because that nigga was two kinds of crazy. Aldeen gave everybody a look as if to say get to work. Just then, KoKo came out the building and stood on the corner adjacent to them. She was sporting a pair of loose fitting jeans, T-shirt, tan Timberland's, and a vest. She wore her hair in a ponytail and had a harder bop to her walk than the niggas in the crew. KoKo was now seventeen. Over the last couple years working with Wise and Aldeen, she had become a beast and because of her fearless attitude and natural mind for business, they had her in charge of several areas in Brooklyn and the Bronx. She stopped at the gate and looked around. She had never met Kayson, so she didn't know why all of a sudden the atmosphere had changed.

"Yo, are y'all muthafuckas working or what? I ain't running a gotdamn babysitting service. Do some shit or get the fuck off the block."

Niggas got busy doing whatever their job was. People

were coming up whispering in her ear trying to let her know the daily count and that Kayson was present. She looked up and spat on the ground and headed toward Kayson and Aldeen.

"Who the fuck is that?" Kayson said to Aldeen.

"That's KoKo," Aldeen said with a smile. He was interested in what Kayson was going to do next.

"We got a fucking dyke out here running shit?"

KoKo could hear him, so she answered the question. "I eat a lot of things, but pussy ain't one of them." Aldeen busted out laughing because he knew that shit was getting ready to get real interesting.

"Is that right?" Kayson responded.

"Does a bear shit in the woods?" She put her hand out then said, "I'm KoKo."

Kayson put his hand out to make the introduction. "Well, I'm Kayson, the Boss." Neither one of them blinked.

Then KoKo said, "Oh, that's what they call you?"

"They? What you mean by 'they?'" Kayson quickly responded.

"I'm just saying. The way I see it, we work in goods and services. You provide the goods. We provide the service. If you didn't have us, you would be out here yo' damn self-hoofing and sweating. So my motto is, Fair exchange ain't no robbery."

Kayson looked at Aldeen. Aldeen shrugged. "So wait a minute, if I ain't the Boss then who the fuck am I?"

"You are going to have to do some soul searching or some shit for that one."

Kayson had to laugh. He could not believe that here he was going back and forth with a bitch, and she worked for him. What the fuck is going on? He couldn't get mad because she was a *female version of him* just like Aldeen had said. All he could see was that with a little training, he had a fucking pit bull on his hands. Kayson didn't know what to say next. But whatever it was would have to wait because what happened next definitely let him know that this little bitch with the mouth was going to be his number one.

As Kayson stood there trying to see what his next move should be, he saw a guy with a crazy look in his eyes approaching. KoKo had the nigga pegged from the corner. It was Ike and he was always trouble. The frown mark on her forehead was deep and her eyebrows rose. Kayson was wondering why her attention was now totally diverted. Then he realized that this nigga must be a problem. He positioned his hand behind him where he kept his nine, but this day, he wouldn't need it.

"Yo, what the fuck is up? I told you what I needed and when I needed it, and you just fucking a nigga around," the guy approaching yelled out.

Kayson was getting ready to say something, but Aldeen touched his arm as if to say, "Watch this."

"Don't even worry. She got it," he whispered.

"Muthafucka, I told you that my office hours are from six to nine. It's 4:30. I don't talk to you muthafuckas a minute before," KoKo growled at him. This was KoKo's favorite line from The Five Heartbeats, she had adapted to her program, and when it was violated, a nigga was in trouble.

"Bitch. What the fuck you think this is? Your office hours! Get the fuck outta here with that bullshit."

"You see a bitch, you slap a bitch." KoKo spit on his brand new sneakers. And looked at him like *nigga what?*

Ike moved under his shirt as if he was going to grab for a burner. In one swift movement, KoKo stepped in front of Kayson, pulled out her nine, and shoved it into Ike's mouth. At the same time, she grabbed him in his collar and swept his feet from under him, knocking him to the ground.

She kneeled over him. "Now, as I said muthafucka. I

don't talk business until six o'clock. Now, what's stopping me from blowing your muthafuckin' head off?"

"Nu . . . tttthing," Ike tried to get out as blood ran down the sides of his mouth." He was scared as hell. That nigga had his hands up in surrender, sweating, eyes popping all out his head.

"You muthafuckin' right."

Boom!

KoKo blew Ike's brains out all over the sidewalk. Looking over at her goons, she gave the nod and they got Ike out of there in thirty seconds flat. Two dudes picked him up as a van pulled up to the curb. They put him inside and then replaced her gun with another one and were gone. People looked on in fear. She kept two cleaning dudes nearby for shit like this. They came pouring solution and spraying water, cleaning the area within minutes. It was like nothing had ever happened. KoKo put her gun in place, looked at Kayson and said, "Now, you were saying something about being my boss."

Kayson was impressed, but had to say something about that dangerous move she just pulled with him out there. He looked her in the eyes.

"Don't ever pull no shit like that again with me out here," he said.

"Well, you better let me know when you coming. 'Cause around these parts, I'm the Boss. Anything else? I got a business to run. You're holding me up."

Kayson had a confused look on his face. Didn't she know who the fuck he was? He made a note just then that he was going to make her submit. *I'm holding her up. Yeah, all right, first chance I get I'm gonna hold them legs up on my shoulders and fuck the shit outta her.*

"That's all for now." Kayson looked over at his right hand man, Aldeen. "Bring her to me later."

"No problem, Boss." He turned to KoKo and said, "Be ready when they come to get you."

She smiled at him and said, "As long as it's not between the hours of 6 and 9."

Kayson chuckled, shook his head, and walked toward his car. He figured that he had been in the hood one minute too long.

Aldeen walked over to KoKo. "You gotta calm your ass down, yo."

"You might be right. But today. Ain't the fucking day." KoKo spat on the ground and walked off.

"Yo, I'll pick you up at 9:30," Aldeen yelled out.

KoKo put the peace sign high in the air and said, "Indeed," and kept on walking.

Wise came over to Aldeen and said, "That was some crazy shit."

"Hell yeah, that bitch is fearless," Aldeen said, thinking about what Kayson was going to do. "She's what Kayson needs to handle these next missions."

"What do you think Kayson is going to do when he get her up to the house?" Wise asked.

Aldeen smiled then answered, "Nothing today, but if I know my nigga like I think I do, he's going to make her call him the boss."

Later that evening...

It was 11 P.M. Aldeen, Wise, Baseem, and KoKo were just arriving at Kayson's mansion. He lived outside the city in the 'burbs. The gate opened and they drove up to the house. When they got within twenty-five feet, the garage opened up and it led to an underground parking area.

KoKo was impressed. It was some straight up Godfather shit. They exited the vehicles and headed for an elevator right by the parking spot. All the way up, everyone was quiet as

hell. KoKo was starting to wonder what type of visit this was going to be.

When they got to the second floor, the doors opened, but no one got out. Baseem put his arm in front of the doors so they wouldn't close and said, "Take a left and go straight. Have a seat. He will be right with you."

KoKo looked at them. "Where the fuck y'all niggas going?"

Aldeen smiled. "Sheeeeit. He wanted to see you. We about to go chill. Catch your happy trigger-finger ass later." Wise cracked up.

"Fuck y'all. You know how I get down," KoKo stated.

Baseem looked at her with that evil ass sneer. He was the type of nigga that never smiled for shit. "Get your ass out the way. I'm about to go downstairs and get my dick sucked. You cock blocking. Now take your I-don't-give-a-fuck ass down the hall and sit the fuck down," he said, giving her a little shove.

"Yeah, all right, the last muthafucka who shoved me can't wear hats." She heard laughter ring out as the elevator doors shut, and then KoKo walked down the hall. It was dark and quiet as hell. *Is this a set up? Shit, this nigga better come correct or it's on. I ain't going out like no sucker.* She sat on the couch admiring the artwork and sculptures that were all around. The aroma of leather and air freshener filled the air. She was sitting there for about thirty minutes when Kayson came out from fucking nowhere.

"Damn, I almost busted a cap in your ass. You can't just sneak up on a bitch."

"You talk a lot of shit for such a little person," Kayson said smoothly.

"Size doesn't mean shit," KoKo continued the exchange.

"We'll see about that," Kayson said with a wicked grin on his face. He already knew that he had to calm that ass down

73

and knew just how he was going to do it. What KoKo didn't know was he had been watching her get big for the last two years. He stood back and let her do what she had to do, and she had become one of his best workers. Up to this point, he never felt the need to make himself known to her, but he needed a female for his next task and the bitch had to be fearless. He also knew that she didn't have a boyfriend and that the last time she had sex was two years ago. He had made that dyke comment earlier just to see where her head was. She was too rough around the edges and he would have to get her to act like a fucking lady in order to pull this heist off without error. So he knew she needed some serious dick control.

"What you drinking?"

"I don't drink. But if you got some sticky you can twist me up something nice."

"Nah. We don't smoke up here." Kayson was real smooth. She didn't know how to receive him. He walked up to her and stood over her. "You know you owe me, right?" he said.

"What the fuck do I owe you?"

"You took out a worker of mine without permission."

"Sheeeitttt. I did you a favor. That muthafucka was weak and always crying like a bitch. He was a liability; we are only after the assets."

Kayson was even more impressed. "I got some shit I need to take care of. You are the only one that I can use."

"No problem. Give me the nigga's name, address, and social and I'll call you when it's done." She stood up to leave. Kayson grabbed her by the arm and made her stay there. Kayson gave her a dirty look that said, all right now; I let you have an inch. Don't take a fucking mile. KoKo was a fool, but she wasn't a damn fool. So she stood right there. Kayson backed her up against the wall hard and pinned her there staring into her eyes with severe intensity. He turned her around and put both her hands on the wall. Then he got all up on her ass and spread her legs with his foot like she was under arrest. "They didn't search you before you came up here?" he whispered.

KoKo was thrown totally off her square. "No, but I guess you're going to take on that post." KoKo was still trying to be tough.

Kayson slid his hands slowly down her arms. He got to her breasts and then whispered, "Keep your hands up."

She could feel his dick getting hard; it had to be half way down his leg. Kayson continued his search, rubbing under her breasts then down her stomach. She twitched with every touch. Kayson smiled, enjoying every moment. He went down and put his hands in the crease of her legs, moving slowly down her calf. When he got to her ankle, he went to the other ankle, moving up calculatingly, making sure this time to get a feel of that pussy as he reached the top of her leg.

KoKo breathed in and out. All Kayson could think was, I am going to tear this ass up when I get a chance. When he got to the top of the other leg, he stood up placing the dick right back where he had it. Then he whispered, "Why you all jumpy, tough guy?"

"Did you find what you were looking for?" KoKo responded.

"Sure did," Kayson said with his warm, soft lips positioned at the back of her ear.

"Well, why the fuck am I still armed with my hands in the air? And why is that on my ass?"

"Oh, him? That's the enforcer. He is in charge of the next mission."

"Is that right?" KoKo tried to mock Kayson's favorite saying.

Kayson was all up on her, checking her out from head to toe and mapping out every position he was going to have her in.

"This shit ain't going to be that easy. We have some planning to do and you have to act like a fucking lady."

"What does your dick have to do with me acting like a lady?" KoKo said, her voice dripping with sarcasm.

That was the last straw. With one quick move, Kayson snatched the .45 from the small of her back, threw it on the couch, then grabbed her by her throat and bit hard into her neck and sucked. Easing his free hand down the front of her pants he whispered, "Keep your hands up."

"What the fuck?" Koko said softly. However, in the back of her mind she was thinking about the rumors she had heard about Kayson's dick being hypnotic. And shit, she wasn't trying to be the bitch on the bench. She was getting ready to be all in his little game.

Kayson slowly but firmly circled his finger on her clit. She was getting ready to put her hands down to stop him.

"Keep them where they are," he commanded.

She was feeling things she had never felt before. "Sssssss . . . damn, you trying to break a bitch. What part of the game is this?" she asked barely able to talk.

"I'm giving you some of this act-right," Kayson answered.

"Mmmmmm," KoKo moaned again.

Kayson had total control just the way he liked it. Then he began his tutoring session. He was instructing her on what he needed from her. She could barely pay attention as her orgasm came on. Kayson moved a little faster. The orgasmic waves were more than she could handle.

"Kaaaayyysooon . . ." rang out in her head, but she wouldn't allow it to leave her lips.

When he realized he had that ass, he didn't say a word,

just kept on handling his business. KoKo came so long and hard, she damn near passed out. She dropped her hands to her sides. Kayson pulled his hand out real slow, turned her around and looked in her eyes. "I'm the fucking boss and don't get it confused again," he said.

KoKo was too spent to say anything. She could not believe what the fuck had just happened. Kayson kissed her lips then said, "Go to the bathroom and clean up. The boys will be up here in a minute." He pointed her in the direction of the bathroom.

She walked away. Mentally, her head was all fucked up. "What the fuck was that?" she mumbled.

When she got to the bathroom, she looked around and found a linen closet. She grabbed a washcloth and went to the sink. As she looked in the mirror, all she saw was pleasure on her face. And a big ass passion mark on her neck. *Oh my god! How the hell am I going to explain this shit?* She washed up and headed back to where she had left Kayson.

Aldeen and Baseem's voices got louder. She did not want to face them. *Shit, I can't stand in the fucking hall forever.* She did the good old walk of shame with her head bowed down and everything. When she reached them, everybody looked at her like she had just stolen cookies from the cookie jar.

Kayson was giving everybody their instructions. Aldeen looked at her and shook his head. For the first time, she didn't have shit to say. Aldeen could see that big ass hickey on her neck and he knew that Kayson had started his process. He never gave a bitch the dick quick. He always made her beg for it. The hickey was a sign of phase one. *Send a bitch home wet and tingling; make her respect your gangsta.*

"I need you to tie shit up on the streets. Let Wise and Aldeen take over for a few weeks so I can train you. I have to have you right here so I can get you ready. I need you to keep your fucking cool. Don't get into shit. Don't make me repeat myself." He gave his final order to KoKo not even blinking.

KoKo couldn't let the guys think she had gotten soft. She went up to Kayson and looked him up and down. "Keep the change. Pretty muthafucka," she said then continued on her way past the crew. She yelled out, "Let's roll niggas. Time is money."

Kayson smiled. "I was planning on it," he yelled as he watched her exit the office with Aldeen and Wise and Baseem were right behind her smiling and shaking their heads. For the next couple of weeks, Kayson would send for her. He hadn't made another move yet. He would just talk slick, get up on her, and get her pussy wet, but he didn't touch her. KoKo was wondering what this cat and mouse shit was that he was playing. However, KoKo was feenin' for the streets. She had decided that she was not coming to his house tonight; she was going to grind.

Chapter 10
Wise

Wise walked into the house prepared to lay down before KoKo came to pick him up. He had just spent seventy-two hours doing surveillance and planning to move on their next targets. He was tired as shit, but he had no such luck. Vanessa was waiting for him and with major attitude.

"You know what? You're going to make me kill one of these bitches, I swear to god," she yelled as she walked from the bedroom to the living room where he was standing.

"Come on, I ain't got time for no bullshit," he said, heading to the loveseat and grabbing the remote. He turned on the TV and sat back.

"Nah, fuck that. We got some shit to talk about," she said, walking over to the plug and yanking it from the wall.

"What the fuck is wrong with you?" Wise jumped up and headed in her direction.

"What? Why you getting up with all that attitude? You don't treat them bitches in the street with all this attitude." Vanessa held the cord behind her back.

"What bitches? Why you always got drama when I get home?" He tried to reach behind her back.

"You know what the fuck I'm talking about. I saw your black ass last night leaving the club with that bitch with the red Jag."

"Come on, stop playing. You know that was business."

"Yeah, it's always business when y'all want to stick your dick in some bitch, but if you catch my black ass out, you want to throw a fucking fit." She pushed him back.

"Put your hands on me again. It's going to be some slow singing and flower bringing," he quoted Biggie and started laughing.

"Fuck you. I'm tired of this shit, Wise." She threw the cord on the floor and headed to the room. Wise picked up the cord and plugged it back in and then headed to the bedroom.

"Look, you ain't got shit to worry about. I handles mine."

"That's what all cheating ass niggas say, then they give you some AIDS or some shit."

"You stupid," Wise said, laughing again, which always pissed her off.

"This is not a joking matter. Everybody in your little world gets respect but me. You shit on me constantly."

Wise stood there smiling. "Believe what you want to believe. I got to get me some rest." He walked out the room heading back to the living room. Vanessa came charging at him, he turned around quickly, and she was now face to face with an angry man. "I told your ass to chill the fuck out. Keep it up and I'ma knock you the fuck out." Vanessa stood there huffing and puffing, tears now coming from her eyes. Wise kept his eyes on her. "I thought so." Then he turned around and walked to his chair.

"I fucking hate you!" she yelled as he walked away. "One of these days, you're going to come home from one of your fuck fests and a bitch is gonna be ghost."

Wise started to respond but the bell rung. He knew it was KoKo. He went to open the door and the look on KoKo's face said it all.

"What the fuck is all that yelling coming from up in

80

here?" she said as she moved past Wise.

"That's your girl acting like a fucking mad woman," he answered as he closed the door.

"What 'sup with that?" she turned her questions to Vanessa.

"Not now, KoKo, this is between me and Wise." Vanessa moved toward the kitchen.

"Bitch, the way you fucking hollering up in here it's between you, Wise, and the whole fucking neighborhood." KoKo spat as the crease in the middle of her forehead deepened.

Vanessa tried to straighten the shit out real quick because she knew KoKo was crazy and she didn't play when it came to Wise. "No disrespect, KoKo, but your brother is living foul."

KoKo looked at Wise then back at Vanessa. "Oh, so you on that bullshit again?"

"Yeah, she stay on that bullshit," Wise said, walking to the bedroom to grab his shit. He realized a nap was not going to be possible.

"What you fussing about? That other bitch again?"

"I don't see how y'all act like that shit is supposed to be normal." Vanessa shot back.

KoKo had this conversation with her before, and the last time she had one of her little blowups she almost blew Wise's cover. "Bitch, play your fucking position. You know what this is. You wifey. Can't nothing change that. That other bitch is for business." KoKo mean mugged her. "Check this, you up in here. You don't have to worry about shit but looking pretty, keeping his house peaceful and fucking this nigga good when he come home. Now you can either continue in the role you are currently in or get the fuck on the block and help him make that money."

Vanessa looked at KoKo as she tried to process the

ultimatum she was just given by her husband's partner in crime. "I know my role, KoKo," she said in a calm voice.

"Well then act like it, because your ass is definitely replaceable. Shit. I was taking applications last night," she said then laughed. "Let's go, nigga. I ain't got time to play Dr. Phil up in this muthafucka. I'm outside." KoKo headed to the door as she mumbled under her breath, "stupid bitches."

Vanessa stood in the kitchen with her arms folded and steam coming out her ears. She hated when Wise let KoKo get in their shit. But she had to admit, she was right; Wise took care of everything and the only time she found out about shit was when she went looking for it. Wise came from the bedroom carrying an overnight bag.

"I'll be back in a couple of days," he said then passed her a fat knot of money. "Behave yourself." He smiled then leaned in to kiss her lips. Vanessa reluctantly puckered up and returned the kiss.

"That's it?" she said with sarcasm in her voice.

Wise grabbed his dick and said, "Well, you could have been laid out, but you wanted to fight instead of fuck. So I'll see you in a couple." He slammed the door on his way out. Vanessa threw the money up against the door then watched it rain all over the floor. She plopped down on the couch, put her face in her hands, and cried. At that moment, she realized she wasn't married to him; she was married to the whole fucking organization. She wanted a normal life; she wanted Wise out and vowed to start planning on just that.

Back to the Block

KoKo was on the block sitting with Baseem in his BMW. They were strategizing and watching how sexy the block looked when niggas were moving product and taking care of business.

"You see those two niggas over there?" He pointed at two young boys that were so-called running shit.

"Yeah. What's the M.O.?" she replied.

"They getting big. Got mad heart and they move smart."

"Anything else?"

"Nothing besides Stokes been talking about he is the next come up. Little nigga a little bigheaded. I think with you being off the streets for the last couple weeks, he getting tough." Baseem got silent. KoKo let him revel in his last statement.

"Yeah? Well, riddle me this, my nigga. Why didn't you tell me he said fuck Koko and he don't know why they got a bitch running things?"

Baseem looked confused. *How the fuck she know that?* While he tried to recover from her last statement, she looked up and saw Al-Java walking up the street. Her blood started to boil. "When I ask you what the fuck is going on, don't put shade on the shit. Give me the whole fucking story," she said as she got out the car.

Baseem was thrown back because she didn't usually talk to him like that, but she didn't play with the reports. She needed her eyes and ears to serve their fucking purpose. Without even thinking, she jumped out the car, ran up to him, and pulled out The Midnight, her gun she used after hours. She busted him right in the head. Java was so caught off guard. He fell to the ground.

"What the fuck, Kok?" She stood over him pointing the gun right in his face.

"Why the fuck you think your punk ass need a raise? I should raise my foot up your ass."

"Hold up, Kok. I was just saying; I been out here on the grind." He was so shook up, plus, he saw Baseem and Darren approaching.

"You ain't on no muthafuckin' grind, nigga." She ran

through his pockets and came up with five hundred dollars. "What the fuck is this bullshit?" Her nostrils flared and her mouth twisted. "You been out here all day and all you got is five hundred funky ass dollars?" She smacked the shit out of him with the gun and then ran his day down to him.

"Your dumb ass got up at around 12 P.M., climbed up in Tanisha's funky ass pussy, rode that for about forty-five minutes. Gotdamn shame. Played Nintendo, showered, got dressed, ate, and didn't hit the block until 4 P.M. Grind, nigga? I'll show you a fucking grind." She busted him in the head again.

"Ahhhh . . . a'ight, Kok. A'ight." Blood poured from four different places on Al-Java's head and face.

"Don't you ever think because you don't see me that I don't know what the fuck is going on. Punk muthafucka!" She kicked him in the mouth and his two front teeth flew out with a stream of blood. Al-Java hollered out in pain. She took the money and threw it at him. "Take this and get your shit fixed and your ass is on vacation. I better not see or hear about you being on the streets. Do I make myself clear?"

He could hardly answer. "A'ight, Kok."

"Get his five dollar ass outta here before I make change." KoKo took the opportunity to spit a line from her favorite movie New Jack City.

Darren signaled to the death squad. "Take him to the emergency room and tell them he got jumped at a party." They picked him up and got him into a nearby van.

KoKo, Baseem, and Darren headed across the street. When they got out of earshot she said, "Get rid of him."

Darren said, "Already on it."

She spotted Wise and Aldeen standing next to a Benz. "Oh shit," KoKo mumbled under her breath. Once she got up on them, Aldeen definitely looked disappointed. He had heard what she was told— Kayson needed her to calm down, which he made perfectly clear.

"Scared workers create disloyalty."

"They are loyal because they fear me."

"Let's go. The Boss wants to see you."

"Why is everybody all serious looking and shit? Y'all need to lighten the fuck up," KoKo said as she opened the car door.

"Just get your hardheaded ass in the car. You are a fucking rebel without a cause. You know good and gotdamn well Kayson don't want you out here smacking niggas around."

"Shit, he ain't my fucking daddy. I thought we cleared that shit up already," she said as she shut the door behind her.

Aldeen looked at her like she was crazy. She slid down in the seat, lit up a blunt, and zoned out. KoKo was tired of all this back and forth shit; she was about the streets. She loved everything about it, the smell, the sounds, and the action. All this other shit about calming down and being a lady, she wasn't about it. She had planned to let Kayson know when she got there that she was flattered that he wanted to work close with her, but maybe he could find someone else. *Plus, that shit he pulled a couple weeks ago fucked my shit up. I'm all catching feelings and shit. Man, I ain't beat.*

During the ride, KoKo was quietly thinking. As they pulled into the garage, her heart started beating faster. She was rehearsing what she was going to say. When they got off the elevator, Kayson stood there shirtless, eight-pack bumping and looking sexy as hell. The fresh haircut and the sweat pants showing off that dick print totally threw her off her game. "Damn," she murmured.

He picked up a towel off the chair and wiped his face. It appeared that he just finished working out.

"What's up, Boss?" Aldeen broke the silence.

"I can't complain. You got any reports?"

Al gave him the look. That let him know that a private conversation would be needed.

"Y'all go chill. I'll get with you in a minute." With that, everybody headed down the hall, except Aldeen.

"I have something I want to talk to you about, Kayson." KoKo was reluctant to give her little speech.

"Yeah? I was going to talk to you, too. I need you to spend the night. Go get the streets off you and we'll talk then. I put a towel, washcloth, and some shit for you to put on when you come out of my bathroom. Get on the elevator and go upstairs. I'll see you in minute." He looked at KoKo as if to say, "Just move, none of this shit is up for discussion." With that, she moved out.

She waited for the elevator. *What the fuck just happened? I was supposed to be on my way back to the Benz and back to the streets. How the fuck did I get sent to the gotdamn shower? I got to put an end to this bullshit.*

Getting off the elevator, all she saw was money. He had his bedroom hooked up. Everything was black. The bed looked like four king-sized beds put together, but it was circular. The headboard was leather with a tinted mirror that went all the way across. Wall-to-wall carpet and floor-to-ceiling drapes. "Daaamn." Mirrors were everywhere. Tall plants sat in every corner. Vases and shit rested all on the dresser. Two lounge chairs and a coffee table decorated a sitting area with a small wet bar. In front of it was the biggest couch she'd ever seen. Across from that, a large black and gray marble fireplace went all around the wall. It was lit and kindling. She guessed he needed all this big shit to go with that big ass dick he had. KoKo looked around to see which door led to the bathroom. First, she walked into the huge walk-in closet.

On one side, he had all suits and dress shirts hanging. It

must have been at least two or three thousand. In the middle of the closet were his shoes in a glass rotating shelf case, which looked like it held four hundred pairs. On the other side were street clothes, jeans, and sweatshirts. Another shoe case had all sneakers and boots; everything looked new. In the corner was a tie rack with about two hundred ties on it. In the center of the room was an island with drawers, they were see thru as well and contained all kinds of jewelry in them. *What the fuck is he into?* She left out impressed as hell.

KoKo finally reached the bathroom. It blew her mind. *This shower is big as hell, a walk-in the size of a fucking bedroom!* The decor was black and burgundy marble and glass. Ten showerheads came from different parts of the walls and ceiling. There was a little bench with a cushion. Across from the shower was a large in-floor tub that looked like a small pool with a headrest pillow that read 'The Boss.' "Well, damn," she said. KoKo undressed and folded her clothes up and put them on the chair. She picked up the body sponge and little shower bucket containing body wash, shampoo, a douche and a razor. "What the fuck is he trying to say? Whatever!" She walked into the shower to begin the process and the water automatically came on forceful and warm.

"I could get used to shit like this. He's trying to spoil a bitch," she said, and began shaving her under arms, legs, and panty line. She douched and sat the empty bottle in the bucket. She washed her body, pouring Victoria's Secret pear body wash on the sponge lathering her whole body. The steam and the aroma had her feeling relaxed. She was in heaven. KoKo turned on the built-in wall unit music system and dimmed the lights. "Sheeiit. A bitch ain't ever going home now!" she said.

While KoKo was in the shower, Aldeen was down there giving Kayson the low. "Yo, you got to speed up the process. KoKo is crazy. She beat the hell out of Al-Java. We got to put his ass to sleep."

"Is that right?" Kayson was quiet for about a minute. He had just planned to tease her again, but he could see she needed the full treatment. "A'ight. Don't worry, I'm about to handle it. Is there anything else?"

"Yeah, one last thing; she loves the streets too much. You have to show her how all this shit is to her benefit. She is a straight up beast out there; she can't live without it. If she don't calm down, somebody is going to kill her."

"She will be a different person in the morning. Trust me. The enforcer got some shit for that ass tonight."

All Aldeen could do was laugh. He knew that once Kayson put that shit on her, she would be seeing shit his way. "I'll see you tomorrow afternoon. Trust me; she'll be straight by then. I'm going to knock that ass out."

Chapter 11
Hard Head Makes a Soft Behind

Meanwhile, KoKo didn't even see or feel Kayson when he entered the bathroom. He watched her perfect petite 5' 6" frame as the water rained all over her body. She put her hands on the wall and let the water run down her back. It slowly ran between the crack of her ass. She turned around, grabbed the shampoo, and washed her hair. Kayson admired her perky erect breasts staring back at him. Her cocoa brown skin was flawless. The bubbles from shampooing her hair ran between her breasts, continuing across her pussy and down her legs.

"Damn, all that was under them baggy jeans?" Kayson stood there stroking his dick. He wanted to make sure 'The Enforcer' was wide-awake once he stepped foot in the shower. He knew once she saw it, that would start his reign of terror. Kayson entered the shower then walked right up on her. She opened her eyes, shocked that he was right there.

"I'm almost done. I will be right out of your way," KoKo stated, trying to get the last of the soap off her body.

"You ain't going nowhere."

KoKo looked down and said, "Damn!"

Kayson smiled. "What's up?"

"Your dick."

"Don't worry about him, he's harmless," he said, moving toward her.

"Shit, I can't tell. He looks like he is more than harmless."

Kayson ignored her, quickly changing the subject. "Why don't you do what I tell you to do?"

"Look, that was what I wanted to talk to you about." She ran her hands over her face. Kayson's eyes roamed all over her body. She put her hand under his chin and brought his eyes back to hers.

"I'm listening. Go on," he said, continuing to stare at her body like she was his next meal.

"As I was saying." She wanted to finish the sentence, but was caught off guard.

Kayson put his strong arm around her back, placed his mouth on one of her nipples, and began to suck gently.

KoKo released a small sound from her lips. The water rained down on them as he gave her chills all over her body. R. Kelly's "Honey Love" blasted from the shower radio.

"There's something in your eyes, baby, its telling me you want me baby, tonight is your night,"

He stopped briefly and said, "And you were saying . . ."

KoKo couldn't get her thoughts together. "I was trying to tell you tha—"

Kayson zoomed in to give the other breast the same treatment. This time, he grabbed her leg and placed it up to his waist so he could slide his dick back and forth starting at her clit and taking it all the way back. "Continue," Kayson said.

How the fuck can I say anything with him doing all this to me? KoKo thought.

Kayson kissed her lips then her shoulders, and back to her breasts. He put her up against the wall and grabbed the other leg so that she was now up in the air and he had full control. Kissing her passionately and roughly at the same time, giving her some of that thug love. He turned and walked her over to the shower bench. "Stand on here," he commanded.

She did just that. Standing there with her hands on his shoulders not knowing where he was going to take it next. Kayson took some time to stare at her naked body and her perfectly shaved pussy staring right in his face. In one move, he put his arms under her legs lifting her up and placing one leg on each one of his shoulders, positioning her pussy right in his face. He took another minute to gaze at it. The lips were pretty and glistening and her clit was calling him, so a nigga had to answer.

"Is there anything else you want to tell me because you're going to be speechless for a while?" He didn't wait for a response; he was now sucking on her clit just right sending electrical shocks up her spine. Putting his hands on the small of her back, he moved over a little to position her right under the showerhead as he began giving her that diesel tongue.

"Aaaaaahhhh . . ." She arched her back and put her head against the wall. He grabbed her hips then stiffened his long tongue and slid it in and out her pussy like a dick.

"Oh my god! What the fuck?" She didn't know what to do with herself.

Kayson knew that he had that ass. She was riding the wave. He went back to sucking her clit hard and shaking his head back and forth. KoKo was now screaming. She had never had an orgasm like this before and he could tell because she couldn't handle it. He thought she was going to break his neck. But he knew that he could not let up. He had to tame that wild horse and with his mission in sight, he was doing just that.

KoKo begged him to stop. "Wait! Wait! I have to go to the bathroom. I need to get down."

Kayson paused to say, "No you don't. That's daddy making you feel good; let that shit go." With that, he went faster and sucked harder, squeezing her butt to keep her in place. She trembled and screamed. "Kaaaaaaaaay.

Kaaaaaaaay."

Reaching up, grabbing the showerhead with both hands, and fully arching her back, she came all over his mouth. Kayson nibbled on her inner thigh then looked up. Water ran down between her breasts and into his face. Kayson was pleased with his handiwork. He pulled her down and stood her up. Her body quivered in front of him as she stared at him with that 'fuck me' gaze. He rinsed his mouth out and said, "Why you so quiet? I thought you had something to tell me."

KoKo couldn't maintain eye contact. She didn't know whether she was coming or going. It didn't matter much to Kayson what she had to say because he was serious as hell and moving to the next step of his plan. He picked her up and headed to the bathroom counter placing her down effortlessly. He stepped between her legs, began sucking, and licking her neck from throat to chin, then reached down to get him a handful of pussy.

"All of this belongs to 'The Boss' now." He took his middle finger and inserted it deep inside, she moaned out in sheer pleasure. He began to pick up the pace; making sure to go in deep with every entrance until her juices flowed plentifully. He then slid his hand out, grabbed his dick, rubbing KoKo's juices all over it. Biting hard into her neck, he inserted his dick inside her. Knowing that his dick was big as hell Kayson used the biting to create a diversion and it worked, because she barely flinched. Plus, Kayson understood that if he got that kitty purring first, she would take that dick like a champ.

Damn, she feels good as shit, Kayson thought. Her pussy was tight as hell and he wanted to enjoy it, but he would have to wait until his work was done.

KoKo squeezed him tight around the neck; he was deep inside and hitting shit, she didn't know she had. So she tried to move back a little, but couldn't get away fast enough. He blocked that attempt by holding her firmly in place by her hips.

"Why you trying to run?" Kayson teased. KoKo's response came out in moans,

"Aaaaaahhh . . . Ooooohhhh . . ."

Kayson stroked fast and deep while licking and sucking her earlobe and back down her neck. Once again he bit down on the back of her neck. She flinched and moaned aloud.

Kayson thought to himself, *Jackpot.* He had found that hot spot. Picking up speed, he sucked hard on her hot spot and fucked the shit out of her G-spot.

"I'm cumming again. Kayson . . . ooooohhhh."

He picked her up and kept the orgasm going as he began walking toward the bedroom bouncing her up and down on his dick. She was trying to climb up his chest in an effort to stop him from going in so deep, but her movements were futile. Strong as hell, he engineered every stroke. Once he got her in the bed, it was on like popcorn. Taking her from one position to the next for over two and a half hours without even letting her catch her breath. KoKo was cumming every few minutes; she was blowing Kayson's mind.

Damn, she's multi-orgasmic, too. I got to keep this pussy for myself, he thought. Kayson took a minute and pulled out of the pussy long enough to execute his final attack when he rose up on his knees. KoKo thought it was over, but she was wrong. Kayson was about to lean back in, but KoKo put her foot on his chest.

"Wait, I'm done," she whispered, barely able to open her eyes.

"Well, that's good, but I'm not." He grabbed her by the ankle, flipped her over on her stomach, and figured it was time to talk shit. "You better do what the fuck I tell you from this day forward." He slid back in the pussy going in deep and coming all the way out. He would keep it right there leaving her anticipating when he would go back in. Then he would repeat the process, going in hard and deep as he worked that pussy, not missing a stroke.

"I'm getting ready to break this pussy down. Brace yourself because 'The Boss' is getting ready to take you on a rough ride." He had her up in the bed like DMX had ole' girl in the movie *Belly*. He whispered in her ear, "You gonna do what I tell you?"

"Yesss . . . Yesss. I promise."

"Who am I?"

"Kaaayson . . . Kaaayson."

"Wrong answer." He growled then went faster.

"What's my name?"

"Aaaahhhh . . . Aaaaahhhh." She knew what he was looking for. Then she yelled out, "The Booossss . . ."

"Am I in charge?"

"Yes. Yeeee . . . ssss," she said in a submissive voice.

"I don't believe you." He picked up speed and went in deeper. She was trying to get away, but it didn't help because Kayson was all up in it.

"You're the boss . . . you're The Boss," was all she could get out when a gut-wrenching orgasm came on and wouldn't stop. It got stronger and stronger with every stroke.

"That's what I'm talking about. Give it to me, baby," he repeated. "This pussy belongs to 'The Boss!'"

She was screaming and crying. "Yes . . . Yes, it's all yours. I submit. I'm going to calm down!" she yelled right before cumming hard as hell and passing out.

Kayson said to himself, *got her*. He smiled and pulled out. Satisfied, he placed tender kisses all down her back. KoKo laid flat, arms stretched out and unable to move. Kayson rose to his knees and began stroking his dick. KoKo could sense he was planning another attack, so she whispered, pleading her case, "I can't take no more."

"You can't tell me what to do with my pussy." He slid on his magnum, flipped her back over on her back, and said in a sexy voice with a wicked smile, "It's my turn." He slid up in KoKo once again grinding nice and slow. Now that he could enjoy her, he closed his eyes and savored the ecstasy dripping from her lips. It got so good he started to moan. He figured he had better switch positions before he lost control; he flipped over so she was straddling his lap.

"No wait, Kayson," she moaned. But he didn't, he was all up in the pussy hitting it from the bottom steady.

"Mmmmm . . . shit . . . Let's go for a ride," he said as he pumped in and out watching his dick disappear in between kissing her lips. He lay back and said, "Do it to me," as he guided her waist to his pleasure.

KoKo was feeling it. She zoned out as she picked up speed when he hit that spot.

"I'm cumming again, Kayson . . . Oh my god!" she yelled out.

"Let it go, baby."

She did just that. He turned her around on his dick clockwise, still pumping without losing contact with the pussy. She was now side straddled and bouncing up and down until he was again hitting that spot and she came again. He turned her again until her back was to him. He sat up so he wouldn't lose control; he was hitting it so hard that she grabbed the sheets trying to get away. "You ain't going nowhere. I got you." Hitting that spot again, KoKo was fucked up in the head after that last one. Kayson pumped a few more times then they both came so hard, she fell forward and he fell back.

"Gotdamn!" he said, slowly rubbing his hands back and forth across her butt. He slid out of her then he pulled her up so she could lay on his chest. He looked at her as she laid on him, then they fell asleep for what seemed like an hour.

Kayson opened his eyes as he realized he had been out for a little over an hour. *That was some good pussy.* Why a nigga would let that go was beyond him, but it was all good because he knew what to do with it. He tapped her so she could get up. "We got to hit the shower."

KoKo looked at him and thought, *shit nigga, I hope you carrying me because I can't walk.* She managed to sit up and get to the edge of the bed. KoKo finally made it to her feet. *No, I didn't just fuck him. What type of relationship are we going to have now?* She thought.

Once they both got up, he changed the sheets and headed to the shower behind her. KoKo was both confused and sex drunk. She looked in the mirror and could not believe what she saw. Hickies were all over her neck, back, and breasts.

Kayson came in the bathroom with a sneaky smile on his face.

"Why you staring at yourself like you don't know your name?"

"I'm good." KoKo tried to sound a little tough.

"You sure are. Real good. I gave you that Boss dick, that's why you all confused." Then he got up behind her. She quickly turned around. "Please Kayson, don't." She was scared as hell.

"Don't what?" he asked, looking in her eyes like he wanted to eat her up.

She put her arms up to his chest. "I can't." Her pussy was throbbing. And he looked like he could go another three hours.

"Look at you, all scared and shit. Where's my solider at?" he teased.

"She's right here." She was hoping he was not going to take any more.

"Give me a kiss," he demanded, standing in front of her

with a semi hard on and his hands behind his back. She kissed him quickly.

"That ain't no kiss," he said as he raised one eyebrow.

"I don't want to wake up your friend."

"It's okay, I told him to relax for a little while. Stop being scared and give me a kiss before I turn green."

She put her hands around his neck and kissed him, sucking on his lips and then sliding him her tongue. He received her in his mouth then said, "See, I know how to be a good boy."

Yeah right, she thought. He smacked her on the ass and said, "Come wash The Boss up." He walked into the shower and she was right on his heels. Sometime later, they got out and oiled each other down. Kayson got in bed butt naked with no covers, lay on his stomach, and was sound asleep. KoKo climbed up under the covers trying to get as far away from him as possible. She didn't want him to feel her moving and start back into his attack. While laying there she thought, *Oh my god! He tried to fuck me to death.* She admired his perfect body, the muscles in his back, ass and legs. *Damn, all this is mine.* With that, she shook her head and allowed herself to doze off.

The next morning, Kayson was close up behind her. She woke up but was afraid to move and she lay there in slight fear.

"Pretending to be sleep can't stop me from getting some pussy. Whenever I want it, I will take it," he said.

"How did you know I wasn't sleep?" she asked.

"Your breathing changed and your heart rate picked up. Things like that will be very important to pay attention to in carrying out this mission. You have to pay attention to his every move."

KoKo was really starting to pay attention to everything Kayson had to teach her. She was now his humble student.

"Let's go get ready for the boys. They will be here in an hour. I don't do late." They showered again and got dressed. Kayson had bought her some more feminine clothes. She put on the dark blue Rock and Republic fitted jeans and the matching body shirt that showed off her cleavage. Her long, healthy looking hair was now wavy from the shower so she pushed it back with a headband. It flowed past her shoulders. She topped it off with the Christian Louboutin red bottom heels. She thought to herself, *how am I going to walk in these?* So she practiced a little before she came out the bathroom.

As they came down on the elevator, Kayson kissed her lips and rubbed her breasts. He slid his hands down on her ass and whispered in her ear, "I want some more of this."

"Don't get carried away; this is just business."

The elevator door opened and she quickly rushed passed him. He had to laugh. "You real tough now that security is here." She turned her head, looked over her shoulder, and winked.

Aldeen and Baseem were sitting on the couch in the office waiting for them. The first thing they both noticed was KoKo's curves. They had never seen her in anything but baggy clothes. She walked behind Kayson while he strutted like he knew he had just put in some serious work. KoKo's walk confirmed that she had got that kitty handled. It was like you could hear it purring with every step.

"Hey KoKo." Aldeen was the first to say something to her. KoKo turned her head slightly.

"What's up, Al?" she said in a relaxed tone. Her eyes were low and not from the weed smoke.

She could tell he knew exactly what had happened and was going to make sure she knew that he was up on it.

Kayson looked serious and was ready to talk business. He began to tell them about the guy they were going to hit, his name was Raul. He was Puerto Rican and he ran Queens. He had done business with Kayson some years back. Kayson told them he was taking shit off the top, but decided to let it slip for the time. He wanted him to come up so when he finally hit him, he would take everything old boy had worked for and then take his life. He needed KoKo to create the diversion and keep him busy while the crew hit all his stash spots. Then KoKo would take his life. Kayson gave everyone their job and told KoKo that her role was the most important and the most dangerous. She would have to convince him that he had to have her.

Raul was fine as hell. 6'1" and 220-pounds of all muscle. Light brown with jet-black hair and green eyes. He was the type of nigga that walked into the room and bitches would just walk up, snatch the pussy out the socket, and give it to him. Kayson had found out that he had one weakness and that was a bitch that was hard to get. He was a collector and he wanted whatever he thought he could not have. KoKo would play that role and it would cause him his fortune and then his life.

The first phase would be to get her to have a 'come fuck me' attitude and walk to match. The hair and nails, and the wardrobe would all be essential for her to play her part. Her wardrobe would have to say: This bitch got class and money and she ain't no fucking pigeon. Kayson knew he had to put her in the right place at the right time, and that nigga would bite at the bait that would prove to be poison.

"Does everybody understand what we have to do?" Everybody shook their heads. They got up to leave to start putting together the crew they would need to hit his five stash spots. "Take her to Lisa's shop to get her hair and shit done. Tell her I want it long, black, and straight. Then take her to the nail shop. Get them short with a French manicure. Then bring her back here. I still have some work to do."

KoKo looked at him like: Please, your work is done. That is all you are getting. He noticed this immediately then told his boys, "She will meet y'all downstairs. I have to tell her something." His boys got up and headed to the elevator.

Kayson got up close to KoKo. She didn't know what he was getting ready to do. *Damn, this nigga's scent is intoxicating.* He turned and then leaned up against his desk, pulling her between his legs. Looking her in the eyes he said, "Bring the Boss back his hot chocolate real soon. I have a sweet tooth."

KoKo smiled. "I was planning on going to the block tonight."

"Didn't I tell you that the block is off limits to you for a while?"

"Oh shit. You were serious about that?" she asked with a seductive smile. Kissing his lips, she pulled back and walked out his office. Kayson knew at that minute he was going to have to pull out the big guns, because Miss KoKo was not going down without a fight.

The rest of the day came and went and when night fell, KoKo was back to her usual self. She had snatched that freshly done hairdo back into her famous ponytail and put back on her street gear. She grabbed her guns to load them up and said, "How the fuck am I going to kill a nigga with these damn nails on?" She turned the gun side-to-side in her hand. "Who the fuck is going to take me seriously? He is cramping my style. Cramping my gotdamn style!" She chuckled then she moved out.

Chapter 12
Feather Fred

KoKo spent the last forty-eight hours ducking Aldeen and the crew out while at the same time closing deals and making sure niggas were doing their job. KoKo was still trying to process what happened between her and Kayson along with the feelings that were developing inside her. Not to mention, she was still conflicted about this so-called mission he was sending her on. Her motto was if a nigga was an enemy, just kill him. Why did she have to seduce him first? Feeling confused about the whole situation, KoKo did the only thing she knew to do when she needed good advice, and that was to go see her mentor, Feather Fred. Fred was a pimp that KoKo first ran for. He sold coke by day and pussy by night. KoKo would hang around him and his group of hoes, listen, and learn. She realized early that anything could be sold and made a hell of a profit if it was marketed correctly.

KoKo threw on her jeans, a t-shirt, and boots and finished it off with her fitted cap, and rolled out. When she got to the end of her block, she stood on the corner smoking a blunt and hailed a cab. She jumped in and sat back and, of course, the Arab driver started his shit.

"You can't smoke in here," he said in his thick accent.

Tossing three hundred in the money slot she said, "Shut the fuck up, Habib, and take me to Marcy." KoKo sat back and kept toking.

The driver quickly grabbed the money and said, "Open the window."

Satisfied with his reply, she smiled and let the window down a little. "All niggas is the same; money talks and bullshit runs a marathon."

Forty-five minutes later, she pulled up and threw another hundred in the hole and said, "Meet me back here in a hour and a half. Don't make me come looking for you, Abdul Khan #45923." She jumped out, pulled her cap down, checked her gun and slammed the door.

True to form, KoKo bopped up in the 'jets getting eyes from everyone in attendance. When she got to a crowd of guys guarding the entrance to the door she was heading toward, she caught eye contact with the one whom they felt was in charge. The stare down was intense. Everybody noticed the interaction and got quiet, curious about whom she was and why their head guy was looking at her like that, then the silence broke.

"Fuck you looking at?" the deep voice bellowed above the crowd.

"I don't know. That's why I'm staring trying to figure it the fuck out," KoKo shot back.

"Bitch, you must have bumped your head," D'low yelled back. The tension was now so thick you could cut it with a knife.

"Muthafucka, you must be ready to die." She reached behind her back walking closer. Niggas started to reach for their metal. Then one of his boys yelled out, "Who this bitch think she is?" As he stepped toward KoKo, D'low put his arm in front of him stopping his movement.

"Nah, let that go, I got something hot for that ass," KoKo spat.

D'low smiled. "You crazy as hell." He put his hands out

and they gave each other the coded handshake of his crew. His boys looked on in disbelief. "You almost got yourself killed," D'low said all casual.

"Shit, I was taking half these muthafuckas with me," she said then gave a half-smile. "Fred in?"

"Yeah, he's expecting you. Go on up, Lil' Will is waiting at the elevator for you."

"A'ight and train these muthafuckas while I'm gone. You know how we do. Rule number one: Shoot first and ask questions later. You were getting ready to be one man short." She looked at his boy, who had just called her a bitch--an insult to the highest order in her book. KoKo headed to the building and walked in.

D'low stood there shaking his head. He and KoKo would play like that every time he saw her. He got a kick out of this little bitch with all the mouth and ready to back it up. "Who is that bitch?" John-John was heated.

"That's KoKo," D' low said then looked at John-John. "That bitch right there is as thorough as they come."

"I don't give a fuck. She betta watch that shit. Fuck around and get fucked up," he said and spat on the ground.

"Nigga, you crazy as hell," Pete said. "That's the Boss' Crew."

"Fuck that bitch, she bleed like I do." John-John grimaced, refusing to take the low.

"We'll see, tough guy. We. Will. See," D' low stated and changed the subject.

KoKo took a quiet ride to the seventh floor, got out, and did the secret knock. A half-dressed female opened the door and waved her in then pointed to the back. KoKo went past her and headed to Fred's room. When she entered, he was sitting in his lounge chair smoking a pipe full of hash and weed, listening to some Isaac Hayes. When he looked up and saw KoKo, a huge smile came across his face.

"KoKooo," he drug her name out.

"What's good, Fred?" she said as she sat down across from him.

"It's tighter than the elastic on a fat bitch's draws." He inhaled and released the smoke from his nose.

KoKo laughed as she looked Fred over. His once muscular frame was now frail, his caramel skin had gotten dark, and his eye's lacked the glow they once had. All she could think was how he went from superstar to bum in a small period of time. Fred had made a major fuck up; he went against his own code. He fucked his main bitch without a condom one night, all high up on that acid. She gave him AIDS and he had been dying slowly ever since.

"Do give me some wisdom, oh great one," KoKo said as she sat back and pulled the other half of her blunt from the back of her ear and lit it up."The streets are saying you snuggling up with the boss, wearing fucking heels and shit. What's up with that?"

"I'm just making a few moves," KoKo said briefly to see where he would go next.

"You know what you doin?" Fred asked, inhaling and releasing smoke.

"I hope so. That's why I'm here."

Fred paused and slowly nodded his head up and down. "Well, I can say this. That nigga is loyal. When you with him you cool. Cross him, you dead. That's it. As far as love goes, I never really heard of a bitch snagging him. He did have a long relationship with this woman named Dominique, but she did some foul shit and he has been doing him ever since."

"Yeah? What happened?"

Fred smiled. "That's between you and that man."

KoKo chuckled and said, "Fair enough."

"I will tell you this. You moving into the big leagues now. Ain't no turning around. So if its power you after, that nigga got plenty. But it's going to cost you big if you fuck up."

"I got you." KoKo rose to her feet, reached in her waistband, pulled out two envelopes of money and sat it on the table. "Take care of yourself, Fred. It will be a while before you see me. If you need anything you know what to do." She turned and walked toward the door.

"You still having those nightmares?" Fred yelled out, referring to the bad dreams she would have about her mom and dad.

KoKo paused with her hand on the doorknob. Without turning around she said, "That shit will haunt me until I settle it, and trust and believe I will settle it, even if it costs me my life."

"Be careful, KoKo. I don't want to read about you. You a bad bitch, no doubt. But remember, even though a broken clock is right twice a day, the fact remains that the muthafucka don't work," Fred said, his whole mood changing.

KoKo turned to look at him. "I'ma live in the moment type bitch, so time don't mean shit unless it's time to pay me my money. Be easy." She walked out of his room, heading to the door thinking about what he had just said. She knew he was giving her a warning, and she got it loud and clear.

KoKo met Will at the elevator and rode down in silence. When the door opened, Will pulled KoKo out the way of the cameras and said, "Don't come down here no more, KoKo."

"What's up?"

"It's some niggas gunning for you, and Fred ass is too frail for a war. I'm just saying."

"Names."

"You already know."

"I got you. You need to relocate."

"KoKo, I can't afford a fall out. My wife and kids are in this building."

"I got you. Tomorrow morning leave like you always do. Meet me at the spot," she told Will not even blinking. "No looking back. No coming back."

Will shook his head and then opened the door for KoKo. "Don't be out here tonight," she said, heading for where D' low was standing.

"A'ight KoKo, same time same place," D' low said as she approached, extending his hand giving her the special shake.

KoKo returned the greeting. While looking into the eyes of John-John, she said, "I have always learned that the best business to mind is your own, and when a nigga wants to die, he always gives you a reason to kill 'im." John-John looked at her dirty. He wanted to flip; here he had a bitch standing on his turf threatening him.

D'Low laughed then said, "Go 'head, KoKo, you always talking slick."

KoKo stared at John-John, wanting to put his ass down right there, but she didn't want to mess up the business she had in progress. She heard the cab blow and broke her trance. "Find me if you need me," she said to D' low and walked off. She jumped in the cab, sat back, and put together a plan to end John-John's life.

At three o'clock in the morning, John-John was sitting in his car leaned back getting Alesha's head game. "Slow down, ma," he said and closed his eyes. The music was playing and the windows were cracked. KoKo was bent down moving along side of the back of his car. When she heard him moan, she knew he was totally distracted. She rose to her feet and put the gun to his neck. John-John was paralyzed. Alesha sat up and got out the car without saying a word. Just as he was about to grab her hand, KoKo put one in his neck. John-John grabbed his neck in an attempt to stop the blood squirting from his neck like a fountain. He struggled for air as his other hand slid over the steering wheel. KoKo watched as he choked and gasped for air. As he was taking his last breaths, she said, "You don't bleed like me, muthafucka. From what I can see, your shit is on the outside. Bitch ass nigga." Then she slid off.

KoKo and Alesha cut through the alley. Then KoKo said, "Muthafucka should have read the label."

"What's that suppose to mean?" Alesha asked.

"That shit read: Warning! Fucking with KoKo is hazardous to your health."

As Alesha turned, she put two in the back of her head. KoKo watched her body hit the ground, then she walked over to her and said, "Thanks for your help, but a dead witness is the best witness." She pulled her hoodie over her head and jogged off. *Mission accomplished.*

Chapter 13
Missing in Action

Three days had passed before the crew caught up with KoKo. She was sitting in the back of the pool hall sucking on a blunt, laughing, and talking shit with Scales. When she looked up and saw Aldeen coming, her whole mood changed. Scales noticed it immediately, got up, and headed to the bar.

"What's up?" she said.

"You know what's up. The Boss sent us for you."

"Damn. A bitch got to change her floor plan 'cause he can't be having all this access to me."

KoKo got up to walk out and Aldeen grabbed her by the arm. She looked at his hand on her arm then back up at him. "Look KoKo, we trying to take care of some important shit. Either you down or you not. We ain't got time to be playing with you. Kayson said yo' ass is the one, so man the fuck up and let's do this shit!" Aldeen said, giving her a stern look. She could see he was serious as hell, and at that moment, she decided to take shit serious as well.

"A'ight, take me to the mansion. Let me go face the music." KoKo took a few more pulls off her blunt then sat it down and walked to the door.

Again, during the whole ride she was thinking, *Why me?* Why did he have to get her caught up in his little plan and then on top of that, put some dick on her that had her pussy wet all day. *One job then I'm out. This nigga is going to have a bitch soft.* They pulled up and she was being marched to Kayson like he was the principal and she had just pulled the fire alarm. They came right up to the third floor as instructed. Kayson sat in his chair in his sitting area looking in their direction. Aldeen said, "We found our little juvenile delinquent."

"Is that right? Well, leave her with me for a minute. Then I'll send her downstairs. I want her to go with y'all to stake out that spot," Kayson said without taking his eyes off KoKo. Everybody left and headed downstairs.

"Didn't I ask you to come back here after you got done?" he said, not cracking a smile. He got up, walked to the other side of the desk, and leaned up against it. Carefully, she watched his every move.

"Sure did, but I had some shit to do," she answered.

"Come over here and let me taste those sweet lips." Reluctantly, she walked over to him and gave him a little peck on the lips.

"Don't play with me. Give me a kiss."

KoKo leaned in to kiss him. He grabbed her tight around her back and rubbed up and down her butt while looking deep in her eyes. Kissing her lips lightly, he grabbed a handful of her hair, pulled her head back, and softly kissed up her neck from the base of her throat, and then up her chin. He began kissing her deep and long, letting their tongues dance to the rhythm of their hearts.

KoKo was getting hot and breathing heavy. When she felt him rise, she wanted to move back, but he had her in a tight grip.

"They're waiting for me," KoKo said between kisses.

"I'm the boss, remember? They will wait."

"Kayson, please don't do this now," she tried to plead, but her request fell on deaf ears.

"Don't do what?" Kayson lifted her shirt, moved her bra

aside, and placed one of her nipples in his mouth and started sucking it, putting her body on fire.

"Kayson don't," she pleaded. He ignored her and kept going as he started to open her pants. She placed her hand on his and again tried to stop him. "Kayson, okay. I'll come right back the next time you tell me."

"Too late. I no longer need you to do that. See, it's like this: I need you to do what I say. When I say it. Remember?" Kayson stood and backed her up into the room. KoKo had a look in her eyes that asked *what the fuck did I just get myself into?*

"I need to introduce you to the electric chair," Kayson said with a sinister look on his face. *Oh god, that does not sound good,* she thought. When they got to the room, Kayson stripped down to his boxers, grabbed a chair from the sitting room, put it by the wall, and sat down. KoKo stood, wondering what he was planning.

"Take your clothes off." She didn't hesitate. She was learning real quick what happens when she didn't listen. KoKo started pulling her shirt over her head with attitude.

"Do it real slow," Kayson ordered. KoKo raised her shirt up inch-by-inch.

"Close your eyes. Think of how good it feels when I touch you." She closed her eyes and started to think about how good it felt when he was eating her pussy in the shower. Once the shirt was over her head, Kayson commanded, "Rub your breasts." She followed his instructions, allowing her hand to glide over her breast and down her stomach. When she got to the top of her pants, she unbuttoned them, and then slid her hand down the front of her panties and gently rubbed. Kayson licked his lips and began massaging his joint. Sliding her hand back up her stomach, she unfastened her bra, allowing those perky breasts to stand at attention.

"Walk over here. But do it slow and sexy."

KoKo tried to sashay over to him, pausing at each step for effect. When she got close, Kayson grabbed her waist and guided her the rest of the way. She placed one of her feet in the chair between his legs and he slid off her shoe and repeated the motion with her other foot.

Kayson pulled her pants all the way down and she stepped out of them. Planting soft kisses on her thighs, he used the tip of his tongue to lick around her panty line, taking time to inhale the scent of paradise. He licked her belly button then began sucking and nibbling on her stomach. "Turn around," he said. Once she was turned around, he planted kisses on each one of her ass cheeks then he pulled her panties all the way down.

"Bend over." She gave in to his every command.

"Spread your legs."

Kayson now had a perfect view of her sweetness. He held her firmly by her hips, leaned forward, and guided his tongue deep inside her. KoKo cried out. Kayson licked around the lips then began nibbling and sucking around the hole.

"Sssss . . . Aaaahhhh . . . Kayson."

Once he had her as hot as he wanted her, he used his legs to spread hers wider. Then he took out his dick and placed her right on top of it. She was now in a split position as he moved her down onto him.

He began to stroke and KoKo closed her eyes, enjoying every inch of him. Gently squeezing her nipples, he sucked her neck, zoning in on her hot spot.

Then the phone rang.

Usually, he would never answer the phone, but he knew it was Aldeen because he had told him to wait for her. He picked it up at the same moment KoKo had started to cum.

"What's up?"

"Do you still want us to wait on KoKo or roll out?" Aldeen didn't even need to wait for an answer because he could hear her moaning in the background like whatever he was doing was feeling real good.

"Kaaaayy . . . I'm about to cum."

"Nah. Go ahead, Al. KoKo is going to be busy for a while. We'll see y'all later."

Aldeen hung up, laughing and shaking his head. "Damn. Boss man is turning KoKo out. Shit, I hope she can keep her head straight to do this job because he is putting that shit on her."

Wise looked over at Aldeen and said, "Man, he got it. When he gets finished with her, she is going to be his star player." They pulled off and headed to size up their mark.

Meanwhile, Kayson had KoKo on the edge of a powerful orgasm. She was riding up and down with her back firmly placed on his chest. She put her head back on his shoulder.

"Sssssss . . . Oh my god, Kayson. This feels so good."

He grinned because he knew he was getting ready to fuck her head up with his next move. He started to stroke up hard, meeting her stroke and going in deeper every time. He put his middle finger on her button and started to circle fast.

"Aaaaahhhh . . . waaaiiit!"

Kayson stroked faster, making his finger match his pace. KoKo grabbed the sides of the chair. Kayson reached his other arm across her chest and held her breast firmly in his hand and then squeezed her tighter as he moved his finger faster on her button. KoKo was coming so hard she couldn't even breathe.

"Kaaaaaaaay . . ." she yelled out.

Kayson was in his glory. She couldn't get away from him if she wanted to. She tried to close her legs and he bit into her back causing her to open them wider. Kayson bit harder. Her legs shook uncontrollably; her head jerked back and forth like she was possessed. Kayson squeezed a little tighter and went a little faster on her button. "Let me have it, baby. Let that

shit go."

"Aaaaaahhhhh!" KoKo groaned and cried. "Aaaaaaaaaahhhhh ..." KoKo skeeted in his hand, then lay in his arms lifeless like a limp rag. Her hands dropped to the side of the chair.

Kayson ran his fingers up and down the lips of her pussy playing in her wetness. Making small circles on her clit, he caused her body to jerk with every movement. "You can't hang with the boss?" Kayson teased as he kept the orgasmic rhythm going. KoKo was out of it. She couldn't move or speak. Kayson repeatedly pumped in and out of her pulsating pussy while applying more pressure to her clit. That got KoKo's attention. She moaned out in exhaustion.

"Damn, you feel good," Kayson said in a sexy tone. Then he started to rock back and forth while holding her firmly in place. His dick was playing a game of hide and seek with her G spot. Placing soft kisses on her shoulders and at the base of her neck, Kayson used her non-lucid state to teach her some more lessons.

"You have to use this pussy to bring the boss his money. You can't fuck him because this now belongs to me. But you tease the hell out of him and then bring the pussy to daddy so I can handle it."

"Yeeesssss . . ." KoKo moaned softly.

"You have to create an illusion to make him drop his guard and at that moment you take that muthafucka's life." He began to stroke faster.

"Yeeeeeesss."

"I've been waiting for you, KoKo. I need you, baby. I need you."

KoKo felt another powerful orgasm coming on as her muscles strangled his dick. He gripped her hips and dug deep.

"Damn girl, this pussy is dangerous," Kayson moaned in pleasure enjoying how good her tight, wet pussy felt. KoKo took one of his hands and placed it on her breast and the other, she guided to her clit. She kept her hand on top of his as he began to circle slowly. Using her other hand, she placed it on the back of his head, turning her head to the side so she could see his eyes. "Do it again," she whispered.

Kayson was more than happy to hook a sista up again. He was taking her there while KoKo sucked and bit on his neck right under his chin. He moaned out in pleasure.

She realized that she had found one of Kayson's sweet spots, so she kept on nibbling and sucking while he was pumping up in her with intense speed and giving her clit a fit. They both started to cum. Kayson was taken off guard by KoKo's last move. He was usually in charge, but she was learning quickly what felt good to him. Because of how good she was making him feel, he came hard and long in what felt like buckets, and then held her tight. Her juices ran down onto him. He held his hand on her pussy as she tongued him deeply.

"I love the boss's electric chair," KoKo purred.

"Is that right?" Kayson said in a satisfied voice.

"Yup, and I found out that The Boss likes to be bitten, too," KoKo said with pride, glad that she was able to make him cum with her just as hard.

"Keep fucking me like this, and I might have to give you a bonus."

"I hope your tongue is involved in that bonus," KoKo shot back.

Kayson laughed. He could see he was getting in touch with KoKo's freaky side, which is what he needed to make her the undetected killer he needed her to be. Barely able to walk, they headed to the shower, and then later passed out.

Chapter 14
Thick as Thieves

Aldeen, Wise, and Baseem were to meet Kayson at one of their spots to go over a few plans to get ready for the upcoming mission. They sat engaged in a deep conversation about what happened at the club last night.

"That bitch was on your dick hard last night, Baseem," Wise said, clearly trying to find out what happened between them.

"Hell yeah, I was going to try and duck her out because Charmaine was there. But she wasn't trying to leave a nigga side."

"What happened?" Aldeen cut in.

"Man, she got to the house and before I could get the door closed she was on her knees pulling my dick out. She sucked my dick, balls, and licked my ass. I was fucked up after that."

"Damn, nigga you a lucky muthafucka," Wise said, leaning over to give Baseem some dap as they cracked up.

Kayson walked in and a silence fell across the room. They could tell he was all about the business. He walked over to the wet bar, poured himself a glass of mineral water, and sat down. He never drank while discussing business so he could keep a cool head. He didn't want to miss shit.

Kayson sat back in his large leather armchair and stared at the wall behind them for a few seconds, which was his

115

practice. He always made them feel like he was trying to read their minds. Kayson broke the silence. "Report." Everyone knew their order and spoke on their turn. Aldeen was always first.

"I checked on my Intel and everything is on point. I got a bitch dealing with each one of his top niggas' that is in charge of the stash spots."

Kayson nodded. Then Wise went.

"The death angels are ready; I got them muthafucka's on a pussy strike just up in the spot simmering waiting to eat these niggas up." Kayson gave him the same nod. Baseem spoke.

"I got all the equipment and ammo. And I have been training those niggas on it every day. We ain't going to have no problems."

Kayson was pleased with what he heard. He again got quiet. If possible, you could see the wheels turning in his head.

Aldeen broke the silence. "How is Koko doing? Will she be ready?"

Kayson gave him a look that said nigga, you know not to question my technique. Everybody was quiet as hell except Aldeen; he knew he could ask him whatever he wanted. They were like brothers and would give their life for each other. Kayson looked at him and said with a serious face, "I have got a girl whose pussy is so good if you threw it up in the air it would turn into sunshine." Sounding like Della Reese in *Harlem Nights*. They all busted out laughing, everyone except Kayson, who gave just a half-smile.

"Nah. On the real, she'll be ready in a few more weeks. I got her out with Benita getting wardrobe and shit tight. I'm hosting our party on Friday after next. We will send her after that nigga Saturday at his usual spot. When KoKo gets a hold of this nigga, he's not going to have any choice but to lay down and surrender.

Terrance

Terrance left his Oakland, California home and headed to the block; it was overdue. While driving and listening to Biggie, he reached in his ashtray and lit a blunt. Inhaling and blowing out smoke to the beat, he figured he'd better stop and get something to eat at the local burger joint. He knew once he got out there, he wouldn't be able to get away. As he pulled in the entrance, he caught something else looking tasty on his right side. He quickly parked his truck, jumped out, and headed in her direction.

When he got close enough, he said, "Hey Shorty."

She turned to look at him and Terrance was thrown back because she reminded him of his mother—beautiful in every sense of the word. Dark brown with light-brown eyes and a perfect smile. Tall and slender with big ass titties and a small waist with a bump in the back that made a nigga want to hit it from the back for days.

"Shorty? Is that how you address a woman?" She turned back around, bringing her attention back to the person behind the counter. "Let me have a grilled chicken salad and a milk shake."

Terrance loved that attitude. "Oh my bad. I didn't realize that a woman was present. You look like a little girl," he said and then flashed that sexy smile.

Star looked at him. *Damn, he is fine as hell.* But she wasn't going to let him off that easy. "Yes. I am a woman. A *real* woman. So when you get your grown man on, then try again." Again, she turned away.

Being the player that he was, he recognized the fake

tough role then called her bluff. When he saw her food coming, he put a hundred dollar bill on the counter and said, "It's on me. Give little mama the change." He turned and walked away.

She didn't know what to think then. *Damn, I was going to give the cocky brother a chance. No he didn't just throw a yard at me and walk away.* She smiled; she had never been approached like that before. Getting her food and her shake, as well as the change she walked out. When she got outside, she saw him standing there smiling.

"Was that grown enough?" he said as she approached him.

Star just wanted to keep on going, but it was something about his smile. "Well, thank you, kind sir. But a sista got her own money." She put her hand out to give him the change.

"Well, my mom taught me to be a gentleman." He closed her hand with his and put it down.

"Oh, so you're a mama's boy?"

"Used to be. My mother got killed when I was five, but she gave me the best of her before she left me." Immediately, she felt bad about what she said. It also made her no longer reflect on having a mother. "I'm sorry to hear that. My mother passed from cancer when I was small as well, so I can relate. I didn't mean to be disrespectful."

"It's all good, ma. Life deals the cards; all we can do is play our hand."

She now felt a connection with this sexy stranger that had just fell onto her path. She wanted to know more about him. They stood at his truck talking for about twenty minutes. They found they had a lot in common. She looked at her watch and said, "Oh my god, I am going to be late for school."

"Can a brother call you sometimes?"

"Sure, I need to see what else is behind that hard

exterior." She took his cell and put her number in it then started to walk away.

"I never got your name," Terrance yelled out. She turned and said, "Star." He was thinking, *You sure are.*

"I'm Terrance. I'ma hit you later."

She gave him that smile. They both got into their cars and drove off. Terrance, for the first time was smitten. He was used to running into hood rats that wanted the money and the dick, but he could tell that this one was different. And he was going to find out just how different she was. When Terrance got to the block, he wasn't focused on nothing but his money.

Motive

It was eleven in the morning. Kayson and KoKo were just waking up. She lay in his arms peaceful and angelic. "I've had you all up in this bed giving you all this good loving and I don't even know your real name or where you live for that matter," he said, wanting to see if she would reveal a little of her hand to him.

KoKo looked up at him then got quiet. She took a deep breath. "My name is Ce'Asia, nosy, and I live here, remember? Mr. I need you here to train you," she said, giving him a pretty smile.

"I like Ce'Asia. That's pretty as hell. Why do you call yourself KoKo? Oh yeah, I live here. You spend the night all the time. It's a difference. Where do you keep your shit?"

"Well, first of all, I keep my guns in a small apartment on Park Avenue. If you must know. And if I get an uninvited guest I know where the leak came from. As for my name, my dad gave me that name. My grandmother told me that I was chocolate and had a little patch of hair on top of my head that my mom would put powder on to keep me cool because I was always hot. So he started to call me his little cup of KoKo and it stuck."

KoKo got quiet and slid into the little shell she went into whenever she had to talk about her parents.

"If you don't mind me asking, what happened to your father?" Kayson asked. She remained quiet, wondering if she should reveal her whole hand to Kayson. Then she thought she had the upper hand with all the shit she had on him so she decided to tell him.

"Did you have sisters and brothers?" He was curious.

"I don't know."

"Were you and your dad close?"

"I don't remember him. All I know is that my dad's name

120

is Malik. He was killed by some greasy ass nigga, who until the day I die is a marked man. This heartless fucka took my mom and my dad, and when I find his ass, he will spend the time from introduction to death in agonizing pain."

Kayson was thrown off. He hadn't expected her to reveal all that, but he was glad she did. He had done his research and her story checked out. Plus, he was falling for her and wanted her to trust him and be able to trust her. "Well, don't worry, baby, because now that nigga got two killahs on his ass, and if I find him first, he will pray that you found him instead of me." Then he leaned over, kissed her forehead, and held her tight. His thoughts reflected to this guy he knew named Malik and wondered if it was the same one. But damn what would be the odds of him ending up lying next to his daughter. He needed to go see his mother and he was taking her with him.

"I want you to go somewhere with me today."

"Okay. Where?"

"I want you to meet my mom."

"Are you sure?"

"Yeah, she cool as hell and I need to know if you up to par. I would hate to have to get rid of all this good lovin'."

"Shut up. You know good and well no bitch you ever been with take dick as good as I do. I see your toes all curled up when a bitch is doing her thang."

Kayson started cracking up. "Oh, you got jokes. I don't know how you can see all that with your eyes closed, yelling 'Kayson stop'."

"Oh, that's the game. Remember you said paint the illusion?" Then she got off the bed. Kayson laughed again as he watched her walk naked to the bathroom. He made a mental note to make her take that back. When KoKo got to the bathroom door, she turned and said, "Come make me arch my back." Kayson's dick hardened.

"You have to make my toes curl first," he said. KoKo gave him that smile and said, "Well, come on, let's not keep momma waiting."

Kayson jumped up and true to his word made, KoKo take back everything she said, and oh yeah, that back was arched and the words "Kayson stop" was music to his ears.

Later, as they rode in the car, KoKo was quietly thinking about what she had told Kayson earlier about her parents. She always tried to keep those feelings under control. However, him bringing them up only put them right back into focus.

When Kayson pulled up to his mother's brownstone, he grabbed her hand and said, "Relax. My mom is good people." KoKo looked at him then opened her door. Kayson went to the trunk to get the bags. He always made it his business to bring his mother something. He took KoKo by the hand, pulling her from the car. They walked up the stairs and he opened the door with his key. As he walked in, his mom stood at the big bay window watering her plants.

"Hey sexy lady," he said as he came into the room. He wrapped his arms around her and kissed her cheek. KoKo stood in the doorway watching the whole exchange.

"Hey yourself." She pinched Kayson's cheek and looked him up and down. "Are you eating?"

"Yes ma'am. I eat. Are you eating and taking your medicine?"

"Yes, I am," she said in her 'don't start' voice. His mom had breast cancer and she had come out of remission twice.

Kayson was always worried about her. He had hired a nurse, a chef, and a maid that came and took care of everything for her.

"Well, who is this lovely young lady? Is this the infamous Miss KoKo?" She walked toward her.

"I don't know about infamous, but you can call me

122

Ce'Asia." Koko met her in the middle of the room.

Kayson watched their first meet and he could not help but see the look his mother had in her eyes when KoKo said her name was Ce'Asia. Monique ran her hands down KoKo's face and looked her up and down like she had been waiting for her. She took her in her arms and held her tight. KoKo gave in to the embrace and closed her eyes. She hadn't had a woman hug her with such love since before her grandmother died.

When they released each other, Monique had a tear in her eye. KoKo was shocked at the emotion this woman she had never met was showing her. Then she asked, "Is everything okay?"

Monique smiled. "You are so beautiful and I've always wanted a daughter. The things Kayson told me about you just overwhelmed me, I guess. Come on in and sit down. Kayson, go get her something to drink," she said.

Puzzled, Kayson went into the kitchen. When he returned, his mother was gone and KoKo was sitting there alone.

"Where did my mother go?" he asked as he passed her a soda.

"She said she had to get her medicine." KoKo felt a little awkward after their exchange.

"Oh, I'll be right back," Kayson said and went upstairs. His mother was sitting on the bed holding her hands together and rocking back and forth.

"Ma, what's the matter?" he said as he went to kneel at her feet.

"That's her. That's Malik's daughter."

"Are you sure?"

"Yes, I'm sure. I suspected it when you said KoKo, but when she said her real name, I knew it, plus she looks just like him." Kayson took a minute to reflect. It took him back to

123

when he was five years old and his dad's friend would bring his mom money every Thursday and the little baby he brought with him a few times. Then he thought about the night he didn't show up, but two other guys did and handed his mother a white envelope and then she started crying. He never saw Malik again.

"Look Ma, let's keep this shit under wraps for right now until I can pull this shit together. She is going through some shit right now and I need her to be on point."

"Okay son, but don't let secrets ruin your life like I did." She put her hands on his face.

"I won't." He kissed her hands and they went back downstairs.

When they returned, KoKo was looking at pictures of Kayson when he was little. "I thought I was going to have to come up and get y'all," she said as she turned to them.

"I'm sorry, sweetie pie. Sometimes all this medication gets me all emotional. I needed a minute."

"It's okay."

"Come sit down with us and eat. You also look like you ain't had a meal in days. Child, you thin as a rail." She took KoKo by the hand and led her to the kitchen.

KoKo took the opportunity to blame her weight on Kayson. "Your son doesn't feed me. He just makes me work."

"Is that right?" his mother asked.

KoKo smiled. She now knew where he got that.

Kayson's mother brought dishes to set the table. "Well, I'll tell you something. My son is a one-track kind of man like his father. See, they are the type of men that are hung like a Shetland pony, so they think as long as they can keep you screaming, you got all the meat you need. However, I keep telling the boy you have to nourish the mind, body, and soul."

KoKo's mouth was on the floor.

Kayson shrugged his shoulders and said, "What can I say? I told you she was real."

They sat down, ate, and talked. Monique was mesmerized. KoKo had grown to be so beautiful, and the fact that she ended up in her son's arms blew her mind.

As the evening closed, she hugged KoKo and made her promise that she would come back soon. She told her that she could even come without him. KoKo laughed and promised she would. Fifteen minutes later, she and Kayson got in the car and headed to see one of their connects.

"Your mother is so nice and the shit that comes out her mouth needs to be on *Def Comedy Jam*. She is funny as hell."

"Yeah, I know. I just pray she can pull through all this and get back to herself." He got quiet. Seeing his mother only fueled his fire to kill Raul. His head would be the ultimate gift and he was hell bent on making sure it was the next one he gave her.

KoKo had not seen him like this before. Kayson was running all his plans repeatedly in his head. Then he said, "KoKo, its killing season."

She looked at him and smiled.

Chapter 15

Aldeen

A week later, Aldeen, Wise, and Baseem were to meet Kayson at one of their meeting spots to go over a few plans. Aldeen was Kayson's best friend since seventh grade. When they were fifteen, they got close after Aldeen killed his stepfather for beating his mother.

One night Aldeen came home and saw his stepfather, Russell, standing over his mother kicking her in the ribs and cursing her out. "Didn't I tell your ass you couldn't leave this house?" he shouted.

His mother crawled into a ball and pleaded for her life. Aldeen slid into the kitchen and got a butcher knife. He ran at Russell with all his might, stabbing him repeatedly in the back, puncturing his lung. Russell swung around out of breath as blood came out the side of his mouth. Aldeen didn't back down. He gritted his teeth and said, "Let's rock, muthafucka." Russell lunged at him and was met with the fate of Aldeen's knife. He stabbed him deep then pulled it up making sure to rip whatever it touched. Russell fell to his knees and Aldeen watched as he perished.

His mother looked on in amazement as Aldeen smiled. "You don't ever have to worry about another beating, mommy." She crawled over to her son and hugged him around his legs like he was her savior. He consoled her for a minute, then he called Kayson to help him get rid of the body. Kayson was right there. The cops were on her hard. When shit cooled off, they got up the money and put his mother on a bus to stay with some family in Boston. He moved in with Kayson and his mother until they got another spot.

They were inseparable ever since. Kayson and Aldeen met Baseem when they went down to Atlantic City to gamble the summer they turned eighteen. Kayson and Aldeen were drunk as hell and trying to hold on to each other. Aldeen was cracking up because Kayson didn't drink. He was fucked up and mad at the same time because they couldn't remember where they parked the car. Somehow, it came to them that they didn't drive, but came in a limo. This information sent Kayson into a laughing fit and he had to pee, so they stopped beside the Tropicana by the dumpster.

"Oh shit, hold me up," Kayson said to Aldeen.

"Shit, I'll put one hand on your back, but if I got to hold your dick, you going home pissy tonight."

They started to laugh again. They heard a faint argument in the background. This woke both of them up. All they could hear was a voice saying, "Y'all niggas thought that I was a punk?"

Kayson put his dick back and zipped his pants. They peeked around the corner and saw this black ass nigga holding two guns, one in each hand and pointing at two cats who looked like they were deer caught in headlights. One responded to the question.

"Nah, my dude, we was just checking your status. We never saw you before."

"Well, y'all need a better welcoming party because this nigga hit me with a gotdamn bottle. That shit felt more like a threat on my life."

Just then, Kayson noticed a nigga creeping up from the corner and coming up behind the guy with the guns. Kayson reached for his gat and put one in the trigger. He usually didn't get in other niggas' business, but from what he could hear, if they hit this nigga with a bottle and he was able to remain standing and get to his guns then turn the tables on them, then he might have run up on a hit man for hire. Kayson was always looking for talent so he could step farther back.

When it looked like it might be over for Baseem, Kayson bust off catching the guy in the head. Baseem immediately put one in the throat of the guy on his left, and one between the eyes of the guy on his right. They both fell like a deck of cards. Baseem turned his attention to Kayson and Aldeen, realizing that they had just saved his life. He went over to them and gave them dap. "Thanks for having a nigga's back," Baseem said, apparently very grateful.

Kayson said, "I have a proposition for you. Let's get the fuck outta here then we can talk." They quickly got to the limo and headed back to New York and Baseem had been paying his debt to Kayson ever since. Shit, the way he figured it, he owed him his life. And for that, he became one of Kayson's most loyal.

Baseem is a beast, but his only weakness is pussy. Often times, when Kayson would be looking for him, he would be holed up in some pussy. Mainly, this chick named Shonda.

Shonda was his freak; she would let him do her in every hole she had, and then suck his dick so good he would pull out his wallet and hand it to her and say, "Keep the change."

Aldeen and Wise would always tell that nigga to stay focused. They couldn't get mad at him up until this point because he was a top earner and a true executioner. This muthafucka would kill mercilessly and without prejudice with no interview, trial, or jury. When they sent him in, even the rodents would be laid out and he would leave the spot traceless. If Kayson said "get 'em," they were got. And the only thing to stop him was if God himself was there to sweet talk the bullets.

Wise was one of those cool cats that never got upset unless it was absolutely necessary. Aldeen and Wise grew up next door to each other and did all their dirt together. That is, until they met Kayson. Wise, at first, was a little taken aback at how close Kayson and Aldeen had gotten and how they were able to put together a dynasty in no time. Sometimes, he felt like a third wheel until he realized that everybody had a role in an organization. The hand can only do what it's natural function is. You can't ask it to be a foot or an elbow, so with that wisdom, he found his natural talent, and that was to teach and train the foot soldiers and then make sure they were running shit correctly.

Kayson had to respect him because he knew he could not be successful in any business unless the workers were on his side. Wise did just that, and his number one project was KoKo. KoKo was more like a little brother than a little sister. She never complained, was always on time, had no attachments, and could take direction and execute plans like a well-oiled machine. It was for that reason that he had suggested her for Kayson's brilliant plan to make a muthafucka leave the same way he came, by the pussy.

The Secret

Monique passed back and forth in front of her bay window trying to decide if she should place the call she had waited patiently for over fifteen years to make. She walked over to the couch, sat down, took a deep breath, reached for her cell phone, and dialed.

"Ring… Ring…Ring."

"Hello?"

"Long time, no hear." Monique said into the phone.

"Moooo." The voice said back. "How have you been?"

"I'm fine and you?"

"I can't complain. What do I owe the honor of this call?"

"It's time to reveal our hand?" Monique answered.

"What are you talking about?"

"You're not going to believe this…but…I seen Malik's daughter today."

"Get the fuck outta here. Where?"

"She is Kayson's woman."

There was a long silence. "Hello?" Monique broke the eerie silence.

"Yeah I'm here Mo." He got silent again. "Does she know?"

"No. but I almost fucked that up by crying and shit. Then Kayson made me promise to wait until they finished handling something he had pending."

"Well, when she is ready, send her my way. Until then, we just wait." He started to smile. "Is she beautiful?"

"Yes, very. I mean, what are the odds she would end up with Kayson?" Monique said then laughed. "And the real funny part is that I think the little nigga is in love." They both busted out laughing.

"Yeah? Not Mr. Heart of steel."

"Yes, him."

They both laughed again. "I don't want her to get hurt." Monique stated.

"Don't worry. I will handle everything."

"Okay. I trust you."

"Aight Mo. If you need me, I'm here."

"Love you."

"Love you too."

They disconnected the call both feeling relieved and afraid that they would finally have an opportunity to release the demons they had been holding and finally seek retribution.

Chapter 16
Too Close for Comfort

They always made it a habit never to meet in the same place twice in a row. They had all arrived at the same time and proceeded inside the building. They would hold meetings in over twenty different spots. Apartments, office buildings, restaurants, and other places they would rent just for meetings. Only one spot was a common place used for shooting pool. They never talked business there nor were they there at the same time as Kayson. Because he was the boss, his motto was: To maintain respect of the men, show up when necessary. That way, a nigga couldn't get it confused because to do so would prove fatal.

"So, my nigga, what happened with you and that red-head bitch?" Aldeen asked Baseem as they exited the elevator and headed to the back office.

"Man, she was crazy as hell. I couldn't mess with her. I was getting ready to hit that shit and she told me that when she came, she wanted me to cut her."

"What?"

"Hell yeah, not cut to kill, but she wanted me to make small incisions on her arms with a razor blade. Sheeitt. My dick retired at that moment."

They cracked up laughing.

"What did you tell her to get out of there?" Wise asked.

"I told her I had somewhere to go. And it wasn't a lie; I

132

did have somewhere to go. The fuck away from her crazy ass."

"Oh shit," Aldeen said as he continued to crack up.

"I told you about those white girls; they be looking like sisters, talking like sisters, and even acting like sisters, but they be some freaks," Wise made a point to say.

"Well, y'all know I'm an equal opportunity employer, but this bitch had the wrong resume," Baseem said as he unlocked the door and they all proceeded inside.

Each one made themselves a drink, sat down, and continued to talk. They were sitting in the big room having a deep conversation. Kayson walked in and silence fell across the room. They could all tell he was all about business. He sat back in his chair and stared at the wall for a few minutes, which was his practice when he went into deep thought. There was so much shit going on, his head was clouded, the room as filled with silence the he said, "Reports?"

"Yeah, that nigga Raul is bragging about this new bitch he has in his stable," Wise revealed.

Kayson nodded. Then Baseem chimed in, "Yeah, I'm a little worried about baby sis. I hope she can pull this shit off. I was following them the other night and that nigga had his hands all over her. I wanted to kill that nigga on the spot."

Kayson squinted and he took a deep breath before saying, "We have to maintain our control of the situation. It's almost over. And trust me, KoKo got it."

Everyone was looking at him trying to figure out how he was really feeling. He was so good at hiding his emotions, but one thing was for sure, he didn't like what he heard about that nigga's hands being all over KoKo. For a minute, they sat in silence then Aldeen said, "On a brighter note, Dominique came by the spot and dropped off the paperwork you were waiting for. She said to ask you to come by when you get a chance. She got ready to ask me something else but

I had a call, so she just waved at me and left out."

"Yeah, she been trying to get at me, but I don't have time for her bullshit right now," Kayson quickly said.

Aldeen heard what he said, but knowing his boy, he could see for the first time that nigga was falling in love, and the woman he was falling in love with was KoKo. Aldeen smiled. Kayson turned sideways in his chair, folded his hands, and gave them their orders. They all agreed about the next step of the mission then Kayson dismissed them.

"A'ight, is that all?" Kayson asked.

"Yeah, for now. I'm getting ready to go check on them uptown niggas."

They all stood to shake hands and the three men left out. Kayson sat back down and went over in his mind what was at hand, and the danger KoKo would be in if she was not careful. Plus, he had begun to catch a feeling or two for her; he knew it would fuck with him if he let something happen to her. Protecting the woman he cared about had become a full-time job—part of the reason he was on Raul's ass like he was. His mother was the fuel that ran his engine.

Kayson's mind went back to that night when he was nine years old and waiting for his mother, Monique to come home from work.

She worked at a big accounting firm in the daytime and would come home and cook and then help him with his homework. Later, she'd work at the Jazz Café down the street for a few hours. Her best friend, Belinda would check on Kayson every hour until she got in. They had a special thing they would do when she came in. Monique would take a break around ten o'clock and come and tuck him in. Kayson would sometimes hide in his closet and she would pretend to look for him. She'd find him, tickle him, then put him to bed, but not before quickly reading him a story. Once he fell asleep, she would go back to work until 2 A.M.

The Pussy Trap

This particular night when she came in, Kayson heard a male voice echoing behind his mother as she walked in. So instead of hiding in his room, he hid in her closet. He would come to find out this was a bad idea. The conversation still haunted him to this day.

Edwin had walked her to the house since it was late. Monique reached into her bag, pulled out her key, and stuck it in the door. She turned to tell him thanks and good night, but he started talking before she could get a chance.

"Look Monique, I'm not trying to take no for an answer," the male voice said with anger and hostility while forcing his way into the house.

"Look, I like you. You're cool people, but I'm not trying to get in a relationship the way you want one."

"I'm not asking for a relationship. I want to be able to get some of that ass once or twice a week on schedule."

"You must be crazy. I think you need to go. You're drunk and talking shit. The kind of shit I'm not trying to hear. My son is here and I have to go back to work."

"Bitch, you done got my dick hard and you ain't going nowhere until you make it go down." He grabbed her by her hands and pulled her to him, kissing and licking all over her face.

"Stop Edwin, you're hurting me."

"Stop being a fucking tease," he snarled.

"Please stop, my son is awake. Don't do this."

"Bitch, we are way past conversation." He ripped her shirt off and put his hand to her throat. With his free hand he went under her skirt and tore her panties.

"No, Edwin, please!" She tried to fight him off, but his 6'1"; 175-pound frame overpowered her 5'5", 125-pound body. "I want you, and you're going to give yourself to me willing or unwillingly." His alcohol breath along with the smell of his sweat mixed with cologne was causing vomit to come up in her throat. He slammed her on the bed and held her down. All she could think was, *my son is somewhere in the house. Is he is awake?* Knowing Edwin was nothing to be played with, and her main concern was protecting her son and not wanting him to find her dead, she tried not to fight him. Plus, she figured since he was drunk, and if she just co-operated he might cum quick and leave.

Edwin opened his pants and released himself. He found his way to her opening and forced himself deep inside her. Pumping and moaning, he held her down on the bed. "Damn baby . . . mmmmmm . . . this is all I wanted . . . You were worth the chase."

She turned her head; tears flowed down the side of her face. Monique just lay there praying that it would soon be over. She wanted to throw up; his grunts and liquor-filled breath mixed with the very idea that he was enjoying himself was killing her soul.

"Edwin, please stop!" she pleaded and began to cry harder, which only turned him on. He put her leg on his shoulder and went in deeper, sucking on her neck and calling her name.

"Mo . . . ssssss . . . Damn girl, you must like to make a nigga take it because it's wet and good as hell," he managed to say nearly out of breath.

"Edwin, stooooop . . ." She was now trying to release her leg, but her movements were futile; he was strong and forceful. Then she thought, *I need to make this muthafucka cum so he can get off me.* She squeezed her pussy muscles tight with his every push.

"Oh shit . . . that's what I'm talking about."

Within seconds he was ready to release. He came long and hard, pushing himself into her as far as he could go, as if he were trying to make a baby. *I can't believe this bastard. Thank God my tubes are tied.* Once he was done, he had the nerve to kiss her on the face. Then run his long tongue down her neck.

"Okay, you got what you wanted, please leave."

Edwin pulled out of her, pulled up his pants, staggering backwards. "This is our little secret. If you tell anyone, you and that boy will be dead."

He left out the same way he came in.

Kayson was crouched down in the closet feeling helpless and scared. Full of anger and hate, he watched his mom lay there and cry in a ball of shame and disgrace. He vowed that Edwin would suffer a pain that no one would be able to heal and Kayson was going to be the one to give it him.

His mother quit that job, moved out within two weeks, and never said anything to him. No explanations, nothing. But he knew that after that night, she was a different person and he was too. Kayson didn't see Edwin again until he was seventeen. He had been waiting to get his revenge and Raul was going to be his vehicle.

Chapter 17
The Party

Friday night. Kayson's party was jumping. Everyone was dressed in all white and looking good. It was definitely a ballers affair. Everyone was there except KoKo and Kayson, but that was all about to change. They arrived a little before eleven in separate vehicles.

Kayson arrived in a black Rolls Royce Phantom just thirty minutes before KoKo. Wearing a two-piece off white Brioni Linen Suit and men's Prada burnt orange patent leather shoes with an iced out Presidential Rolex. He began to socialize. This function was organized solely for putting different members of the crew together. The room was filled with one hundred-fifty of his top workers who all had an expertise in a certain field. Kayson held one of these parties twice a year. His workers would come from everywhere in the country and network, so if anyone needed anything at any time they would know where to go and get it, dealing with only the ones that Kayson trusted.

When KoKo arrived in a dark green Maybach, she had niggas tongues dragging on the ground. Her all white Roberto Cavalli dress stopped mid-thigh. Low cut back, and a deep V in the front showed off her perky 38C's. Her legs glistened and accented by a pair of color-block platform sling back patent leather shoes. She was the signature of elegance and class. Her hair was just the way Kayson liked it, long with a

Chinese cut bang. Her lips were shining and an orgasmic fragrance that would assault a nigga's nostrils before she got to him making him weak in the knees scented her skin. Strutting with confidence and arrogance, all eyes were on her as she went straight to the bar and ordered a half a glass of wine. Caressing the glass with her petite manicured fingers, she slowly turned. KoKo's eyes scanned the room for Kayson. When she caught his gaze, he winked in approval. She walked through the crowd and began socializing. The men in the room were eating out of her hand. Using the stick and move method, she gave them just enough conversation but not too much. Kayson watched her captivate everyone's attention by the way she moved and spoke. He couldn't help but wonder where the fuck she was hiding her piece, but he damn sure was going to find out later. His attention was sidetracked when he saw Danielle heading his way. She was a chick Kayson had cut off from the dick and made their relationship business only because she didn't know how to act.

"Hey Kayson," Danielle said in a seductive tone, leaning in and kissing him on the check.

"What's up, Dee?" Kayson replied in a serious voice.

"Do you ever smile, Kayson? Damn, it's a party. Loosen up a little," she said in hopes of changing his mood.

"It's only a party for y'all; it's always business for me."

"It's always business for you, huh? Well, can you write into your business plan about Dee Dee licking that magic rod?" She took a chance throwing that on the table. Shit, all he could do was say no and just as the words left her lips, she slid her hand slowly up and down the length of his dick. Kayson looked at her then looked up and saw KoKo staring at them. He didn't change his facial expression.

"That ship has sailed. The Boss got something hot waiting on him," he whispered, moving her hand.

"Damn. Well, she must be a bad bitch because no man turns down good pussy when it's staring them in the face."

"It's not about the pussy. It's about the power. Excuse me." Kayson moved past Dee. She sucked her teeth, realizing she wasn't getting anymore of Kayson, so she just moved toward the next nigga.

Just as Kayson got close to KoKo, this nigga named Moe from Yonkers came up on her. KoKo wanted to use this moment to give Kayson a taste of his own medicine. She was laughing and touching Moe while he was rubbing up and down her back and whispering in her ear. She made sure she spent sufficient time to fuck with Kayson's head; not too much to get him upset but enough to make a point. She placed her hand on the back of his neck and whispered in his ear, "Thanks for the conversation."

Moe smiled big. As she turned to walk away, she made sure her butt swished against his dick, giving a nigga fever. Kayson saw the look in Moe's eyes, knowing Moe was a hunter. He was no doubt about to go after KoKo. However, right before he started in for the kill, Moe saw Kayson looking at him like nigga don't do it. At that moment, he knew she belonged to the boss. Moe immediately backed off; he knew not to ever try Kayson. After that little encounter, KoKo moved through the party mesmerizing all the men in attendance, making sure not to go near Kayson. He was enjoying the little cat and mouse chase. After she saw that woman rub his dick, she was determined to stay away from him all night, leaving him no choice but to watch her flirt with and touch different men.

The thing that got Kayson's attention was KoKo standing by the wine closet and this nigga named Slim walking over to her. He was one of Kayson's strongest workers and was the overseer of most of Kayson's crews out west. Slim was smooth as hell; if he wanted it, he would get it. He was a pussy hound, but he wasn't getting KoKo. Kayson knew he had created a monster by fucking her good and then cutting her off. He hadn't touched her in weeks—the pussy was hot. Kayson had made it clear that she was his, but when the kitty purred, it called for someone to scratch it.

KoKo saw Kayson moving across the room in her direction, so she took Slim by the hand. "Come over here so I can hear you better," she said, walking him to the entrance of the hallway. Slim's eyes were glued to her ass.

When they got to the hallway, she made sure Slim's back was turned to Kayson so he couldn't see his face and run away. But, Slim was too busy putting the moves on her to think of any repercussions. He had heard her name ringing in the streets and this was his first meeting. What he heard and what he saw didn't match, but he was damn sure overwhelmed with everything he saw. Slim had his hand on KoKo's waist and kept leaning in to talk to her. She was giggling and taking him all in. Kayson had to admire her swagger. He had taught KoKo a few tricks and she was pulling them all out the bag. Yes, he had to admit she was talented, but he was a genius. And as he always said "talent borrows, but genius steals." He was getting ready to steal up in that ass. Just as Slim was getting ready to make his next move, he felt a hand on his shoulder. He turned to see Kayson wearing a look on his face that Slim had never seen before.

"What's up, Boss? You need me for something?" he asked in his usual smooth way.

"Nah. My nigga, I don't need you for shit, but I do need that right there," he said, giving KoKo an intense stare. Slim looked back and forth at both of them and could see just like Moe had that KoKo was off limits.

"Oh a'ight, Boss man. Let me let you handle your business," Slim said, smoothing off.

"You trying to make me fuck you up?" Kayson asked KoKo.

"What are you talking about?" KoKo asked as she tried to move past him. Her move was futile because he grabbed her by the arm and pulled her back.

"You leave after I say you can. And I didn't dismiss you." Kayson pulled her close to him.

"I'm trying to enjoy the party. Can we talk about this later?"

"Nah, we gonna talk about this right now. Step into my office. I need you to take some dick . . . tations."

"Why don't you get that bitch who was feeling all over you to take some dick . . . tations?

"She don't take dick like you do." He chuckled, thinking her little jealous attitude was cute.

"Fuck you, Kayson."

"My thoughts exactly," he said as he pushed her into the wine closet.

When they got inside, Kayson hit the light. All she saw was wall-to-wall Champagne and wine bottles. At the end of the long closet was a small bar with two stools. KoKo had her arms crossed, looking at him like: What's up?

"You look real sexy tonight," he said, trying to lighten the mood. He placed his hands on her hips and moved in to her. KoKo removed his hands, but that shit didn't bother Kayson. He knew what he was getting ready to do and her little attitude wasn't going to stop him. He gave her that sexy 'I'm about to tear this ass up' look. "Are you going to be mad all night?" he asked. Then he put his hands back on her waist, leaned in and kissed her lips softly.

"Why don't you go be concerned with the bitch who was rubbing all over your dick?"

"You turning me on with all this sarcasm." He placed light kisses on her collar bone.

"Well, I'm glad to amuse you, but if you will excuse me, I have a party to attend." She tried to push him back, but that was the last move. Kayson grabbed her tight in his arms, bit into her neck, and started to walk to the back of the closet where he saw the stool.

"Kayson you're hurting me," KoKo whined.

He stopped long enough to say, "I know, but I'm getting ready to make you feel real good and forget all about it." He placed her onto the stool and started to lift her dress.

"Kayson, please don't. Wait. Not here." Her plea fell on deaf ears. Kayson was kissing all the right places and touching them, too. When he got her dress over her thighs, he looked down and marveled at the pearl handled baby .22 attached to her garter belt strap. He put her hand on his rock hard dick and said, "I came with my own steel so you won't be needing this." As he removed it and placed it aside, KoKo moved his hand trying to get him to stop.

"Kayson, take me to the house so you can get a real fix," she said, trying to get off the stool.

"Nah ma, I want mine right now." He unzipped his pants and released the enforcer. KoKo was still trying to resist; she knew how he got down and was scared that someone would hear her. Kayson again bit into her, moved her panties to the side then slid in fast and hard. She let out a moan and he went to work. At one point, he heard a knock come on the door, but they left when they heard KoKo moaning and calling out his name as Kayson was hitting it from the back. An hour later, they came stumbling out the closet and everything outside the door was still going on as normal, but KoKo was embarrassed as hell. She felt like everyone knew what had gone on in the closet.

Kayson was the one with a sly smirk on his face as he headed to the bar and got a drink. KoKo stood next to him, ordered herself a double shot of Bacardi Red, and threw it back. Getting up behind her, Kayson whispered in her ear, "Meet me at the house. The boss needs something to eat."

KoKo's kitty tingled so she crossed her legs and said, "Only if you promise to let me sit on your face while you do it."

Kayson finished his drink. "You going to make a nigga act the fuck up tonight, huh?"

"Sure am, and bring your A-game because a bitch is trying to get her hair pulled and her ass slapped." Excited, she headed to the door not wanting to waste another moment.

Kayson moved through the room saying his good-byes and then left the party. Turned on by KoKo's new sexual attitude, he wanted to get home and enjoy his 'something hot.'

Chapter 18
Raul

It was 11:30 P.M. and KoKo strutted her fine ass in the club. Strippers would be posted up at the VIP section trying to catch some loaded pockets this night. KoKo's informant had told her this was Raul's night to get lap dances and jaw breakers from all the baddest bitches in attendance.

KoKo wore all Alexander Wang, a black fitted crop top showing off her toned stomach a pair of Black fitted jeans, accented with a pair of dark red four-inch heels with the deep arch and leather tassels and a small clutch to match.

She made her way to the bar and ordered a glass of wine. KoKo turned to make contact with her mark. Just as she was told, he was posted up in the glass enclosed VIP section getting a lap dance by a stripper named Sugar.

KoKo made her way through the crowd and posted herself next to the window, leaning up against the rail on the balcony with her back turned to Raul. Raul was trying to enjoy his lap dance, but KoKo's curves caught his eye and his attention was diverted. Sugar was putting her best moves down and became aggravated because his undivided attention that usually was on her was now on KoKo.

KoKo turned slowly and looked Raul right in the eyes, flashing him a sexy smile, showing dimples and all. Then she switched away with her perfect heart-shaped ass rocking to the music and giving a nigga fever. Raul looked at Jose and said, "Go get that for me."

Jose headed after KoKo. When he got close to her, he put his hand on her shoulder. KoKo said to herself, *Got 'im.*

"Excuse me, mommie. My boss wants to holler at you," he tried to relate over the loud music.

"Is that right?" KoKo said back in a nonchalant attitude

"Yes. Do you mind coming into the VIP room with him?" Jose asked with a smile. He knew she would go because no bitch turned Raul down.

"Yes, I do mind. I don't want no nasty bitch's pussy all in my face. Tell him if he needs to see me, I'll be over there." KoKo walked off, leaving Jose standing there. He scratched his head and laughed. *That bitch is a trip.* Jose shook his head. *She must don't know who the fuck we are.* Jose turned around and headed back to VIP.

"What's up? Where she at?" Raul questioned.

"She said she didn't want no bitch's pussy in her face and if you want her, she would be over there." Jose pointed to the side of the bar where she stood sipping her wine. When she was sure that they would be watching, she began to wind her waist to the reggae song by DMX and Sean Paul "Here Comes the Boom." Dudes were pushing up on her, but she was ignoring them as she kept on teasing the shit out of Raul, who was watching her every move. She closed her eyes, winding her hips slowly then faster, going to the floor then coming back up. Raul's mouth watered.

"Who the fuck is she? Have you seen her before?" Raul grabbed his dick and squeezed it as he continued to watch.

"Nah, but she is sexy as hell," Jose said, wanting to go after her himself. But he knew once Raul put the hunt out, they had better stay the fuck back.

"Let me out," Raul said to Sugar and pushed her away at the same time.

Sugar was mad as hell. Her money was getting ready to walk out the door.

Raul got up and pulled himself together. Walking over to the wet bar, he washed his hands then ran some water over his face and headed to where KoKo was.

When he got up on her, he said in her ear, "What's up, mommie?" She turned to face him and his green eyes pierced her brown eyes. Koko caught a little tingle. Then she smiled and said, "How may I help you?" as she continued to wind that waist.

"Help me? Oh, okay. You got jokes." Raul chuckled then said, "You can't help me. But I can help you with that wind. It usually works better if you got something in place to support it."

"Is that right? Is that why you just had all those nasty bitches winding up on your dick?" Then she turned her back on him and asked the bartender for another glass of wine. Raul put some money on the counter in an attempt to pay for her drink.

"I got it."

"That's okay; I pay for my own shit. I don't want a nigga thinking I owe him something." She slid a $100 bill on the counter and said, "Keep the change." Raul was impressed with the sexy ass woman, cocky as hell, and not trying to fall for his bullshit.

"Is that all?" KoKo said as she was about to walk away.

"Hold up, ma. Let a brother get your number so I can take you out and without all this noise and shit." Raul was reaching; he never gave a fuck if a bitch wouldn't bite. He would dismiss her and move on. But it was something about her that intrigued him and he wasn't letting her get away.

"Nah. Give me your number and I'll get at you."

Raul looked at her, smiled, and licked his lips. "Oh, so you're going to play hard to get?"

"I'm not playing. I am hard to get." KoKo pointed to the many bitches posted up around the VIP section. "You see them bitches, all they are going to get is a dick and a smile. I want a dick, a smile, and a nigga with an apron on asking me what I want to eat in the morning."

Raul started laughing. "Give me your phone." She handed it to him and he entered his number. *Yeah, I'll play along for now.*

KoKo took back her phone as he ran his fingers across hers. KoKo thought, *Stupid muthafucka.* Just then, another song started playing. She used it as another opportunity to let him see her in action. She started to dance again. He got close to her and she said, "Space is needed," as she moved a little.

"You never know, you might like all this once you try it," he said, gently caressing his dick.

KoKo looked him up and down. "Do you really get girls with those bullshit lines?" Then looked at him all complex. Raul smiled and licked his lips.

"You like teasing a brother?"

"Not teasing. Just tempting," KoKo shot back.

"Temptation can be dangerous," Raul stated, fixing his gaze on KoKo's hips.

She turned and watched as he was caught up in her hip action. "So I've heard, but the anticipation of it all is well worth it," she said. KoKo briefly stopped dancing then leaned up against him to get the bartender's attention, signaling for two drinks.

Raul took that opportunity to inhale her scent and was actually pleased. He was turned on because not only did she have a cocky, confident attitude. She looked and smelled edible. And being the pussy eating professional he was, he was always interviewing prospects.

The bartender slid the two drinks to her and Raul picked his up and downed it, slamming the shot glass on the bar. The bartender filled it back up and he downed the next one just as fast as the first then looked at KoKo like she was on the menu. KoKo was trying her hardest to be hard, but it was something about his eyes. She had to quickly run her mission through her mind and remember that this muthafucka is a dead man and she was his assassin. She said, "You did all that to say what? I am not impressed."

Raul gave her a half-smile. "I didn't do it to impress you. I just happen to like something hot in my mouth then feel it run smooth down my throat."

KoKo had to chuckle. *This nigga is crazy*, she thought to herself. *Who the fuck says shit like that to a bitch they don't know? I could be the walking poster child for the good AIDS and this dumb muthafucka wants to put me in his mouth. Well, shit, I ain't no dream killah. If he wants some of this hot KoKo, I'm going to heat him up, then put something hot in him, but it damn sure ain't going as smooth as he think it will.*

KoKo interrupted his fantasy. "Look, I can see you're interested in a sista and I am damn sure wanting to find out what is hiding behind those eyes, so I'll get with you later."

"Later, what about right now?" he said without taking his eyes off her. KoKo looked him up and down this time.

"I got shit to do, so I will have to check my schedule and see if I can get you penciled in."

Raul couldn't believe what he was hearing. Never in his whole history of trying to get a bitch on his team had he ever been told that they would try to pencil him in. This only made him want to chase her even more.

KoKo could feel the intensity of his stare. She knew she had to hurry up and end it or this little meeting would not be effective. She grabbed her drink, downed it, and slammed it on the bar. Looking him in the eyes she said, "I like the way hard shit hits the back of my throat, too. I'll be in touch." She pulled out another hundred-dollar bill to pay for the three drinks then turned and walked away, making sure to put a lot of sexy attitude in her walk. She didn't even need to turn around to see if he was watching because she knew that he was.

Raul stood paused for the first time. Conflicted. He didn't know whether to stand there or go after her. Looking at the bartender, he shrugged his shoulders. The bartender tried to slide the change to him. Raul looked at him as if to say, don't insult me. So the bartender quickly snatched up the money and tucked it away in his pocket. Raul headed back to the booth in an effort to have a good time, but he could not get KoKo out of his mind. He could only hope that she would call because he was definitely going to get that if she gave him half a chance. Shit, he wasn't no slouch; he knew she would call. Then he vowed *I'm going to fuck the shit out her first chance I get.*

Two weeks later...

KoKo called him two weeks later at four in the morning. "What's up, papi?" Her voice came through the phone, catching Raul off guard because this was the first time he had heard her voice since that night at the club. Plus, he had his baby mother, Maria, over. She had just woke up and was giving him deep throat while he lay back and smoked a blunt.

"What's up, mommie?" Raul said with a smooth and relaxed tone.

"Did I catch you at a bad time?"

"Nah. I was waiting to hear your sexy voice. What do I owe the pleasure?"

Maria was getting upset that he had the nerve to answer the phone, and then talk to some bitch, so she slid his dick out her mouth and got ready to get off the bed. He grabbed her by the arm and mouthed, "Don't play. Finish." She went back to work, attitude and all. She knew not to play with Raul because that nigga was crazy and would fuck a bitch up in a New York minute.

"I told you that I would call and being a woman of my word, hence the phone call."

"Well, I'm glad you called. I have been thinking about you ever since we met. I want to take you out." Just then, he felt the urge to cum approaching fast so he motioned to Maria to get on top of him. She climbed on top and slid down on his dick.

"Why don't you take out the bitch that's sucking your dick?" KoKo said.

"I took her out already. I want to take you out."

"What are you doing later?" KoKo asked.

"You. If you let me." Raul was cocky as hell.

"Well, I think you better make sure you bust a good one because all I'm planning on giving you is some time and conversation." KoKo's stomach started to turn as she could hear the woman in the background start to moan out in pleasure.

"I'll take that for today, sexy lady. What time do you want to meet?"

"I'll call you later." KoKo hung up, not giving him a chance to respond. With a grimy look on her face, she spat, "Nasty muthafucka,"

Raul looked at the phone and smiled. "I can't wait to make her moan." He flipped Maria over and dug in deep with thoughts of KoKo filling his head. Maria got the fuck of a lifetime and she had KoKo to thank.

****

KoKo had been out with Raul several times and to her surprise, he was a perfect gentleman. This particular night, he had bought KoKo this badass Alberta Ferretti dress and shoes to match. He also threw in a David Yarman necklace,

151

bracelet, and earrings. KoKo knew she should have gone to the apartment she kept for herself to get dressed, but hey, she figured she didn't have shit to hide so she got dressed at Kayson's. She stood in the bathroom in her panties and bra combing her hair and brushing her teeth. She had on Kayson's favorite fragrance and it filled the room. Once he entered, she watched in the mirror as he checked out the things she had on the bed. She could see in his eyes that he wasn't feeling this little date she was going on with Raul, but it was almost the end. KoKo had found out everything they needed to know, and now all she had to do was make plans to get him to a certain place at a certain time, cut off his phone then complete her part of the mission.

"Be careful, KoKo," Kayson said. It was fucking with him that he was sending his woman into the next niggas arms. And sooner or later, that nigga was going to try something. She might even have to succumb to a few advances. That thought had him wanting to call the shit off and just do it himself. But the bigger picture kept him calm.

KoKo grabbed him around his neck and tongued him down. Slowly, she unzipped his pants and pulled him close to her. Hopping up on the sink, she wrapped her legs around him and pulled her panties aside and forced him inside her. Kayson welcomed the invite and began to please her.

"See, it's all yours, Kayson, and only yours," she said, leaning back, allowing him to hit the bottom.

"Sssssss . . . Shit . . . I know what's mine. You better not forget." Sliding out of her, he pulled her down, bent her over the counter, and made her scream his name until she couldn't take any more. He leaned in and whispered, "Remember, don't give that nigga my pussy." Then he came. Satisfied, KoKo looked back at him and said, "I won't."

Minutes later, she jumped in the shower, douched, and got dressed. She was running late so she had to hurry.

Raul picked her up at the empty apartment she had set up. Thank God he was late or he would have seen her pulling up. She jumped in his car and they were off. First, they went to eat at a Spanish restaurant, then he took her to a club in Spanish Harlem. They danced and danced and yes, they had a ball. Shit almost got fucked up when she looked up and saw Slim staring at her from a booth he was sharing with this Spanish chick. She quickly told Raul she had to go to the bathroom.

"Shit. Think fast KoKo," she said to herself, staring in the mirror as she came up with a plan. She washed her hands and headed back to the table. When she got close to the bar, Slim was at the end of the bar right by the bathroom posted up ready to defend his boy. When she got up close, he grabbed her by the hand and said, "Does my nigga know you here with the next man?"

KoKo was going to say something, but Raul was already over there. "Is there a muthafuckin' problem?"

"You tell me?" Slim reached for his gun. Raul followed suit. KoKo put her hand in both of their chest. She turned to Raul and said, "Let me handle this."

"You know this muthafucka?" he yelled over the music.

"No, I don't. It's just a big misunderstanding," she said. Grabbing Raul's gun, she smacked the shit out of Slim. He fell back to the bar. She got up on him, put the gun under his chin, and pulled his head to her. "I'm on a mission, dumb ass. Get the fuck outta here before we have to fill two boxes instead of one," she said. KoKo was taking a hell of a chance because Slim was a bonifide nut. Being that he saw sincerity in KoKo's eyes, he put his hands up in surrender and said, "You got it." KoKo moved back, allowing him an opportunity to smooth off, but not without losing eye contact with Raul. It was something about him that he didn't like, and if her story didn't check out with the boss, it would be them in boxes by morning.

Raul stood back looking at the whole scene. He was so turned on that he wanted to rip her clothes off right there and handle that wild stallion. KoKo turned to him, handed him his gun and said, "Let's get outta here." She walked past him and toward the door. He was right behind her.

As they were driving, she noticed the office that Raul had that Kayson could not get the code to, was two blocks away from the highway he was getting ready to get on to take her home.

"Damn, I have to pee." She started to squirm in her seat. "I think there is a gas station a few blocks from here."

"My office is right up the street," he said. They pulled up and got out. He punched in the codes and KoKo and her elephant memory had them all.

They got on the elevator and went upstairs. She'd mapped out the whole area then went to the bathroom. She came out and was ready to go, unwilling to stay too long and arise any suspicions. Getting back on the elevator, Raul stopped it. "I want to taste you," he said, which came across as a whisper in KoKo's ear.

"You want to taste me? You don't even know me. You could be sucking the next nigga's dick."

"Well, if another nigga's dick is hiding in your pussy when I get down there, then I guess I'll be sucking it," he said, lowering himself to KoKo's waist.

"You are so nasty," KoKo said, watching him slide his hands up her thighs reaching under her dress and then grabbing at her panties. She wanted to stop him, but shit, she had never been the type of bitch to stop a nigga from putting in work. Plus, he had been talking a lot of shit and she wanted to see if a nigga could back it up. Not to mention, this would seal the deal. "I'm not giving you no pussy, Raul," she said, grabbing his hand.

Raul looked up with those sexy ass green eyes. "I said I just want to taste you. Satisfy my tongue for a little while and we'll talk about it." Then he started placing soft kisses on her thighs, placing his face between her legs and inhaling. Pulling her panties down, he ran his tongue lightly across her clit. "Damn, you smell good," he said, reaching down and grabbing her ankle and placing it on his shoulder going to work. He was way different from Kayson; he treated the shit like an art. Every movement was slow and accurate. His mouth was so hot and wet and his tongue was soft. He was moaning with every lick and sucking her clit like a lollipop. And before KoKo could even think of stopping him, she was cumming. After her third orgasm, she reached down, put her hand on his forehead, and said, "Thank you, I'm good." She removed her leg from his shoulder.

"Damn, you going to just cut me off like that?" he said. While thinking, *Damn, I ain't never had a woman cum like that.*

"Yes, I think you have had enough. I don't want you to get a cavity from all this sweet chocolate." She pulled her skirt down and reached for her underwear.

Raul grabbed her around her waist and said, "You know you're walking around with an atomic bomb between your legs and a nigga wants to blow the fuck up."

"Well, you are going to have to wait for that 'cause a bitch don't just jump in the bed with every nigga that wants to give his tongue some exercise."

Raul started laughing. "Your mouth is slick as hell. Well, can a brotha have a kiss?"

"I don't kiss in the mouth," she said and turned her cheek to him.

He placed a nice soft kiss on her cheek then asked, "Why not?"

"Cause, I don't suck dick and I damn sure don't eat

pussy."

"Well, it was your pussy I was eating."

"Yeah, that's all good. I only want to know how it look, feel, and smell not how it taste."

"I need to use the bathroom again," KoKo stated.

Raul smiled then turned the elevator back on heading upstairs. KoKo went right to his bathroom, grabbed a handful of paper towels by the sink, and washed up. She retrieved her gun from the back of the toilet where she had stashed it. Having some suspicion that he was going to try something, thank God she followed her instincts. She placed it in the small of her back. She washed her hands, her face and then looked in the mirror. Instantly, the guilt of letting Raul taste her and how good that nigga's head game was had set in. She could hear Kayson's words ringing in her head: "Don't fuck that nigga." Still, the thought of him finding out and being mad at her made her stomach sick. "Shit!" she said in a low tone. She leaned on the sink contemplating for a minute. *Fuck it, this is business and if this nigga is going to trust me enough to get comfortable so I can kill his ass, then I have to take some risks.* She quickly pulled herself together and came out ready to go.

When they got in the car, he kept looking over at her. She was saying to herself, *I hope I don't have to kill this nigga right now because if he tries something, Kayson's whole little carefully thought out plan is going right down the tubes.* He must have noticed it because he took her home like a good boy and dropped her off. Raul came around the car and let her out, but not before saying, "Next time you ain't going to be so lucky." He hugged her, kissed her cheek, got back in his car and drove off.

KoKo went inside then later left out the back. Hopping in her other car, she headed to the mansion.

When KoKo pulled up to the mansion, she just wanted to

go jump in the shower and wash the whole night away. She parked the car and then hopped on the elevator, hoping Kayson was in the basement. She didn't see him and she wasn't going to look either. Quickly, KoKo tried to put on her game face, but she wouldn't have enough time for that. As soon as the doors opened, Kayson was standing there waiting on her. Frightened, she jumped when she saw him, which caused him to say, "What the fuck are you jumping for?"

"Shit, you scared me," she said, grabbing her chest.

"What? You scared of me, or what I'm thinking?"

"Neither, I was just caught off guard. We need to speed this shit up, this nigga is starting to fall for a bitch," she said as she moved past Kayson. He was no fool. He could tell something had happened. He was just hoping it wasn't what he thought it was.

"We need another week then it's over." He watched KoKo undress and head to the shower, which confirmed that what he was thinking was correct. But how far did she go?

Kayson came in the bathroom watching KoKo wash everything as if she felt dirty. He walked over to the shower and said, "Did he touch you?"

"What?" she answered, taking her face out the water and looking at him.

"You heard me. Did. He. Touch. You?" he said with a hint of jealousy.

KoKo rinsed her face and mouth out then turned back to him and said, "Of course, he touched me. He thinks I'm his fucking girlfriend, remember?" Then she turned around, yet feeling Kayson's eyes beaming through her back. She continued to wash herself, but was interrupted by his next question.

"You didn't fuck that nigga, did you?"

"Hold the fuck up." She got in his face, finger pointing

and all. "Let me tell you something. This shit is business and as usual, a bitch is doing what it takes to get the job done. So don't come up in here questioning what it is that I have to do to get shit done for you." She stood there looking in his eyes.

Kayson smiled. "He ate your pussy, didn't he?" he asked.

"Fuck you!" KoKo spat, turning around and cutting off the water. She headed out the bathroom, bumping the shit out of Kayson as she passed him. From the closet, she grabbed her underwear and bra, jeans and T-shirt, and started to get dressed. As she was putting her leg in her pants, Kayson came up behind her.

"At least let me finish what he started," he said, grabbing her around the waist.

"Get the fuck off me!" She pushed his hands away forcefully. "Look, I'm going to handle the rest of this shit then all this shit we got going is over." She buttoned her pants, snatched up her shirt and tried to put it on.

Kayson grabbed her by her shoulders. "Don't fucking fall apart on me. This is what I was trying to avoid. That nigga ain't no joke, KoKo. You have to tuck all these feelings away and handle your business. No attachments. When you get this high in the game, being in love with anyone or anything can cost you your life. You have to hide that shit from your enemy, and when you can no longer hold it, you turn the love into revenge. Then use it to kill your enemy."

KoKo folded her arms across her chest and looked at him. She had to admit he was right; she was having all kinds of feelings and had fallen in love with Kayson. Now she'd involved herself in a fake relationship with a mark that was turning her out with every date. In actuality, she needed this little interaction with Kayson to get her head right. Kayson took her in his arms and kissed her forehead. "Baby, I know what I'm asking of you ain't easy. But it's necessary. When I get done with you, ain't nobody going to be able to fuck with you."

KoKo stood there trying to calm down. Kayson looked into her eyes. At that moment, he watched her turn into the ruthless bitch he was training her to be. They stood there quiet for a minute. Kayson said, "Standing here all mad at the boss. I know what you need after you get that kitty tongue kissed. Come in this lion's den and let me make you think you making love to a god." Going for her zipper, Kayson unbuttoned her pants, then he put his lips to hers looking her in the eyes.

KoKo looked at him and shook her head. "You still think that you're the boss?"

Kayson picked her up and carried her to his bed. "No, you are, and you can pay me in pussy."

Chapter 19
Terrance and Star

It was a Wednesday night and Terrance decided he should give Star a call. He was playing it real cool, knowing that she was mad shy so he tried to play his cards right. He didn't want to turn her off.

"Hello," Star said, coming out of the bathroom from washing her hair.

"What's up, pretty lady?"

"Who is this?"

"This is Terrance. Did you forget me that fast?"

"Oh yeah, Mr. Money bags."

"Oh, you got jokes. What you doing tonight?"

"Nothing, I just washed my hair and I was planning on chilling out. I have a ton of homework."

"Can I come help you with that?"

"How good are you at math?"

"I'm good with adding and subtracting, but I specialize in dividing things," Terrance said in a very flirtatious tone.

Star was thrown off by his openness. "Well, I don't know. I don't want you to distract me."

"Look. I'm going to pick up something to eat and come over. I promise to be good."

"All right," she said in a suspicious voice. She thought he had something up his sleeve.

"A'ight, I will see you in an hour or so." He hung up and headed over to the address Star gave him. After he picked up

160

some chicken breast sandwiches, macaroni and cheese, and salad with peach cobbler on the side from the local soul food restaurant, he pulled into Star's parking lot and headed upstairs. When he got to the third floor, he found the apartment at the end of the hall, knocked then heard that sexy ass voice say, "Who is it?"

"Terrance." She opened the door and was pleasantly surprised. He stood there in baggy True Religion jeans, a t-shirt, and a pair of Prada sneakers. His muscular shoulders, chest, and arms showed through the shirt.

"Can a brother come in or are we going to eat in the hall?" Terrance was turned on by the sight of her in booty shorts and tank top with no bra. *Damn* was all he could think.

"Oh, my bad come in," she said.

He walked in and set the food down on the coffee table. She had her books spread all over the couch and quickly moved them allowing him to have a seat. She ran into the kitchen, got two plates and two bottles of soda, and then began opening the bags.

"Awww, I love these sandwiches from Sylvester's. Thank you."

"No problem, I try to do what I can," he said, looking at her like she was on the menu.

"Let's eat before you start acting up."

They sat and ate and laughed for over an hour. In that time, they learned they had a lot in common. They were both raised by their grandparents and both of their mothers were dead. Also, they had both never met their fathers, Terrance's being killed when he was a baby. Terrance had taken off his shirt and was getting comfortable. They were sitting side by side and when Terrance saw how comfortable she was, he leaned in and kissed her lips lightly. She closed her eyes and received his tongue in her mouth. They began to kiss deeply and passionately. She wanted to stop him, but it felt so good. He decided to take it a little further, rubbing and gently pinching her nipples, causing a slight moan to escape from her lips. Just then, she grabbed his wrist. "Terrance, wait."

"What's the matter?" he asked between kisses.

"I don't think I'm ready for all this yet."

"You feel ready," he managed to get out. He put his hand up her shirt and started to kiss and suck her neck and in one move, he was on top of her.

"Terrance, I can't do this."

"We ain't doing anything but kissing." He lifted her shirt and sucked on her nipple.

"Sssss . . . you have to stop." He ignored her and slid his hand between her legs. That must have freaked her out because she grabbed his hand and moved back.

"What's the matter? Why you stop me? I thought we were having fun."

"I can't go there with you."

"Talk to me. What's up? You ain't got no man, do you?"

"No. I just . . ." She was scared to continue.

"Just what?" Terrance stared at her, anticipating what bone was going to fall out her closet. She sat up, pulled her shirt down, looked him in the eyes and said, "I have never given myself to a man before."

Terrance looked at her like she was an alien. "You're a virgin?"

"There are still virgins out here. They're not an endangered species. But that's not what I'm saying. I said I never gave myself to a man before. There is a difference." As she tried to get up, Terrance grabbed her arm. He needed to know what it was she was trying to say.

"Talk to me," Terrance said, concerned.

"Nothing."

"Nah ma, if it's something I should understand about you

then I want to know."

Star took a deep breath and recounted that fucked up night that changed her life forever. Then she started to pour her soul out to Terrance.

"I was sixteen and started to hang out with these three girls from the local college because I was taking a class that transferred into college credits while still in high school. One weekend, they invited me to a party, so I got all dressed up and they picked me up and drove way out to Compton to this guy's house. It was filled with all kinds of suspect looking guys, smoking and drinking. People were yelling and playing domino's and cards. Girls were posted up dancing nasty and allowing dudes to feel all over them—putting their hands up their dresses and feeling all over their breasts. I knew at that moment that I had come into a situation that was way out of my league. The so-called "innocent" college girls I had been studying and hanging with instantly turned into first class whores. They walked over to this dude named Sisco and grabbed the bottle of Hennessey out his hand and started to guzzle it down. I wanted to run right then, but I had no idea where I was, and lied to my mom so I sure didn't want to call home.

'Janet grabbed my arm and said, 'Girl loosen up. Get a drink and have some fun.' She pulled me along to a bar where some guy was making drinks and yelled over the music, 'Give me a rum and coke.'

'I don't drink. I'll just take the soda.' I tried to inform her but she shot that down.

'Girl please, this is a big girl party. You're out with the big girls so act like it.'

"Then Janet forced the drink in my hand. I took a couple of sips and immediately got sick. I ran down the hall to the bathroom and threw up. I washed my face and when I got back to the living room, my girls were gone. I was dizzy and disorientated. This guy asked me if I wanted to lie down then led me to a room. Then next thing I know I was being undressed. His hands and mouth were all over me. I wanted to get up, but I couldn't move. He undressed and put on a condom before I could regain my composure. Then without patience or care, that nigga took the most innocent part of me. Without permission, he took my virginity. I just lay there in pain and cried. I waited for the pause in the music then I yelled out. At first, no one came, then Karl came busting in the room. We only had one class together and hardly spoke, but he liked me and saw me being led into the room. He came right in time and pushed the guy off me and helped me up and took me home. We have been friends ever since." Star wiped the tear that ran down her face.

"I have been trying to focus on school. And I never wanted some lame talking about me with his friends. So I've just been saving it for someone I feel really deserves me. I started not to give you the time of day, but it's something about you." she smiled.

Terrance kissed her again and then said, "It's like that? In that case I can wait."

"Who said you were the one who deserves it?" She smiled.

"Oh, don't worry. By the time I get done with you, you're going to be begging me to take it." He said trying to lighten the mood.

"You are a trip." Star lay across his lap. Terrance rubbed her hair and looked down at the woman he was now developing feelings for. He could definitely make her his number one.

For the rest of the night, they just talked and laughed. Then he pulled out around 1 A.M. The block was calling.

Over the next couple weeks, he came over faithfully. He always made sure she had everything she needed. He had started spending the night and had bought her a king-size bed and all kinds of new shit for her apartment. Their relationship was growing and as Terrance saw it, everything was right on schedule because he was going to be the first one she gave herself to.

Chapter 20
Taking Chances

Star and her best friend Sha'Reese and a white classmate named Lindsey from college were sitting at an outside café in LA having lunch when the infamous Terrance became the topic of conversation.

"So what's going on with you and your little thug?" Lindsey asked.

Star was taken off guard because she had not talked about Terrance with anyone but Sha'Reese. She thought very carefully about how to answer. "I have someone I'm interested in." Then she got quiet and looked at Sha'Resse over her glasses.

"Bitch, don't look at me like that. Shit I shared, is that a crime? We just want to know if you getting that ass spanked," She blurted out then laughed hard.

"Shut up." Star threw the straw paper at Sha'Reese. "Everybody is not like you."

"Whatever, bitch, just give up the dirt."

"There isn't anything to tell. He is a perfect gentleman. He treats me very nice and we are taking it slow," Star said in a low tone, as if she was trying to convince herself that her words were true.

"I heard he was a killah," Lindsey said nonchalantly.

"Where did you get that from?" Star asked. Sha'Reese was all ears.

166

"Weeell. I don't really know for sure, but I overheard his name being mentioned when I went to see Tyrese. And from what I hear he is a boss on the streets." Lindsey was the Kim Kardashian type—hooked on that black dick. She spent more time in the hood than the average sister.

Star was now getting agitated; she breathed in and out real hard and sucked her jaws in as she tapped her fork on the side of her plate. Up until this point, she was in denial about how he made his money. She knew he spent dough like water, but she didn't really question it because she was so blinded by the way he treated her. Star sat there with Sha'Reese and Lindsey staring at her. She felt like a kid being questioned by her parents.

"We are not going to talk about this right now," Star said.

"Shit, ain't no time like the present. I see y'all getting serious and I know you ain't no hood chick. I just want you to be sure this is a chance you want to take," Sha'Reese said.

"Look, I know what I'm doing. We are just taking it slow." Star tried to assert herself.

"Well, I hear he got a lot of females on his dick," Lindsey said. Sha'Reese busted out laughing. It always cracked her up when white girls talked hood.

"Well, I'm not on his dick. So I wouldn't know," Star said and sucked her teeth.

"Bitch please, stop the innocent act. You know you want to fuck just like everybody else. Be trying to play the good girl roll, and your ass is going to be turned the fuck out when you finally stop being scared and give that fine nigga some ass," Sha'Reese said.

"Your mouth is so filthy. Let's act like we are educated women," Star said with her face torn up.

"You didn't give him none yet?" Lindsey asked.

"No. Is that a crime? I want to make sure the time is right," she said. Star moved around in her seat feeling very uncomfortable.

"Shit. Hell yeah, it's a crime. I seen what that nigga is working with when he came out the room that day with his pants open. Plus, when I stayed the night, I heard you in there calling for Jesus, and if he can make you moan like that and it's no dick involved, I know he is going to have you climbing the walls. Plus, remember this. All that good dick ain't going to waste cause the strongest and most in love nigga ain't just eating no pussy. At some point, he is going to want to slide in something wet and it ain't no gotdamn shower," Sha'Reese said, eyes rolling and moving her neck and high-fiving Lindsey. And as always, she sat there, laughed and turned red. She enjoyed how they would go back and forth.

"Whatever! That's why I got all I have and you're always at my house and riding in my car and borrowing money off me that he gives me 'cause I don't have to work. And how many times a week you fucking?" It got real quiet. "Oh. I thought so," Star shot back then she high-fived Lindsey.

"Bitch please, I fuck because I like to. See, there's two types of fuck." She had everybody's attention. "It's a need to fuck and a want to fuck. He got them both. That sexy muthafucka needs to fuck. But he wants to fuck you. But you are playing with the pussy, being a fucking tease. All I'm saying is how long you think that nigga is going to take a tease before his needs catch up with his wants?" Star looked at her. "You take heed to what I say. Laugh now. Cry later," she said in her slave voice. They all started to crack up.

"You are so stupid with your so-called dickology," Star said, turning her attention to her salad.

But in the back of Star's mind, she knew that Sha'Reese was right. Some nights, Terrance would come in tired as hell and smelling like some woman's perfume. One night, she had even noticed a few scratches on his back. Then there were the codes that would come into his phone by text that would make him smile and lead to the nights that he would not come back over. But shit, she couldn't say anything; she wasn't giving up any pussy. And at some point, she would have to stop all this scared shit and let him give her what she had heard about from so many of her girls called 'the good shit.'

New York Bound

Terrance got out his car in front of the bar and grill and walked inside. He had a meeting with this guy named Boobie who was setting shit up for him to go to New York. Terrance didn't just want to take a trip. He wanted to take over.

Terrance walked over to the bar, ordered a shot of Patron, and stood waiting for Boobie. When he showed up, he was all about business. He had Terrance's description so he came right over to him.

"You ready to make this trip or what?" he asked. "Let me have a double of whatever he's drinking," he said to the bartender.

"Did you make the connection with the head guy out there?"

"Yeah, it's all set up. But the question is, are you ready?"

"Fuck kinda question is that. I came to you." Terrance was getting agitated with his line of questioning.

"Nigga, don't get all out of pocket. This my reputation on the line." Boobie looked at him with a screwed face. "It is going to take a couple weeks to set everything in motion. I'll hit you with the final plan in a couple of days."

"A'ight," Terrance replied, then he walked off.

Terrance hopped in his car, turned up his music, and drove off. All he could think was *this is going to be a hell of a move*. He didn't know anybody out East, and really he would be going on the word of this nigga he really didn't know. He drove, contemplating for a while then said, "Fuck it, I'm in too deep. Turning around now would be pussy. I'm about to show these East coast niggas how the West gets down." He picked up his phone and dialed Star. After three rings, she answered.

"Hello," she said, sounding half-asleep.

"What's up, pretty girl? Did I wake you?" he asked.

"You know you can wake me up anytime. Where are you?" she said, trying to sound awake.

"I'm on my way. I'll see you in about thirty minutes."

"Okay." The phone disconnected and Star jumped up and went to the bathroom to wash her face and brush her teeth. She hadn't seen Terrance in two days and she had to admit she missed him. She thought again about what Sha'Reese had said to her. They had been dating for a couple of months, and although he had been turning her out with the power of the tongue, she had managed to escape giving him all the luscious. However, after not seeing him for a couple days, she had vowed that the next time he came home; it was going to be on.

Later that night ...

Terrance and Star had just gotten out the shower and were lying in the bed naked. Star was her usual nervous self. "You sure you want to do this?" Terrance asked.

"Yes. I want to please you," Star said.

"Just having you in my life pleases me." He kissed her lips. She was extra jumpy. He knew he had better get her extremely wet or she would not be able to handle all that steel he was packing. He continued to kiss her as he reached down and inserted two fingers inside her moistness.

"Don't worry, baby. I got you. But let me get those

170

peaches creamy," as he lowered himself to do what Star had come to love. Terrance licked and sucked her until she was glistening, then he came back up. Terrance was so emotionally charged that he could barely pay attention. Terrance started to glide into her hot, wet pussy inch by inch.

"Oohhhh . . . Terrance," she moaned as she held on tight to his neck.

Terrance finally got all the way in and started to stroke. He went all the way in so he could feel her deeper. Her every exhale became his inhale. He became intoxicated by her scent. The room was filled with the essence of her innocence and love. "Ahhhhh . . . Terrance . . . Ssss . . . Right there."

Star began to cum and shake. Terrance rode her orgasm until she could no longer remain conscious. Once he saw that she was satisfied, he picked up a little pace and brought himself to the same ecstasy. Then he just lay deep inside her and closed his eyes. In that moment, nothing else existed. Time passed slow and still. Star broke his trance with soft kisses on his lips. Terrance slowly opened his eyes and met her gaze. No words were needed; the stare spoke volumes.

Star slowly wound her waist; his dick was still in full agreement as he started to slide slow and deep, hitting her walls from every angle.

"Ssss . . . ummm." Star was enjoying every inch of him. Each stroke opened up her inhibitions. Her body was asking for more and Terrance answered every demand. She gave him every drop of her and he drank her up.

For the first time, Terrance was caught up in the feeling of making love. He was tuned into her every want and need. His stroke was matched by her every desire. Her moans were releasing all kinds of pleasure and passion in him. Terrance had never let himself actually enjoy a woman. He was used to going in and knocking a bitch down, getting some head, and moving on. But Star had him by the heartstrings. Strumming them, causing a rhythmic combination that he had never felt before, combined with soft moans rising up in his throat and coming from his lips with every thrust. Star's tightness hugged his dick like a glove, as if she were made just for him. Her touch was tender and her lips sweet. He began raining soft kisses up and down her throat and then her lips and shoulders.

It was safe to say that Star had him by the balls and he was willingly giving his whole self to her.

Chapter 21
Killing Session

'm a bad bitch." KoKo stood in the bathroom in her peach lace bra and panty set looking in the mirror trying to clean her face, comb her hair, and apply her lip-gloss. Kayson walked into the bedroom and saw the $2,000 Ce'line Short cotton Khaki Trench dress that KoKo had laid out on the bed. Apparently, Raul had bought it for her. Kayson was feeling a certain way, concerned that Raul was going to get KoKo to come up off some pussy before she could get a chance to take him out. He walked up to her and asked, "Are you ready?"

KoKo looked at him through the mirror and said, "As ready as I'm going to be."

"If that nigga seem like he ain't going to bite and try to do something to you. Get out of there KoKo and the boys will run up in there and handle it."

"Do you trust me?" she asked without taking her eyes off him.

"Yes, I trust you. But it's that nigga that I definitely don't trust." He paused for a minute. "I need you to come home to me tonight, safe."

For the first time, KoKo could see the fear for her safety in his eyes. "Baby, I'll be home by 11 P.M. so wait up. Killing this muthafucka for you is going to make my pussy wet and then I'm going to need you to handle it."

"Keep it up and you're going to make me fuck up the

173

whole mission," Kayson said as he wrapped her in his arms.

KoKo turned and kissed him long and deep then moved from his embrace. "Go ahead, Boss. I have to get mentally ready for this mission."

Kayson left the room. He needed to make sure everyone was on point, especially the backup crew. He needed to make sure them niggas knew if they felt the least bit uncomfortable about her safety, to move in, kill everything, and bring him his KoKo.

The plot thickens...

Raul picked her up from the apartment where he had met her for their last couple of dates. He was drooling at the mouth and awaiting the moment he would be blessed to taste her once again. They went to a restaurant and ate, then he brought her back to his apartment. Within minutes, he had KoKo undressed and moaning out his name as he licked her into euphoria. He was getting ready to slide his fingers deep inside her when she stopped him.

"Nah, mommie you ain't getting away from me tonight," Raul said, grabbing her hand.

"I want to taste you. Let me do you. Let me make you feel as good as you make me feel," KoKo said, panting and moving down toward his stiff pole. Raul immediately released her arm and stood in front of her as he watched her get into position. She pushed him into the chair that she once sat in and began placing kisses on his inner thighs. His eyes would open and close as he anticipated the head game she was getting ready to put down.

KoKo was teasing all around his dick never making contact with it. However, she was squeezing and stroking it, driving him crazy. KoKo reached down and began to rub her clit in a circular motion. This action was turning Raul on even more. He watched KoKo slide two fingers inside herself and began to moan. Raul knew that KoKo was sexy and figured she would be a great lay, but he had no idea she was a freak. KoKo carefully slid her fingers out with the razor in-between the first two. Raul closed his eyes as she lowered her head. This gave her an opportunity to put her two fingers in her mouth, using her tongue and teeth to position the razor. KoKo stopped stroking him and prepared to stand up, but was stopped by Raul.

"Hold up. I need you to finish what you started," he said, trying to lower her back into position.

KoKo looked at him and smiled. "Okay." She kneeled. "Close your eyes. I want you to be relaxed and surprised."

Raul closed his eyes and laid his head back. KoKo grabbed his dick and began stroking. Massaging his balls next, she started to blow on them. He moaned and whispered something in Spanish that she could not understand. When he was totally distracted, she released the razor and ran it across the top of his balls separating them from his dick. Raul jumped, and then grabbed his dick leaving the rest of himself exposed. "You stupid bitch!" he yelled.

KoKo slit his throat twice.

Raul moved his hands from his dick and placed them on his throat, struggling for air as he fell to the floor. KoKo grabbed her purse and retrieved her handgun and cell phone. She stood over Raul watching him gurgle on his blood with a hand on his throat and one on his dick. "Can I have a cab to 56 Long Road?" That was the code for the boys to move in. She closed the cell phone and said her final words to Raul.

"Look at you. Greed got you leaking from both ends. Stupid muthafucka, you could have had some pussy." Then she put two in his head, grabbed all her shit and headed to the door. When she looked out the door, the cab was pulling up. She calmly got in. The cab drove off headed to the mansion. The rest of the crew moved in, swept the house, cleaning out all of the safes, and then set the house on fire. At the same time, all his stash houses were being swept clean of both lives, profit, and set on fire.

Once back at the mansion, she quickly showered and then went to where Kayson was. She found him seated in his chair having a drink. Walking over to him, she sat in his lap and hugged him around his neck. Kayson put his arm around her waist. They sat quietly for a while then KoKo spoke first.

"I brought the boss his money. And. Brought back his pussy so he could handle it."

Kayson was quiet. KoKo sat up and kissed his lips then moved her hands to his zipper and released the iron rod. She lifted up, exposing her bare pussy to him, which only made him harder. She carefully eased down on him and began to ride him just the way he liked it. Kayson had a serious look on his face as he watched her move so graceful and lovingly on him. Then he lightly began to moan. KoKo closed her eyes and enjoyed the feeling. She leaned her head back and picked up the pace. Kayson seized the moment, attached his mouth to one of her breasts, and sucked gently. KoKo could feel the orgasm coming on. Kayson moved to her neck, sucking and kissing it while enjoying her every movement.

"You ready to make this all mine?" he said, guiding her ride to pleasure her to the core.

"I want to…but…I'm afraid."

"I need you." Kayson responded while fighting the urge to cum.

"Why me Kayson?" KoKo asked as she continued to ride

Kayson paused for a minute and then said, "Sometimes a nigga needs to be rescued."

"I'll be yours just don't hurt me." KoKo managed to say on a whisper.

"I promise." He said kissing her lips and holding her firm in place hitting her spot just right.

KoKo moaned louder and louder then she climaxed. Kayson held her tight in his arms. As she went limp, he placed soft kisses on her face. "Kayson, I need to know that the shit I did for you today was it. I will kill any one of these greasy ass fuckers out here, but I don't want anyone else touching me but you."

"Baby, what you did today was both business and personal. I am forever in your debt and whatever you want, you got it."

KoKo paused briefly. "I want half of tonight's take and 10% of each of the stash houses every week."

Kayson chuckled. "Half? That's all you think you're worth?"

KoKo looked into his eyes. "No, I'm worth all of it. But a bitch knows the difference between greed and justice. I think that you are worth a lot more to me if I am fair and just. A greedy muthafucka eats now, but a hungry muthafucka carefully plans their meals and eats well. I'm hungry."

Kayson thought about what she said. He saw nothing but sincerity in her words and actions. Raul was a test. If he couldn't get her to flip on a nigga then she just might be the loyal bitch he needed on his side. Now he realized it was time to show her what he really did for a living, but first he had to pay Raul's dad a visit.

Chapter 22

Kayson sat in his car for over twenty minutes conflicted as to whether he wanted to get out or just drive off. He knew he needed to get out but his heart was heavy which caused his feet to become heavier by the second. He rolled the window down and scooped the area; he turned to the seat next to him, grabbed a bottle, took a deep breath, opened the door, and stepped out. Closing it behind himself, he walked towards his uncle's tombstone. His heart grew heavy with every step.

There he stood staring at the hard cold stone that read Rabb Ali. He stared at the stone and became choked up at the thought that here his uncle lay in a hole in the ground. This was Kayson's second time visiting his uncle's grave site. The guilt that he carried over not being there the day he was gunned down haunted him every waking day. The night that he was supposed to go with his uncle, he cancelled at the last minute to go out with Dominique. It was the next morning before he found out that he was murdered in the front of a club in New York.

Kayson opened the bottle of Jagermeister and poured some on the grave before taking some to the head. "Happy birthday Unc." He said then took another swig.

"I know it's been a while since I came to visit you." He managed to say with his head hung low. "I just didn't know what to say." He paused as a tear fell from his eye. He reached up and caught it with the back of his hand before it rolled all the way down his face. "I let you down. I fucked up." The words left his mouth and a sharp pain hit his heart. He wanted to hold back his tears but he couldn't, they began to come one after another. He took his arm and wiped it across his face and nose then took another long drink.

"You were like a dad to me. Thank you." Kayson went to one knee and placed his hand on the tombstone then ran his fingers over the letters.

"I can't believe it's been six years. A lot of things have changed. For one, I'm rich than a muthafucka." he said then chuckled. His uncle always stressed the importance of stacking his money and having a future, "Because this shit don't last forever." He would say every time he saw Kayson buying something big. Kayson poured a little more liquor out then stood up. Taking another deep breath, he said, "Save me a spot."

Kayson poured the remains out then sat the bottle up against the headstone and turned to walk away. He turned back with a smile, "Oh yeah, I met one. She fine as hell. I know you said don't get fucked up. Too late I think a nigga feeling that 'L' word." He put his head down and shook it, "Don't laugh nigga. It was bound to happen." He paused. "Rest easy." Kayson turned walking towards his car listening to the leaves crunch under his feet; he felt a little better with every step. A smile came across his face and just as he reached the car the sun begun to shine bright. He looked up at the clouds and said, "I love you too Unc." He grabbed his car handle, jumped in his car, and drove off.

Payback

Kayson pulled up to the side of the Hudson River where he would meet Edwin. He sat in his truck thinking about how long he had known Edwin had raped his mother. When Kayson was eighteen, his uncle was killed over some gambling debt. Kayson had handled the niggas responsible for that, but his uncle's connect refused to work with anyone else in the crew.

This event forced Kayson to find his own connections. Edwin always propositioned him, but because he hated the man's guts, he never took him up on his deal. However, his uncle's misfortune would prove to be a very fortunate situation for him. He befriended Edwin and put a plan into action. Carefully, he plotted Edwin's demise many days and nights. While he sat at the same table with this heartless rapist, he thought of pulling out his nine and just doing him right there, but he figured he would let him suffer long and slow.

When Kayson was twenty, he created a riff between the Russians and Edwin's older sons, which ended in bloodshed. Then he took joy in watching him suffer day in and day out. Edwin would come to him and talk about the plans he had for his sons and how he was ready to walk away and leave it all to them and was robbed of that. Kayson would think to himself, *yeah, just like you robbed my mom of her dignity.* Edwin had one last hope, his youngest son, Raul. Until he was mature enough, Edwin had given a lot of control to Kayson, saying he was like a son to him. However, all that did was allow Kayson to get close to him to find out what he needed to know to destroy him. Being the wise individual he was, he took the opportunity and ran with it, getting his hands into all kinds of business. All the while, waiting for the opportune moment to make him pay with the life of his youngest son and then his own life.

Kayson was brought out of his daydream by Edwin's headlights. He turned off his car, walked over to Edwin's Benz, and got in. The sorrow and pain was so thick, you could cut it with a knife.

"So how you making out these days?" Kayson broke the

silence.

"I feel like someone pulled my heart out, cut it up, and then poured hot pepper and alcohol on it then put it back in my chest," Edwin said in his thick Spanish accent.

"Damn. How is the wife?"

"Shit, I wish I could take her pain and bear mine and hers. She cries all day. She can't eat or sleep. She said she just wants to die and be with her sons." A tear rolled down his face as Kayson sat thinking, *well; she is getting ready to feel more pain. After tonight, she will spend the rest of her days in sorrow and agony.*

"Well, here is the last of the money that I owe you. I'm getting out. I have something else I need to concentrate on." Kayson handed him a small attaché case.

As Edwin put his hand out to take the money, he said, "Well, I wish you well. I just hope that you will still come around and see an old man. You are all I have left."

Is this muthafucka serious? Kayson thought. "Only time will tell," he responded.

They sat silently in the car looking out at the city over the river. A hooker came over to them knocking on the window, trying to solicit them. Edwin rolled the window down and stared at the long caramel legs on her. "No thank you, Mommie," he said, handing her a yard. "Be safe," he told her.

"Come on, daddy, at least let me earn it. Maybe I can do you both. I can't go home to my daddy without more money."

"Look, I gave you something. Now get the fuck on."

The woman looked at him with pain in her eyes. She said, "No means no, muthafucka!" Then filled his chest with some hot shit.

Kayson jumped out then ran over to the woman. She slowly looked up at him and said, "Thank you, son. It's over now."

Kayson nodded. His mother grabbed the money and they jumped in his car and pulled off. They had successfully killed all his sons and allowed him to live to feel the pain, and took him out leaving his wife a childless widow. Not to mention all his connects were now with Kayson making him $10 million richer in just a few hours. He could move on, leaving the bad memories of Edwin behind.

When Kayson got home, he showered and crawled up next to KoKo and held her tightly in his arms. "Sleep well, baby. We have a flight to Vegas in the morning."

"Vegas? What's in Vegas?"

Kayson smiled. "Just get some sleep. Everything will all be clear in the morning."

KoKo and Kayson arrived in Las Vegas and were greeted by Mr. Lu Chi's assistant. When they got to his penthouse suite in the MGM Grand Hotel, KoKo couldn't help but feel overwhelmed. She was excited about the lights and view of the city from the huge windows. Kayson could see the childlike excitement in her eyes. He smiled. They sat down and then he whispered in her ear, "Don't worry we have one, too."

KoKo started to smile. "You get on my nerves," she responded.

When they looked up, Mr. Lu Chi entered the room. Kayson got up and gave him the proper greeting. They sat down to talk. He introduced KoKo to him and he was a little thrown off that a man of his caliber would have a woman running things. Mr. Lu Chi was old school, so a woman being in charge was beyond his comprehension. However, he proceeded. Once the meeting was over, KoKo's head was swimming with questions and confusion. All this time, she had thought that all Kayson did was deal drugs, when in fact it was all a front to wash Mr. Lu Chi's counterfeit money operation. Kayson would make major purchases from top distributors then sell the dope and turn clean money over to Mr. Lu Chi for half the profit. So in reality, he was getting free dope, cutting it up and flipping it, then turning half the money over to Mr. Lu Chi. Only to get half of that back as well as whatever the streets were making on the cut down. Sheeiit, that was brilliant.

As KoKo got into the elevator she asked, "Does anyone else know about this?"

Kayson put his finger up to his lips to hush her up. Then he placed her up against the elevator wall and kissed her lips and her neck, his favorite spot. He whispered in her ear, "Don't talk about shit in here. These Vegas cats can see and hear everything." He continued to kiss her, slid his hand between her thighs, and began rubbing in her wetness.

"I thought you said they can see everything," KoKo moaned.

"I did, so let's give them a little show." With that, he slid the enforcer out of his zipper, lifted KoKo up a little, and went to work. He pressed the button to several floors to slow them down from getting to the bottom. Knowing they only had a short time, he went right for her spot. The elevator stopped on the fifth floor, and a young white couple got in just as KoKo was climaxing.

"Ahhhh . . ." KoKo moaned holding him tight.

"Mmmmm . . . Damn, baby," Kayson said just as the couple got on and went to the opposite corner, looking on in amazement. KoKo looked up at him with glossy eyes as Kayson placed himself back in his pants and slowly pulled down KoKo's dress. She, unlike him was embarrassed as hell and failed to make eye contact with the other couple. However, he was smiling from ear to ear then planted a few kisses on her lips.

"Why you looking like that?"

KoKo looked at him like, *are you serious?* "You keep me

in some bullshit," she said.

"Yeah, that may be true, but as DMX said, 'I will keep you with a smile and walking funny.'" All she could do was laugh.

The elevator doors opened. They exited and headed toward the limo, and then to their suite to finish what they started.

For the next year, KoKo had been all over the States making connections and meeting people. She now had a new respect for what he did. Kayson and KoKo were becoming thicker than thieves. He had never had feelings for a woman that could compare to the way he felt about KoKo and was definitely not trying to let her go anywhere. KoKo was almost nineteen and had matured into a brilliant businesswoman, not to mention a trigger finger to match, making her a double threat. Everywhere he took her, people would fall in love with her and she made his trips easier. However, he didn't want her overseas. It was time for him to renegotiate deals with his overseas connects, so he sent her home to check on things and get a little break from all those road trips and she was glad for it. He dropped her off at the airport and said, "Love you, baby. I'll see you in a couple days."

KoKo kissed him. "Be careful, baby. Love you, too." With that, he headed to the international airport and she headed to domestic.

Chapter 23
If a Bitch can't keep her Mouth Shut, Close it for her!

Wednesday night, KoKo was feeling a little bored just sitting in the house so she decided to hit the club with Aldeen and Wise. They had been trying to see her, so when they called and invited her out, she took them up on their offer. She got dressed and headed out. When she got there, she saw all of them sitting in a booth and it appeared that they were having much fun. She walked right over to them.

"What's up, my niggas?" She gave each one some dap.

"What's up, sis?" The boss let you out to play," Baseem said.

"Oooooohhhh," everyone chimed in.

"Shut the fuck up. You know who wears the pants around here," she said, reaching for the blunt in Aldeen's hand.

"Yeah, okay, don't let your mouth write a check your ass can't cash." He took the blunt from her.

"Stop playing. I came out to have a good time. Shit, I'm still the same KoKo," she said, trying to get in the booth.

"Damn KoKo, you're going to be blocking and shit," Baseem said sarcastically.

"No I'm not. Y'all can still try to fuck these drippy pussy bitches, and if they get out of line, I can run in their mouth. Now shut up and pass me something to smoke."

Then they all said, "Yeah, same old KoKo." They sat there reminiscing and laughing and tossing drinks back. The bitch from Kayson's party came over to the table with her two little running partners.

"Hey guys, what's up?"

"Nothing, ma. What y'all up to?" Aldeen responded. Everyone else just looked at Dee Dee. No one in Kayson's immediate crew liked her. Kayson tried to use her for a mission, but she got all caught up in the mark and backed out at the last minute, costing them millions. The only reason Kayson kept her around was because she could handle her business with the little shit he put her on, but as for major jobs, she could not be trusted.

"We are just out trying to unwind." She kept eye contact with KoKo since she had heard that Kayson was sweet on her and she was now the recipient of all that good dick. She was not pleased. Aldeen could feel the tension building between them and thought it best to dismiss the ladies before shit got ugly.

"A'ight. Well, order a couple on me and have a good night," he said looking at her like, 'go ahead.'

"We sure will. Catch y'all later." She turned to leave, but stopped. "Tell Kayson I miss him and hit a bitch up when he gets a chance so I can show him how much." Deviously, she smiled and walked away. Her girls started to laugh.

Aldeen saw that line form in the middle of KoKo's forehead then sweat formed on her nose. He already knew. "Don't sweat that shit, KoKo. That bitch is crazy. Kayson is going to put his foot in her ass when he finds out about this bullshit she just pulled," Aldeen said. That shit was out of line and Kayson didn't play that putting him on blast shit. But it would be too late when he found out because KoKo was getting ready to handle it right now.

KoKo kept her eyes on them until she saw them head

towards the bathroom. "I have to go to the bathroom," KoKo said, leaving the table.

Once KoKo got to the bathroom, she went straight in the stall. The three bitches were posted up and plotting on how they were going to fuck with KoKo. Little did they know, they were in for a rude awakening?

"I can't wait until Kayson gets back. I'm going to suck that sweet dick until he comes hard," Dee Dee said.

"You still messing with Kayson like that?" one of her girls' asked.

"Shit, you know how the boss is. Once he hit that spot, you belong to him." They giggled.

KoKo emerged from the stall with an evil look on her face. "Let me get this shit straight. Y'all bitches thought it was wise to come up in here and fuck with a bitch?" she asked, pulling both guns from the holster. All jokes went right out the window. "Nah muthafucka, you were saying something about you and Kayson."

Dee Dee was scared as hell, but she didn't want to show it.

"What's up? You the flava of the month. So you think you the shit?"

"You tell me. You claim you been sucking his dick so you must have been tasting pussy. So you tell me what's the flava he savors? Oh, I know. KoKo."

Dee Dee stood there in a full stare down with KoKo and the bitch with her wanted to shit a brick. "Look, I'm not trying to get in no shit with the second string," Dee Dee said.

"You know, it surprises me that in spite of the fact that you are getting ready to spend the remainder of your life in agonizing pain, you can still find the strength to try and insult me."

"Well, it amazes me that you still think this is about you." Two girls came busting in the bathroom, stumbling drunk and talking loud and giggling. KoKo turned her head and said, "This bathroom is out of order."

The lead chick looked at her and said, "Girl please, I have to pee," and tried to brush past KoKo. KoKo smacked the girl in the face with her gun. As she fell back, she heard KoKo say, "Bitch, you can either pee somewhere else, or in a bag for the rest of your life. You draw it up." Her friends caught her then made eye contact with the gun slinging female.

"Oh shit! That's KoKo. No disrespect," one of the females said. They staggered out the same way they came in.

KoKo turned her attention back to Dee Dee. "And you were saying?"

Dee Dee felt the first drop of sweat run down the side of her face. Her stomach knotted up and she wanted to try and defuse the situation, but because she felt strong in her spot, she didn't want to lose face in front of her girls.

"Look, I ain't trying to get into no shit with you like I just stated. What me and Kayson had is over and bedsides, you're his bitch. Me and you ain't got shit between us." Dee Dee was feeling tough off those shots of Hypnotic. However, all the drinks in the world couldn't prepare her for what was about to happen next.

KoKo tilted her head and said, "Is that right?" Taking a minute to ponder the situation, KoKo figured she could just smack her around because Kayson would definitely be upset if she killed a good worker over some bullshit. But she at least had to teach this bitch a lesson. She ordered the other chicks to leave the bathroom and because they weren't built like Dee Dee, they got out of there as fast as possible. Putting her guns back in the holster, she jumped on top of Dee Dee and commenced to giving her a good ass whipping. She was fucking her up all over the bathroom, pushing her into one of the stalls and kicking her in the stomach. Grabbing her by the hair, KoKo slung her into the sink banging her head on it. KoKo rained punches all over her face and head then slammed her on the floor. That was it for Dee Dee, she was laid out. Dazed.

KoKo pulled her gun from the holster, kneeled over her, and rammed the gun in her mouth knocking out four of her front teeth.

"So you wanted something long, black, and hard in your mouth?" KoKo slid the gun in and out her mouth.

"Argggg . . ." Dee Dee cried out with tears running from her eyes. "Please don't."

"What? You said you wanted to suck some dick. Well, this is what KoKo's dick feels like." She continued to slide the gun in and out her mouth faster causing the broken teeth to chip more. "Come on, suck it and talk some more shit so I can make it cum and blow to the back of your fucking throat." KoKo could see she took the bitches heart and that was all she wanted to do. She pulled the gun out her mouth, stood up, and grabbed a paper towel. She wet it and wiped the gun off.

"Was it as good for you as it was for me? Next time you see me, bitch, you stay the fuck out my way. And remember, never play with two things of mine. My money or my dick."

Dee Dee lay on the floor in agonizing pain. Every part of her body hurt and now she was missing teeth and spitting out blood. As KoKo placed her gun back, she laughed. "You were going to suck Kayson's dick. Sheeeit, you got a better chance at running through hell with a gasoline thong on with grenades in your pocket. But look at it this way, the next muthafucka is going to feel real good when you put those gums on him." She spit on her, "Stupid bitch!" As KoKo left, Dee's girls came back to check on her. She shot a dirty look at her girls who didn't even try to help her. "Punk ass." KoKo walked out the bathroom. As KoKo walked back to the table, she saw a woman standing at the bar staring at her like she saw a ghost. KoKo made a mental note to remember this woman then she kept going as she thought that she looked a lot like her.

All the guys were looking at her curiously when KoKo got back to the table. KoKo looked back at them. "I didn't kill the bitch, but y'all need to go get her some medical attention." She grabbed Aldeen's drink and took it to the head. She placed the glass down and said, "I'll catch y'all later." Then she bounced.

Aldeen looked over at Baseem and said, "Well, old girl asked for it. Go get her, Ak." Akbar got up and headed to the ladies room to clean up KoKo's mess.

Later that night...

Kayson came in from his trip and all he wanted to do was climb in a hot shower and some wet pussy. When he got upstairs to his bedroom, he didn't see KoKo. He figured she had run downstairs to smoke some trees so he jumped in the shower. When he came out, he went to the monitors to see where she was. To his surprise, she was fast asleep in the guest room. "What daddy do now?" he asked aloud as he headed to the guest room. When he tried the door, it was locked. "What the fuck?" he spat then went to get the key. He opened the door as she lay in bed staring at him.

"You're not sleeping in here. Go back to your room."

"What the fuck is wrong with you?" Kayson said, face all torn up heading to where she lay.

"I had a run in with one of your little bitches at the club tonight. Apparently, she can't wait to suck your dick."

Kayson paused then he chuckled. "Man, get the fuck outta here. How a bitch going to suck my dick from across the fucking world?"

"Shit, I don't know. But from how she put it, once the

190

boss hit it, you belong to him forever," she said with anger in her voice.

"That bitch must have been Dee," he said, then laughed.

"What the fuck is so funny? Is that how you do it? You sex all the bitches into your little organization?"

"Are you serious right now?"

She looked at him for an answer.

"Look, I'm not going to lie to you. Yes, I fucked Dee. She was supposed to handle some other shit for me similar to what you did, but she fell for the guy and cost me millions. I was going to kill her ass, but she is such a good worker on other projects that I decided to keep her on the team. But access to me was immediately cut off. When I saw her at the party, she was testing the waters, but I shot that ass down. Everybody knows the Boss is in love with Miss KoKo, so she tried to play you out," he said, rubbing her leg. "Now stop acting like you don't know it's all about you and make love to the Boss. I missed you." He gave her that sexy smile.

KoKo sat quietly with her arms folded. "Well, all of that is cool, but I still need to sleep alone tonight so I will see you in the morning," she said, now playing hard to get. She turned her back and slid under the cover.

Kayson snatched the cover off her and said, "You crazy as hell if you think I'm not getting some of the luscious." He ran his hand up her inner thigh.

"Stop Kayson. I'm not in the mood. Mooooove!" He had already climbed on the bed and was pulling at her clothes causing them to tear in different places. "Stop! You're not getting anything. Go in your own room." She insisted while wiggling and squirming, this allowed him to insert two fingers inside her and began moving them just the way she liked it.

"Kayson stop. Get off me," she said with both anger and pleasure dripping from her vocals.

"Stop what?" he asked, picking up the pace and bringing on her orgasm.

KoKo squirmed around until his fingers were no longer inside her as she tried to get closer to the top of the bed. Wrong move. Now she had nowhere to run. Focused, Kayson grabbed her ankle and pulled her under him. Pinning her arms to the bed and opening her legs with his knee, he started to suck and nibble all over her neck and breasts.

"Get off me!" KoKo struggled under him, preventing him from penetrating her.

"Why you fighting me? You know how good it's going to feel once you surrender," he teased, letting her tire herself out. When she was on the verge of surrender, he bit into her neck hard. He held her firmly down to the bed and commanded, "Be still."

"Ouch! You're hurting me," she moaned as she tried to comply.

Kayson eased himself inside her. He had been away for a couple weeks and her tightness prevented him from going all the way in like he wanted. So he slowly thrust in and out until she fit all of him like a glove. The more he stroked, the wetter she became.

KoKo was still trying to be tough. She moaned and made her last attempt. "Stop, Kayson, I'm not giving you none."

He released her neck from his mouth. "I know you're not giving it to me. I'm taking it." He kissed her lips, but she moved her face from side to side.

"Kayson stop!" she said with her mouth, but her body told a different story.

When he realized she was still trying not to cooperate, he bit into the other side of her neck. KoKo yelled out, "Ooooouch . . . Stooop . . ."

Kayson then commanded, "Do it to me."

"Okay. Okay. Stop biting me."

He lessened the pressure as she began rolling her hips and sliding back and forth on his thick, long pole. Kayson was enjoying every movement. She tightened her muscles with his every thrust.

"Is this how you want it?" she asked, talking shit. Grinding against him, calculating every stroke.

"Sssss . . . ummmm. Just like that baby." He was in a push up position and she was riding him like a champ from the bottom.

"See, I told you that you would enjoy it as soon as you surrendered." He released her arms and she wrapped them around his neck. Then he took over, went in deep, and fast. Kayson found her spot and brought her to a powerful climax then found one of his own. They both lay there satisfied.

"Damn, a man just wanted to come home and climb in some nice, tight, wet pussy and get some lovin', but you had to make me fight for it."

KoKo said, "If it ain't rough, it ain't right." She smiled.

Kayson kissed her lips. "I love you, baby."

"I love you, too."

"I'm taking you on vacation tomorrow."

"Vacation? I don't have shit packed."

"Rich people just carry plastic, remember? Now come wash the boss up and let me hit it from the back in the shower so we can get a good night's sleep."

"Don't get carried away," KoKo said, trying to get off the bed.

"There you go again telling me what I can't do. Tell me again when I'm all in your spinal column."

"Boy, you swear you so tough. I bet your boys don't know KoKo be having you up in here singing old Negro spirituals."

Kayson busted out laughing "Sheeit, them niggas know that poltergeist pussy have a muthafucka up in here getting exorcized."

"You so stupid." They both busted out laughing heading to the shower.

Chapter 24
The Vacation

can't believe you talked me into riding on this damn plane when we got a private jet," Kayson complained for the fiftieth time.

"Kayson, it's not that bad. We're in first class. Plus, we don't ever get to do shit like everybody else. Just relax and enjoy the flight."

"I don't do it like everybody else, remember?" Kayson said, giving her that sexy look of his.

"Ooooh. That's what I'm talking about. Let's get it on," KoKo said as she undid her seat belt.

"Nah, don't get all excited. You wanted to ride with everybody else and we could be in the jet in bed hurting something right now. But no, we up here with the fucking get-along gang."

KoKo rubbed and massaged his dick. "I need you. Let's go in the bathroom." KoKo raised her eyebrows and looked at him like, come on.

"Behave," Kayson said, trying to take control of the situation.

"Well, sit here and act like you don't know. I'll just handle it by myself."

Then headed toward the bathroom.

"Shit, I ain't no fool," he mumbled then followed her.

Once inside, they were all over each other. He put her up on the sink and then unzipped his pants. Wasting no time, he slid deep inside KoKo hitting the walls from side-to-side searching for that spot and within minutes, she was cumming. Kayson went deep and held it there kissing and sucking on her lips.

"Why wouldn't you wait so I could handle this monster the way it needs to be handled?"

"You know I hadn't had my fix this morning. Stop holding out and I wouldn't have to put a gun to your head for my stuff."

"Is that right? Well, when we land, make sure I get the same offer so I can tear it up."

"Promise?" KoKo said, nibbling on his bottom lip.

Kayson started to stroke in and out again then they heard a knock on the door, but it was too late. KoKo's wetness made him go faster and faster. Kayson grabbed her butt cheeks, lifted her up, and stroked more rapidly. She moaned out in pleasure, cumming again. Kayson released deep inside her, following it with sweet kisses on her lips and neck. Their euphoria was interrupted when several more knocks rang out on the door.

"See," Kayson said.

Embarrassed she yelled out, "Just a minute." They quickly freshened up and pulled themselves together. When they opened the door, a line of people was looking at them. Some were shaking their heads. A woman with her child glared at them with disgust. Her husband, however, was smiling from ear-to-ear. They slid past every one. KoKo held her head held high and said to herself *fuck it. What's the use of being embarrassed; I just got my shit off. I'm going to have a drink and fall asleep.* Kayson shrugged and pointed at KoKo as if she made him do it. When he got to the end of the line, a young boy said, "Man, I feel you. If I had all that, they would have had to treat me like the Taliban, drag me out of there kicking and screaming."

Kayson smiled and said, "What can I say. When the kitty

196

purrs you have to stroke it." He headed to his seat.

Within a few hours, they were landing. Kayson woke KoKo up so she could see the beauty of the sun and water accompanied by the sight of the islands. She looked out the window. All she saw were beautiful islands in the shape of palm trees and then other smaller islands.

"Oh my god, Kayson, it's beautiful."

"I know. I love it here; it's my home away from home."

KoKo turned to Kayson and kissed him. "Thank you, baby. We need this."

A limo was waiting once they exited the plane. "Hello, Mr. Wells. Welcome home. Madam KoKo, good to see you. I hope you enjoy the island." He took her hand and kissed it.

"She ain't going outside," Kayson made it a point to say. He and the chauffeur started laughing.

"Thank you, sir. Don't listen to him." She gave Kayson a soft elbow to the stomach.

"Is the helicopter waiting?" Kayson asked his chauffeur.

"Yes sir."

"Helicopter?" KoKo said with excitement.

"Yes, one of the personal islands you saw is mine and we have to fly to it."

"Damn, you got it like that, Boss," she said sarcastically.

Kayson smiled. "*We* got it like that." They got in the limo and headed to the helicopter. KoKo felt like a celebrity once they boarded. Minutes later, they landed and were greeted by a man and a woman.

"Welcome home, Mr. Wells," the woman said and did a little bow.

"It's good to be home. This is my baby, Miss KoKo. Take good care of her. I have to go take care of something."

"Where you going?" KoKo asked with disappointment.

"I have to go meet somebody. Don't worry. I'll be right back. Shower and change then I'll be back to take you to dinner." He kissed her and then got back in the helicopter.

"Miss KoKo, I have a bath ready for you and a massage set up," the woman said, taking her by the arm and leading her down the walkway to the house.

The man was right on their heels. As she went towards the house, she was blown away. Glass, lights, trees, and beautiful flowers were all around. A pond sat right in front with huge tropical fish in it and floating lilies. As she walked up the long white marble walkway, she felt like royalty. The gentleman opened the glass doors and there were large black marble floor tiles and indoor palm trees in the corners and glass vases with fresh flowers and marbles at the bottom. All the furniture was white soft leather with glass tables all around. Even the ceiling fans were clear like glass. She was led down the hallway to the room. The door opened and KoKo stepped on a glass see-thru floor, which had a gigantic bed with a white comforter decorated with black and red pillows. Floating candles hung from the ceiling over the bed and the view from the window was breathtaking. KoKo was trying to take it all in she stood still, closed her eyes, and took a deep breath.

"The bathroom is on the left. I will be downstairs when you're ready," the woman said. She left out shutting the door and leaving KoKo standing in the middle of the floor looking at everything. *Damn, I didn't know this nigga's money was this long.* She was in awe and retreated to the bathroom. The in-floor Jacuzzi was filled with bubbles and yellow rose pedals. Everything was white and glass, and pretty, very different from the décor of the mansion.

KoKo took her clothes off and stepped in. Minutes had passed and she fell asleep. She woke up some time later, stepped into the glass shower, and rinsed off. Putting the thick robe on, she headed downstairs for her massage. As she passed the bed, she saw an Emilio Pucci Bohemian dress lying there and a pair of Monolo Blahnik heels lay next to it. She smiled. She had gotten very used to Kayson dressing her. He loved her body and would pick out only the best.

Once she was done with the massage, she had a glass of wine and walked around a little. Out of one window, she saw a tennis court and pool. On the other side, about a quarter mile from the house was a small house where the people who helped maintain the house lived. On the opposite side of the house was a dock, which housed a small boat and a large boat. There was also a Tiki bar with tables all around for small parties. She stood gazing at the water. It was now dark and off in the distance, the sky and ocean looked like one. Hearing a helicopter coming in, she watched it land. Kayson got out and walked up the walkway.

Once in the house, he looked at the pile of mail then headed to his room he walked right over to KoKo. "Did you miss me?" He wrapped his arms around her waist and kissed her lips.

"Yes and no."

"What does that mean?"

"Well, I had a nap in that Jacuzzi and then a hell of a massage and this house is gorgeous. So yes, I missed you being here, but I enjoyed the serenity."

"Shit, I hear that. That's why I brought you here. We've been working hard as hell and we needed this vacation. Why aren't you dressed?"

"I figured you had to come and get showered and changed so I didn't want to sit around in my clothes, but I see you already handled your shit." She looked him up and down.

He had changed his clothes wherever he was, which gave KoKo a little pause. Again, Kayson made the type of statement that always made his crew think he could read their minds. "Yes. I changed. What up?" He looked at her with those eyes. "Go get dressed so I can take you to dinner." He released her from his arms then headed to his office so he could check on some paperwork.

Twenty minutes later, KoKo stood before him looking edible. "That's what I'm talking about." He rubbed his hands together and stood up. "Come on, ma. We about to hit the water."

"I see there were no panties or bra with the dress."

"You're not going to need them." He took her hand and led her to the door. They walked in the direction of the boats. A crew was waiting to take them out to sea. They stepped on, got comfortable, and were off. They spent the whole night on the boat eating, drinking, and dancing and oh yeah, making love.

In the morning, they arrived back to the house. KoKo had a whole new love for Kayson. He was now introducing her to things she never would have dreamed about doing.

They spent a whole week doing everything the island had to offer, paragliding, scuba diving, horseback riding, and sky diving. They even went skiing at an indoor lodge and it was the bomb. One night, they went to the opera in a futuristically shaped building that sat on an island by itself. The highway had two very thin bridges that led to the island. Inside the building looked like an indoor paradise and the music brought chills to her body and tears to her eyes. It was powerful. KoKo and Kayson sat holding hands and periodically gazing at each other. KoKo sat thinking how could this roofless killer have such an appreciation for such arts. Being there with him only intensified her love. By the end of the week, they were spent. They lay around just enjoying each other's company. "Get dressed I have something special planned for the evening," Kayson said.

One hour later, KoKo came out dressed in a light blue Bohemian dress. Her skin glowed from the tan she had gotten and she wore her hair in a bun. Kayson looked up

from where he was sitting and all he could say was, "Damn, you look beautiful."

"Thank you, Mr. Wells," KoKo said as she slowly turned to show off the dress.

Kayson smiled. "Are you ready, baby?"

"Yes, I am."

They went down to the beach where a table was all set up with candle light sitting right by the water and under the moonlight. They walked over to the table holding hands and smiling. When KoKo saw everything that he set up, she put her hand to her mouth and said, "Awwww. You're trying to spoil me?"

"Nah, just trying to love you." He gave her a sexy look.

"I want to be loved by you, Kayson." Her heart beat fast; she had never felt this way before.

"Sit down and let's enjoy this evening." They sat, ate, and laughed. Kayson spent time touching her face and staring into her eyes.

"Why you looking at me like that?" KoKo asked in her little girl voice.

Just then, the waiter came over to the table. "Will there be anything else, Mr. Wells?"

Kayson put his hand up and said, "Leave us," as he continued to stare at her.

"I want to see your body in this moonlight," he said.

"What?" KoKo asked a little taken aback.

"Stand up." He took her hand and led her in front of him. "Take that dress off."

"Kayson, somebody is going to see me," she said, glancing around.

"This is my island. I got this. Now let daddy see his twin lovelies glow in this darkness."

She released the tie holding the dress together and it fell to her feet. Kayson admired her curves from head to toe. He undressed and led her into the water. They stood in the water looking at each other and sharing a conversation without using words. Kayson released her hair from the clip and pulled her hair down and she shook it out. Naked, KoKo wrapped up in his arms with the warm breeze blowing her hair she felt so innocent and pure. Kayson ran his hand down the side of her face and when he got to her lips, she put her hand on his, placed it to her mouth, and kissed it. Turning her head slightly, she let her face rest in his palm. Kayson took a deep breath then placed kisses on her forehead and rained them down her face until he got to her lips, placing gentle kisses on them. She slipped her tongue in his mouth and then he started sucking her lips. KoKo loved every second. He handled her so tender and lovingly, running his fingers down the small of her back and gazing at her like she was the last woman on earth. He whispered in her ear, "I love you, KoKo."

"I love you too, Kayson."

He picked her up out the water and held her tight for a few seconds, breathing in all her essence. Allowing her body to slide down his chest, once at his waist, she wrapped her legs around him. Kayson took her by the hips and slid up in her, releasing a slight moan. He lowered them both to the crystal sand and lay on top of her. Their bodies were half in the water and half out. Kayson stroked her effortlessly while waves washed up on his back. The mood was just right.

"Mmmmm . . . sssss . . . You feel good, baby," Kayson whispered in her ear.

KoKo stared into the star lit sky, taking in the whole scene. She closed her eyes as a tear ran down the side of her face and held on tight to his neck. "Kayson, you're the best thing that has ever happened to me. I could be like this with you forever."

With that, Kayson stroked and stroked until they were

202

both satisfied. When they got back to the house, KoKo was quiet and thinking she and Kayson had been sexual in so many ways in so many places, but tonight was different. She was feeling things for him that she had never felt.

"Why you so quiet?" Kayson interrupted her thoughts.

"I'm seeing sides of you that I am falling in love with."

"Is that right? Well, let's take a shower so I can show you another side of me."

"I have a feeling that you are going to do something to me," KoKo said with great suspicion.

"Don't get scared now." Kayson chuckled.

Chapter 25

When KoKo opened her eyes, Kayson was sitting next to her completely dressed and smiling. A brief silence passed. He broke it with "Marry me."

KoKo's eyes widened as she sat straight up. "Are you serious?"

"Yes. You my world, KoKo. A nigga can't wake up to the idea of not having you in my life." KoKo rubbed the side of his face. He turned slightly and kissed her palm.

"You are the only one who can make a bitch cry." She chuckled, wiping away a single tear that ran down the side of her face.

"You didn't answer me," he said, maintaining eye contact.

"I have been your wife from the day you first laid your hands on me. The only thing left is the paperwork." She got quiet then she said, "Baby, of course I'll marry you. I believe that our souls have been dancing together since the beginning of time."

"I love you and thank you for letting me love you."

Kayson hugged her tight then reached in his pocket and pulled out a ring that looked like it cost a million dollars and in actuality, it did. He placed it on her finger; it was beautiful. She turned it back and forth and watched it shimmer. KoKo hugged him tight then broke their embraces to kiss his lips. She smiled, glancing at her ring again.

He stood and pulled her to her feet and again hugged her

tight. "I'm going out to take care of some things. Someone will be here to pick you up in the morning to help you get ready." The moonlight shined on them through the big bay window, accompanied by the breeze coming off the water. Kayson was the happiest man in the world.

The next morning, KoKo called Kayson's phone. "You are really taking this not seeing the bride before the wedding stuff serious."

"Good morning beautiful."

"I missed waking up to you this morning," KoKo said in her naughty voice.

"Is that right?"

"Yes. I woke up wanting to be a bad girl, but I had to do it solo."

"Oh shit. That's a good thing. You know I like it real hot and real wet."

"I can't wait to see you."

"Well, go ahead and get ready. The day is all about you and tonight is about the Boss. Love you."

"Love you, too."

KoKo sat eating the fruit and yogurt set out for her along with the freshly squeezed orange juice. Then she showered. This day, she wore her hair out long and curly, and threw on a strapless sundress. Grabbing the black card Kayson left for her, she then heard the bell ring as she applied her lip-gloss and headed to the door. Once in the car, she sat enjoying the breeze and scenery. The two assistants he hired took her for a full body massage, mani and pedi. Then she was off to get her hair done and pick out a dress. She was out all day and was exhausted.

Late that afternoon, KoKo walked into her room, hung up the dress, and laid out the shoes and bra, figuring she'd better not wear panties. Because knowing Kayson she wasn't going to need them. At six P.M. KoKo decided to take a nap until it was time to get dressed. Kayson called around 8 P.M. and woke her up. The phone rang four times then she answered, "Hello."

"The driver will be there at 9:30."

"Where are you?" she said in a sleepy tone.

"Waiting to make you my wife. Be ready."

"I can't wait to see you."

"Me too. Let me finish getting things together. I'll see you in a minute."

KoKo rose up and stretched, looking over at her dress. She showered and oiled her skin, putting some glaze on her shoulders, arms, and legs. She put on her robe then fixed her hair and poured herself a glass of wine and tried to relax.

At 9 P.M., she heard the maid knock on the door to help her get dressed. Fully dressed and skin scented with Marc Jacob, she looked flawless. KoKo slid that rock on her finger, which made everything real. She felt so tickled inside she couldn't stop grinning. Taking one last look in the mirror, she headed to the living room.

On a Mission

Kayson sat in the back of the Maybach looking out the window at the night sky as his bodyguard headed to their destination. When they pulled up to the remote location on the island and the car came to a stop, he got his mind ready for his mission at hand. Kayson exited the car and walked to the driver side window. "I will be out in thirty minutes." he said.

"A'ight, handle your business," the deep voice replied.

Kayson walked up the driveway and rang the bell. The door opened and he was greeted by Dominique. She wore a pair of tight red boy shorts and a tank top. She appeared to have just showered. When she saw Kayson, her nipples hardened and she smiled.

Kayson had gone to the island for more than pleasure, he had a contract to fullfil and Dominique was keeping the nigga occupied for him while he set him up for his demise. Dominique was just happy that Kayson was talking to her, so she decided to take advantage of her invitation to his island.

"I didn't think you would be able to break away from your little girlfriend."

"I'm not here to talk about KoKo, you said you had something to tell me, so start talking," Kayson said, walking past her.

Dominique shut the door and followed him to the living room. Kayson went to his favorite seat and she sat Indian style next to him. "I missed you."

"Is that right?"

"Yes, that's right. Don't play. You know how I feel about you," she said, staring at him like she wanted to jump on him.

Kayson looked her up and down. He had to admit she looked good and that her pussy print in those shorts was looking sweet, but the memory of their last meeting still had him vexed at her. "Tell me what's on your mind. I got shit to do."

"Look, I don't want to fight with you anymore. I love you and I know that the feelings you had for me didn't just disappear. I want another chance."

Kayson sat there thinking, *is this bitch crazy?* "Is that what you called me all the way over here for?"

"Kayson, I'm not going to let you just throw away all the years we shared," she said as she started to rub up and down his leg moving toward that steel. Kayson grabbed her hand.

"Don't play yourself. Al said you had some info for me. That's all I want."

"You're serious?" she said with shock and disappointment.

Kayson rose to his feet. "From now on, deal with Al or

Wise, don't reach out to me. As a matter of fact, this is your last job." He then walked to the door.

Dominique ran to the door and stood in front of it. "Kayson, please don't leave like this," she said with her arm extended to stop his movement. "Just give me another chance."

"You had all the chances I'm willing to give you. Move."

"I guess playing house with that little bitch got you all soft." She flipped the script.

Kayson took a deep breath trying to keep his composure. "If you don't get the fuck out the way, you are going to regret the day you met me," he said with evil in his eyes.

"I already regret the day I met you. You fucked up my life." She was yelling and semi hyperventilating.

"How the fuck did I fuck up your life? Your black ass betrayed me," he said, pounding on his chest. She had hit that button and there was no turning back.

"You know what? Fuck you. You are so hateful."

"I'm hateful?" Kayson yelled. "You killed my fucking baby. And I'm hateful?"

"How many people have you murdered?" She spit back.

Kayson chuckled. "Bitch, you crazy. Get the fuck out the way."

"I'm sorry, Kayson. I was confused." She started to cry.

"I asked you . . . No, correction—I fucking begged you not to kill my seed. What the fuck was there to be confused about?"

"What security did I have? You were on your way to the prison or the grave."

"I'm not having this conversation with you. Get. The fuck. Out. My. Way."

She put her hand up to his chest. "Please let me make it up to you. Please." She was now crying hysterically. Kayson stood there looking at her with pure disgust, heavily breathing

in and out. All the hurt and pain he felt when he got knocked in Vegas came rushing back. He went out there to expand and someone snitched and he ended up spending almost three months before getting released. When he finally called home, Dominique told him she killed his baby. Immediately, evil thoughts flashed through his mind accompanied by the fact that it was her who he was with the night his uncle got murdered; he never forgave himself for that.

"You want to make it up to me?" he asked in a sinister voice.

"Yes please. I'll do anything." She was desperate.

Kayson unzipped his pants, grabbed a condom from his pocket, and slid it on. "Get on your knees," he said.

Wanting to have any way back in, she lowered herself and took him in her hands. She began to lick and kiss the head and took him in her mouth. Closing her eyes, she went to work. Kayson stood over her watching her actually enjoying herself. Once she was totally distracted, he reached into his back pocket and pulled out a piece of fishing wire. The thought of taking this bitch's life for her betrayal made his dick harder. Dominique felt him swell in her mouth and sucked harder. She heard a hiss slip from his lips and took him to the back of her throat. Just as he released, she pulled back. Kayson slipped the line around her neck and proceeded to choke the shit out of her. Dominique struggled for air, grabbing at the wire but to no avail. All the hatred he had for her pulled on both ends of the wire. When she stopped struggling, he pulled hard a few more times just to make sure she was dead. He dropped her to the floor and pulled off the condom. Grabbing a small Ziploc bag from his waistband, Kayson put the condom he had in the bag and pushed it in his front pocket straightened his clothes then headed for the back door. He grabbed a hand towel, opened it and left out. *A grimey bitch ain't good for shit but a mouth full of dick or death.*

Chapter 26
Ready for Love

At 9:30 P.M. sharp, the chauffeur knocked at the door. KoKo answered and the gentleman's eyes told it all. He looked at her like she was a goddess. "Your king awaits, Madam," he said in his island accent. He put out his elbow and she placed her hand on it and was led to a black Maybach. The ride to the destination was thirty-five minutes and as they approached, she began fiddling with her dress and hair. They pulled up to a gate that opened with a code then proceeded up a long winding road that ended at a large place on a cliff. Breathtaking. Once they parked, the driver opened her door and walked her to the entrance. She was met by two island women. "Come this way, please." They handed her a bouquet of flowers and took her by each arm.

Pink and white rose petals were at her feet, which cushioned her walk down the long hallway. Two large glass doors were at the end of the hallway. Each woman grabbed a handle and opened it wide. KoKo choked up at a view of the patio. Large white glass candles and flowers were everywhere. On each side of the walkway were black marble ponds with lilies floating in them. At the end, Kayson stood in a white gazebo dressed in an all-white two-piece linen Issey Miyake suit smiling from ear to ear. Standing across from him was a man holding a flute. As KoKo approached him, she heard Mariah Carey's song playing.

211

I'd give my all to have just one more night with you, I'd risk my life to feel your body next to mine . . .

As she got closer, her eyes started to water. The moon appeared to be sitting right on top of the gazebo and she could hear the waves crashing against the rocks below. When she reached Kayson, the music faded. He walked down and assisted her up the two steps. They stood there looking at each other as the Imam and the witness walked up to officiate the ceremony. A man with a flute began playing "I am Ready for Love" by India Arie. KoKo could hear it in her head.

I am ready for love, why are you hiding from me? I'd quickly give my freedom, to be held in your captivity.

Kayson mouthed, "I love you."

KoKo mouthed, "I love you more."

The minister began the ceremony then asked each of them did they have anything to say to each other. KoKo went first.

"You came into my life and changed my world. Life without you is not an option. I want to continue to learn and grow with you. Take this sacred part of me and fill it with your love and in return, I will do the same."

Kayson smiled and brushed away her tears. He took a minute and embodied her words.

As the flute continued to play, Kayson took a deep breath. "You are the best thing that has ever happened to me. You showed me that love can be pure and that it doesn't hurt. If you can continue to love me and be patient, I'm going to give you the world."

"By the power vested in me, I now pronounce you man and wife. You may kiss your bride."

Kayson took KoKo by her face as she stared into his eyes, tears and all. Then he placed the first kiss softly and accurately on her lips. He also kissed the tears running down her face. Their lips met again and he kissed her with such

212

passion and emotion. KoKo was so overtaken by the exchange, she felt as if she were floating. When his lips broke from hers and he saw his wife's eyes closed and at the same time tears streamed from the corners, he smiled and held her in his arms. The sound of light applause and emotion from the small crowd privy to witness their union filled the area. But to KoKo and Kayson they were the only two on earth.

They were interrupted by a woman who brought them two glasses of champagne. They toasted to their newfound bond. "Here's to taking over the world," Kayson said.

"Indeed," KoKo added.

The newlyweds were then taken to a room below for a candle light dinner. Walking onto a balcony, they saw the table decorated with petite clear glass vases with floating candles and two small plates of fruit cut in various shapes. They were seated and brought a bottle of wine and two glasses. They gazed out at the ocean. Kayson grabbed her hand.

"I can't believe I'm your wife," she said.

"Is that a good thing?" he asked.

"It's a great thing." She leaned in and kissed him.

"Keep that up and we're going to miss dinner," he said, going into fuck mode.

"You are so freaky." She looked at him, giving him her 'take it' vibe.

Just then, one of the chefs came in with their meal, fresh salmon with a side of yellow rice and steamed asparagus with butter sauce.

"You betta be glad my ribs are touching or I'd be rearranging your organs."

"That's what your mouth say."

"We'll see about all that tough talk." He bit into his salmon.

KoKo giggled then followed suit.

After about forty minutes, the chef came back and cleared the plates. He gave them a rinse bowl to wash their hands and mouth and some mint leaf. Kayson took KoKo by the hand, sat her on his lap, and put his arms around her and began kissing and nibbling on her shoulder. KoKo put her arms around his neck and began kissing him. "I think we better get going because Mrs. Kitty is beginning to purr," she said.

"Let me check on her," Kayson said, sliding his hand up her dress only to find out she was soaking wet. "Stand up." He walked her to the edge of the balcony and she sat on the ledge. He stood between her legs.

"Oh shit, Kayson, I'm scared. You betta not drop me," she said, looking down at the sharp rocks below.

"I got you." He kissed her soft lips. "Put him where he needs to be." KoKo grabbed his dick and guided him to home plate. He slid inside her letting out a small moan then went to pleasing his wife. The whole atmosphere was perfect. The excitement of being up that high and the emotion of danger as she could hear the water crashing up against the rocks along with the newness of being his wife brought KoKo's orgasm on strong one after the next. Kayson started to stroke faster and faster as she held on for dear life. He went in deep and grinded until he busted long and hard. Then he stood there enjoying her muscles tightening around him.

"Damn. That's what I'm talking about," Kayson said out of breath.

"I want some more. Let's go home so you can fuck my brains out," KoKo responded.

"We are home. I own this shit, too. And don't be trying to kill me 'cause your name is on shit now."

KoKo laughed. "Shieet. You the one got me all on the cliff."

"Let's go break this new shit in. I saw a counter and a few walls that look like they need a good waxing." He let her

down and they headed to the room to complete their evening.

Kayson woke up at about 7:00 and looked around the room. He ran his hand over his face then sat up in the bed. Looking over at KoKo, he smiled and rubbed her back. She was so worn out she didn't even move. He swung his legs over the edge and stepped off the bed headed for the bathroom. Once he returned to the room, he sat in the chair next to the bed and picked up the phone.

"Hello." His mother answered.

"We did it." Kayson said with a smile on his face.

"Awww. Son, how did it go?" Monique asked as she sat up in her bed.

"She was the most beautiful bride I ever saw. It was perfect."

Monique took a deep breath and closed her eyes in an attempt to imagine the event. "I wish I could have been there."

"Me too." Kayson said staring at KoKo.

"Don't worry, I will be feeling much better by the time you get home."

"I'm praying for you. Me and KoKo are going to take you out to celebrate as soon as we get back."

"I look forward to it. Kiss my daughter in law and tell her I love her."

"Love you ma."

"Love you too. Kayson?"

"Yes."

"Make her happy."

"I will." With that, they disconnected the call. He sat for a while just watching her sleep, then he got in the bed and snuggled up next to her.

For the next couple of days, Kayson met with several people and took care of some shit before they headed back to New York. This time, they flew in the jet. He wanted to make sure he rode that ass all the way home.

Chapter 27
Traitor

"Stop Kayson." KoKo whined as she tried to move Kayson's hand from her face and go back to sleep.

Kayson laughed as he began planting kisses on her face and lips. He had been messing with her while she was trying to take a nap in the limo. "Wake up ma. We about to pull up." KoKo sat up and stretched.

"Is this what I have to look forward to for the rest of my life?" She said then chuckled.

"Yup." He said leaning in and kissing her again. The car came to a stop and the driver got out and opened the door.

When they walked up to the door, they were exhausted. They opened the door and allowed the chauffeur to carry in the bags. Kayson tipped him three hundred dollars and proceeded to carry KoKo over the threshold. He placed her down softly on the coach then went to close the door.

"Thank you, baby. If all this shit ended tomorrow, I would have no regrets."

"Don't even try it. You're not getting rid of me that quick," KoKo shot back.

"I'm not trying to get rid of you. Sheeit, you see that ring? You got a lot of work to do to pay me back."

"What?" KoKo said, punching him in the arm.

Kayson laughed. "I'm just playing, Mrs. Wells."

"That sounds so sweet. Say it again."

Kayson kissed her lips lightly then looked her in her eyes. "You. Are. Mrs. Kayson Wells."

KoKo closed her eyes and took a deep breath. "Ce'Asia Wells. That is crazy."

"You are so beautiful," Kayson said, gazing into her eyes.

"You ain't too bad on the eyes either." KoKo smiled.

"Well, let's go upstairs and let me put my baby in a nice hot tub then give him a massage."

"Yeah, I need to soak in the tub and get a massage. I'm still sore from when you were holding on to a brotha's neck all tight up on that balcony," he said, standing up and pulling her to her feet.

"Hell yeah, I was holding on tight. Your dick is good, but not good enough to fall off a fucking cliff."

"Damn." Kayson looked at his dick and said, "See how she do you?" He cuffed his ear with his hand. "I know she hurt your feelings. I'll make her apologize."

"You need help. You and your dick." She turned to head for the elevator. Kayson came up behind her, grabbed her around the waist, and kissed her on the neck.

"You should be very satisfied already, Mr. Sugar Monster," she said in a very calm voice.

"Well, I own all this now so you can't deny me."

"I was never able to deny you before because when I say no, you just take it." She chuckled.

"Just like I'm getting ready to do right now." He walked her to the elevator.

The maid interrupted. "Excuse me, Mr. Wells. Baseem and Aldeen are here to see you," she said.

"Damn. Didn't I teach them niggas timing?" he said aloud.

"Well, go play with your friends. I'm going to start unpacking and hop in the shower," KoKo stated as they got on the elevator.

218

Kayson stopped on the second floor and went straight to his office. His partners were already seated. Aldeen got up and gave Kayson some dap and sat back down. Baseem stood up and did the same. Kayson sat in his big leather chair. Aldeen was the first to speak.

"What's up, my nigga? You look all relaxed and shit," he said with a big Kool Aid smile.

"I'm good," he said, thinking of the two weeks he'd just spent with KoKo. True to form, he went right into business. "Any updates?" he asked casually.

"Nah, I ain't got no news. But I do have a question," Aldeen said, looking Kayson in the eyes.

"What's up?" Kayson asked.

"What the fuck is that on your finger, nigga?" Aldeen started laughing.

Kayson looked at his hand and smiled. "Oh this?"

"Yeah nigga, that."

"Me and KoKo got married."

"Get the fuck outta here! How the fuck did she get you to do that?"

"Nah, how did I get her to do it?" Kayson said, going into his memory bank for all the happy thoughts of how good he felt from the time she said yes.

Baseem busted out with, "Daaaamn. Y'all went and got married?"

"Yeah, she blessed a brotha. I have a lifetime supply of hot KoKo."

Baseem and Aldeen started to laugh and shake their heads.

"I thought you were just training her?" Aldeen reminded him of a conversation they had two years ago.

"Yeah, and I trained her well and I can't let the next nigga benefit from all that good lovin'."

"Shit, I know that's right," Aldeen said, agreeing with

Kayson.

"So enough of my business. What's going on in the streets?"

Aldeen quickly got serious. "The streets are good, and everybody rolled over nice after the takeover. I haven't seen or heard any ill will," Aldeen reported.

Kayson squinted, giving him that death stare. "What do you mean you haven't heard or seen any ill will? When is the last time you ran the beat and checked pulses?" Aldeen was off his square because he wasn't used to Kayson talking to him like that.

"I sent Akbar," he answered.

Kayson leaned his head slightly to the right and looked at Aldeen like he'd lost his fucking mind. "What the fuck is that supposed to mean to me?" he responded. The color in Aldeen's face faded.

"Look, Kayson. Either you trust me or you don't. I been keeping up with shit the way I know how for years." He got quiet like he was waiting for the other shoe to drop.

Kayson said his infamous line, "Is that right?"

"Come on, man, you know me. I'm loyal as hell and I handle everything you ask of me," Aldeen explained with the quickness.

"Yeah that's true, but sometimes comfort can sign a nigga's death certificate." Kayson sat forward making serious eye contact with Aldeen. Meanwhile, Baseem looked back and forth at them wondering where this shit was going next.

Kayson walked to his wet bar and poured himself a shot of Hennessey Black then turned around and said, "Make better runs. It's no way every muthafucka that works for us is happy. It's always a muthafucka trying to come up. How the fuck do you think we got where we are? Never second guess the next nigga's greed."

Aldeen nodded in agreement. "Yeah, you right."

Kayson took his glass to the head, turned back to the bar, and set it down. Taking a deep breath, he turned back to Aldeen. "I have never guided you wrong. And I don't have to doubt a nigga because when I feel like they ain't worthy, the last thing they see is black." He took another shot to the head and looked over at Aldeen. He glanced back at Kayson and for the first time, he was scared of him; he saw something in those eyes that he could only explain as terror. The room went silent for a few seconds. Kayson moved next to Baseem, put his hand on Aldeen's shoulder, and locked eyes with him.

"Never question my trust in you." After a short pause he said, "The streets are waiting."

Aldeen and Baseem headed to the door. Once they were on the elevator, Baseem asked, "What the fuck was that about?"

Aldeen was still caught in the moment. "All this shit we are into is all about business. The moment you think it ain't, you're a muthafuckin dead man." The elevator doors opened and they hopped in the BMW and were out.

Kayson watched the monitors to make sure they were gone. He hit all the locks and security system and then went upstairs. Exiting the elevator, he saw KoKo standing in the mirror fully dressed in jeans, a hoodie, boots, a bulletproof vest, and gun holster. She had snatched her hair into a ponytail and put on a baseball cap.

"Where the fuck do you think you going?" he asked.

KoKo heard his voice ring through the bedroom.

"I got to check on the streets," she said, loading her two guns into the holsters.

"Nah baby, you ain't going out there. I got them niggas on it."

"That's not what I heard." She moved around continuing to get ready.

Kayson looked at her like, hold the fuck up. "What do you mean that's not what you heard?" he asked.

KoKo bent over and placed her .22 in the ankle holster then said, "I came downstairs to see what you wanted to eat and I overheard Aldeen say some uncertain type shit and Baseem didn't have a report at all. That nigga just sat up there co-signing. What kind of bullshit is that?" She turned around, went to the table to grab a gwap of money and two blunts she had rolled. Kissing Kayson on the lips, she said, "I'll see you in a little while," and headed to the door.

Kayson yelled out, "You're going to have to give these streets up, KoKo."

She turned to him and said, "When we get a reliable nigga to run shit, I will." Winking at him, she said, "I love you," and bounced.

At first, Kayson was going to make her come back, but then he remembered why he hired her in the first place. He had to admit she was the most loyal member on the team and if shit needed to be found out, she damn sure was going to find it. He had to remind himself that she signed up for the same mission he did. He couldn't let his personal feelings get in the way of business because that is how muthafuckas end up dirt napping.

KoKo had been gone for about fifteen minutes. Kayson had already got into character and got dressed and was on her heels. Shit, he was no fool. He had the same taste for the streets that she did and he could feel something wasn't right.

Once KoKo got to the block, she saw Akbar out there doing what she interpreted as negotiating with a nigga and it looked like Moe.

"What the fuck?" she said to herself. Her frown line deepened, and her heart was racing. Grabbing both guns out the holster, she prepared for a little killing time.

KoKo emerged from between two cars catching both

men off guard. "Let me find out we got some snakes in our camp."

Akbar put all his attention on KoKo then said, "Sheeit. Bitch, I ain't Dee. If you're going to pull a gun on me you betta use it," he spat as he reached for a gat of his own.

Too late. KoKo shot him in the hand causing his gun to go flying.

"Just like Dee, you sleeping on a bitch."

"What the fuck is wrong with you? Bitch, you betta kill me." Akbar bent over, holding his hand and moaning in pain.

"Oh, be patient. It's coming." She turned her energy to Moe. "I knew you were a bitch made nigga, but damn, plotting behind our back with this no account nigga is weak as hell."

Moe took a long pull from his blunt, careful not to do too much too fast. Then he spat out, "Our back? You ain't got no investment in my money. My only loyalty is to Kayson, not the bitch he lay pipe to. As far as I'm concerned, I put my work in. Now I'm moving on."

"Is that right?"

"Yeah bitch, it is right," Moe said, plucking the blunt into KoKo's face trying to get her off guard. He was successful. That move brought him a small window, so he leaped at her going for her guns. They tussled back and forth. He head butted her causing her to fall to the ground. KoKo was a little dazed. When she looked up, Moe stood over her with both of her guns pointed at her.

Akbar stood up in pride and smiled at the situation. "Yeah bitch, it don't feel good staring down the barrel of two guns, now does it?"

"Fuck you! I ain't scared to take a life and I damn sure ain't afraid to lose one. All I can say is, don't miss, muthafucka."

"You know what? You sexy as hell. Laying up there trying

to be tough with death hovering over your head. I see why Kayson is pimping you so hard." He clicked the gun back releasing one in the chamber.

KoKo started laughing, then shook her head from side to side. "Yeah, all y'all niggas is the same. It's all about good pussy. If you weren't such a bitch ass nigga, you could have found out for yourself." Slowly, she raised her left leg, giving him a shot of her pussy print. Moe took a minute to look then said, "Damn shame all that good pussy is about to go to waste."

In one move, she grabbed the .22 and squeezed, hitting him in the pelvis. He yelled out in pain then tried to squeeze off a shot that hit the sidewalk inches from KoKo's face. He went to release again but was stopped in his tracks. The whistle of the bullet that hit his head was from Kayson's gun. He had shown up just in time. Moe's lifeless body fell right beside KoKo. As Akbar hit the ground taking cover, he went to KoKo's side. "You a'ight?" Kayson asked.

"Yeah." She rubbed her forehead and felt a small cut from the head butt. There was a little blood but no need for the hospital.

"Go get in my truck. Go over to the twin's house so she can look at that cut. Call all them muthafuckas and tell them to meet me at the uptown underground spot in an hour and not one of them had better not show up late. I want you there, too." He helped her up, gave her a nasty look, then turned his attention back to Akbar, who had taken a shot and was on the ground pleading for his life.

Kayson helped him up and then called a cab. An hour later, he was walking into the building. Everyone was sitting around looking paranoid. Kayson held a black duffle bag. He was quiet as hell with an evil look in his eyes that no one had ever witnessed. In his hand was a 12-inch machete. He walked over to KoKo and looked at her forehead. Twin had

put a butterfly stitch in her forehead and gave her an antibiotic and pain medication. Kayson kissed her forehead and that would be the last moment of kindness the room would witness. Kayson then went into rare form.

"I had you muthafuckas at my house asking you what the fuck was going on and everybody was acting like everything was gravy." He paused, placing the duffle bag in the middle of the table. He unzipped it, pulled Akbar's head out, and placed it on the table. All you could hear was "oh shit!" ringing out of several people's mouths. One of his top dogs threw up.

Kayson yelled at the top of his lungs, "Y'all tell me why the fuck this punk muthafucka almost killed my wife? My wife!" He looked around the table for a sign. "Nobody? Not a one of you can explain to me why Akbar and Moe was plotting a side deal right up under y'all nose?"

The only sound in the room was breathing and heartbeats. Kayson waved his machete and growled out, "Can't. None. Of y'all niggas tell me why this dead muthafucka right here was plotting behind my fucking back?" He looked around the room and then caught the eye of Justice; he was the one that ran Harlem. He had a look in his eye that Kayson wasn't comfortable with. It screamed guilt and fear. Kayson pointed the machete at Justice and said, "Why the fuck is you so jumpy?"

"I'm good. I'm just trying to see where all this shit is going?" He tried to sound concerned, but Kayson could see right through him.

"Who hired that nigga, Akbar?"

Aldeen spoke up. "Justice brought him in."

"Is that right?" Kayson said as he began to walk slowly around the table. When he got to Justice, he said, "Did you know this muthafucka was plotting on me?"

"Nah Kayson, I swear. He never talked to me about

Ne Ne Capri

nothing." Justice was trying to look over his shoulder, but just as he got ready to turn around, Kayson grabbed him by his dreads and cut his head off. Then he sat it next to Akbar's head and said, "Well, now y'all can talk about it. Greasy muthafuckas."

As Kayson looked around the room, the fear and uncertainty was heavy. He could see that everyone in attendance was fucked up over what they had just witnessed.

Kayson walked around the table and stopped at Aldeen. "I got mad love for you and that's the only reason why I am counting two instead of three. I don't know what the fuck got your head all fucked up, but you betta right this wrong." Kayson walked back over to KoKo. She had a look in her eyes that read: this nigga ain't no joke. Kayson didn't want her scared of him, but he definitely needed her to be there to see he had stepped back but not off. Kayson turned to the rest of the crew. "Remember. I run this shit. I know what the fuck is going on before it happens. Don't make me come down here again because the next time, I'm a hit y'all so hard you'll think I blessed y'all the first time. Now go and reorganize Harlem and tighten this shit up. If you think we got an enemy, kill 'em." As he walked out the door, he yelled back, "Aldeen. Fix this shit."

"I got you boss."

Kayson headed home. When they arrived, KoKo still hadn't said anything to him. She didn't really know what to say. She knew his rep was thorough, but she didn't expect to see him in that type of action. The night's events made her take on a whole new respect for Kayson as well as the empire they were building. As they got off the elevator, Kayson spoke first, "I have been telling you that when I tell you to do something, I need you to do it when I tell you. I say shit for a reason. I have been in this game since I was fifteen. I knew about Akbar. I was trying to see if Aldeen caught it, but he

226

didn't. That shit is still bothering me. He's starting to slip. I need some new eyes. I'm going to have to bring some nigga's out here to handle shit for me when I'm out the country."

"What are you going to do about Aldeen?"

"I don't know yet, but after he fixes shit, I'm going to sit him down. Him and Wise."

"What about Baseem?"

"Who do you think told me about Akbar?"

KoKo was quiet. Then she said, "I'm sorry. From now on, I will take your lead." She walked over and hugged him tight.

"It's all good, baby. Sometimes experience is the best teacher."

They walked into the bathroom, undressed, showered, and hit the sack. Over the next couple of days, Kayson helped get shit in order and prepared for a trip out of town to bring in what he called fresh eyes.

Chapter 28
Caught by Surprise

After that shit happened that almost took KoKo's life, Kayson went back into the streets. He was moving niggas around, kicking ass, and taking numbers. The whole organization was uptight. They were use to handling their shit and just reporting in, but now with him breathing down their necks, niggas was trying to get Boy Scout merits. KoKo was banned from all street activity. Her ass was in the house being what he had made her, his wife.

KoKo was going crazy in that mansion all day, but he wasn't trying to hear shit. He wasn't taking any chances. Missing Kayson as he was out on one of his many ventures, KoKo decided to run herself a hot tub of water and relax. Once it was full, she lit a couple candles and a blunt then poured herself a glass of wine and climbed in. She took a couple hits of her blunt and a few sips of wine, grabbed the remote, and turned on the CD player. Closing her eyes, she enjoyed the mood. Thoughts of Kayson filled her mind and she found herself feeling horny as hell. Opening her eyes, she sat up and grabbed the showerhead turning it on and adjusting the speed. Placing it between her legs so it was directly on her clit, she began to move it back and forth. Laying her head back, she imagined Kayson licking her just the way she liked it, and within seconds, she felt an orgasm coming on. She bit down on her bottom lip, took her other hand, grabbed the side of the tub, and released.

"You couldn't wait for daddy," Kayson said in his deep voice.

KoKo jumped, "Shit, you scared me." She looked over to the bathroom door where he was standing.

"Why you fucking my showerhead?" he asked then smiled.

"Shut up and come handle this." Kayson undressed and entered the Jacuzzi.

"I created a monster." As he leaned down to kiss her, KoKo looked deep into his eyes and said, "Sure did, now give me some of that good-good."

A few hours had passed and Kayson and KoKo came staggering out the bathroom laughing and playing.

"Get up on the bed. I have to give you a belated wedding present."

"What you talking about?" Kayson asked in his curious tone. "What you got for the Boss?"

"I want to talk to the enforcer."

"Oh shit. Is that right?" Kayson grabbed his dick with excitement.

"Nigga, don't get stupid. You know good and well the enforcer got this kitty tamed and I want to slay your dragon." She looked at him with hunger in her eyes and said, "I'm going to thank him up close and personal."

Kayson's dick jumped at the thought. KoKo wasn't the 'giving head' type. She would always tell him, "When a bitch got pussy power she don't need to suck dick." Kayson grinned. Shit, if she was getting ready to do what he thought she was getting ready to do, then he was giving her the keys to the safe. After she led Kayson to the bed, he got in place.

"Just lay back and relax so Mrs. Wells can take care of you."

Kayson put both arms behind his head like the king he was. KoKo went over to prepare to hook a brotha up. He watched in anticipation. KoKo oiled her skin then grabbed a bottle of clear liquid, a towel, and the small ice bucket from the wet bar and headed to the bed. Kayson watched her coming toward him with a sexy, freaky look in her eyes. He could also feel the love. It was pure and real. It was shining through her body, coming from the depth of her soul. KoKo exuded confidence and strength. Kayson was amazed at the sight of his wife that he had watched grow into a woman. The fact that she was all his was orgasmic in itself.

Kayson's dick swelled to full potential. KoKo crawled between his legs, kissing his ankles moving up his leg and stopping to nibble on his inner thigh. She paid close attention to the crease of his leg. She rose up, drizzling liquid all over his pulsating rod. Taking his dick in her two fingers, KoKo slowly stroked him and lowered herself closer to him. What happened next was magic.

KoKo slipped a piece of ice in her mouth, ran the tip of her cold tongue up the line between his balls, and lightly sucked the main vein. She felt Kayson jump then put his hand on her head.

"Relax and let me be in control and I promise I will blow your mind," she instructed.

"It's your show, ma."

KoKo slowly ran her wet tongue up and down the line and sucked at the spot where the dick and balls met. Once more, she felt him jump and his leg shook. She continued while slowly stroking him, applying small amounts of pressure. Kayson grabbed at the sheets. Taking one of his balls into her mouth, she rocked it gently back and forth with her tongue while releasing her now warm breath. Letting it slide out her mouth, she paid the same attention to the other one, but this time she gave him a little hum action. Causing it to vibrate in her mouth as she sucked lightly. She slid him out her mouth then zoned in on that massive hard on.

With his base tight in her hand, she sucked her way up the main vein, continuing to squeeze, jerking, and turning her wrist in a circular motion. When she got to the head, she ran her tongue around the rim then across the top and slid the tip back and forth across the hole.

Kayson moaned. "Damn baby." Never taking his eyes off her, he watched her handle his dick like she loved it. Slowly, she began to take the head into her soft lips and sucked gently yet firm. Taking a little more of him in her mouth, she gave each inch special attention until she took him in her mouth completely. He could feel the warmth and depth of her throat accompanied by the tightness of her jaws. She squeezed and released as her head bobbed up and down at the same time. She made short and fast strokes at the base of his dick.

She used her free hand to tickle his balls.

"Oh shit . . . mmmmm."

She went faster, sucking and slurping and making soft moans of her own as if she were enjoying it as much as he was.

Kayson thought, *damn, I want to grab her head.* But he didn't want to fuck up her flow. Shit, he knew his dick was big and he was surprised she was handling it like she was. He wasn't trying to fuck up the chance of him getting hooked up again so he just grabbed the sheets tight and held on.

"Baby. Baby. Baby . . . Oh my god!"

Kayson was trying to hold back, but she was going hard on a brotha. She took him out her mouth, grabbed his dick with her hand, and jerked it firm and fast, allowing it to hit her lips and tongue. Grabbing another piece of ice, she slid it in her mouth and let it drip on him. Then she slowed down, held him tight, and sucked only the head. Her mouth was wet and soft. Kayson felt the intensity of his orgasm rising hard from the bottom of his stomach and he was ready to let that shit go.

"You love somebody?" she asked using her naughty voice.

"Hell yeah," he managed to say out of breath.

Beginning her final attack, she placed him back and forth in her wet mouth sending chills up his spine. He closed his eyes and sank his head deep into the pillow as she went faster tightening her jaws. He could no longer resist. He grabbed the back of her head; she deep throated his whole 10 ½ inches. All that did was make her go faster and suck harder.

"I'm about to cum," he yelled out.

She was right in tune with him because just as he began releasing she took him out her mouth, giving one last firm suck to the head and then jerked him firmly in her hand as he exploded. Stroking him until every drop was out; she rubbed his wetness up and down his dick as he stared at her. She caressed it causing his legs to shake as she kissed the head. Then she rained kisses up his stomach and his chest.

KoKo looked him in his eyes and said, "I'm going in the shower. You coming?"

"I'll meet you in there because right now you got a nigga's knees weak."

KoKo got off the bed smiling. She looked back at Kayson and marveled at her handy work. Usually she was the one knocked out. "Fucked you up, huh?" she said.

Kayson laughed. "Don't worry, I will redeem myself."

"I'm counting on it." She entered the bathroom and brushed her teeth. Kayson lay there for a few more minutes then he got up and headed in the bathroom. He knew he was going to have to hook her up properly for all that good head action and he was well capable. He walked up behind her and looked at her. "I thought you said you never gave head before," he said.

"What you tryna say?" she asked with a smile on her face.

232

Apparently, she had succeeded at pleasing him thoroughly.

"Nothing, you just gave me better head than I've paid for."

"Yeah, well I wasn't there when the first sticks were rubbed together, but a bitch can start a fire."

"You damn sure can. Shit, if I had known you were going to handle a brotha like that I would have given you that $2 million ring the first day I met you."

"Well, if I had gave you that the first night I met you, I guess you would be outside begging for change. 'Cause a bitch is bad."

****

Kayson's annual party went well as usual. He and KoKo worked the room, made deals, and of course slipped off to get them a quickie. They had a habit of going places and having sex somewhere they felt they would be caught. They always got a charge out of it. By the end of the night, they were spent. KoKo had handled everything. Kayson wanted her to start taking over all street connects because he had other shit to handle and he was proud as hell watching his wife work the room. All that money she just made him had his dick hard as hell. Kayson went over to her and whispered in her ear, "Let's bounce. The Boss wants to go home and do some damage." KoKo smiled and then began saying her good-byes.

Kayson went over to Aldeen and let him know that he and KoKo were about to make their exit. They gave each other a pound and Kayson met KoKo at the door. As they walked down the steps, Kayson said in his sexy voice, "Daddy might need a snack in the car." He stopped a few steps down from her, slid his hand up her dress, and ran his fingers back and forth between the lips of her pussy.

"Well, I must be real special if you're going to let me drip chocolate all over your $400 thousand dollar car seats," KoKo said in a sexy voice.

"Sheeit, as sweet as you are you can cum on anything I got. As long as you cum on my tongue first," Kayson said, giving her that look that said he was getting ready to handle his business.

"You so sexy when you talk nasty," KoKo said, flashing that pretty smile. They continued to the car. He opened the door for her and paused, looking her in the eyes.

"What? Why you looking at me like that?" KoKo asked.

"You are so beautiful." He wrapped his arms around her. Kayson took a minute to gaze at KoKo. He took a deep breath. "I love you more than life itself. I'm so thankful that the gods wrote you into my history. Thank you for walking this journey with me."

KoKo's eyes started to water. She didn't know what to say next. It always bugged her out how this man that would take a nigga's air on GP could then be so gentle with her and say the sweetest things. Once she got herself together she said, "I love you, too, Kayson, and no matter what time or place you will always be right here." She pointed at her heart, and then kissed him very light on his lips. The taste of KoKo's sugary lips along with her salty tears seeped into his. The enforcer was sending messages that he had better get him inside KoKo before he started a riot.

Kayson broke the kiss and said, "Let's get to the house before I have you on the hood of this car." He put his hands on her waist and began moving her toward the car. KoKo giggled. "Oh wait! Let me grab my flats from the trunk. They walked to the trunk and opened it. Kayson grabbed a towel he kept in there because he had the feeling they weren't going to make it to the house. KoKo took off her shoes and put on her Prada slide ons.

KoKo saw the towel in his hands then asked, "What's that for?" She smiled from ear-to-ear.

"What you think?" he said with his wicked grin. Just as Kayson was closing the trunk, a car came up on the side of them and the window slowly rolled down. Kayson pulled KoKo behind him. She immediately tensed up and reached for her burner. Then they heard a voice from the passenger side ask, "You got the time?"

Kayson locked eyes with the stranger. He heard the click of the gun and then a blast, but not before he reached for his gun and let one off in the driver's head causing the car to propel and crash into three cars before coming to a complete stop. The force of the shot caused Kayson to fall back and knock KoKo to the ground. When she was able to look at him, she saw blood dripping from his stomach and chest. KoKo quickly grabbed the towel from his hand and tried to apply pressure. Kayson passed her his gun and said, "Don't let them surround you."

She moved from under him, crawled three cars down, and looked under the cars to see if she could see any one moving. Just then, she saw the guy from the passenger seat stagger out and then the other one from the back seat. She cocked her gun and Kayson's and held them firm, one in each hand. As both guys approached Kayson's body, KoKo rose up and began shooting, dropping both of them with a head shot. She ran over to them and emptied on them then dropped her hands to her sides. Breathing hard and crying at the same time, she felt a burning sensation in her shoulder. Looking down, she realized she was bleeding.

She looked over at Kayson, who was still breathing. As the voices in the back of her got closer she headed to Kayson's side, dropped to her knees, pulled his head on her lap and started to cry. "You'll be okay, just hold on." Turning to the bystanders she yelled, "Get him some fucking help!"

Kayson smiled. "I love you," he said as he coughed up blood.

"Kayson, don't do this to me. This shit don't work without you." She cried harder.

"It's okay, baby. You . . . Always . . . Thought . . . You Were . . . The . . . boss . . . It's all yours now," he said as he began fading away.

"Noooooooo . . ." she yelled, watching him fade just as smooth out of her life as he had come in. She sat there rubbing his face. "Help is on the way, Kayson. Hold on, baby. Please hold on." Rocking back and forth, she held him close.

Aldeen kneeled next to KoKo and tears came down his face. He put his hand over his heart and bowed his head. Wise came over with a gun in each hand, saw Kayson laid out, put his hands up to his head, and began pacing back and forth. "What the fuck! Oh man. No. No. No."

Baseem stood there looking at what he called his savior bleeding to death. He grabbed his gun and went to each body filling them with bullets while everyone watched in fear.

KoKo held Kayson's head and rubbed his hair. She looked down at her hand and her wedding ring was covered in blood. "Why Aldeen?" She looked at him with such helplessness and desperation.

Aldeen put his arm around her and noticed the blood on her shoulder was coming from her. Apparently, the bullet that went in Kayson's chest tore through his heart and hit KoKo.

"KoKo, you bleeding," he said like a concerned dad. KoKo looked down then back at Aldeen then began feeling dizzy. The next thing she saw was black.

Chapter 29
Vendetta

Nine Months Later...

For the next nine months, KoKo spent all of her time in Dubai, in the very house that she and Kayson had spent the best time of their life. She would put on his robe and sit in the big chair on the balcony overlooking the water and cry. She would even talk to him. "Kayson, what am I going to do without you?" she asked, wiping away the tears. "We were supposed to spend the rest of our lives together? How the fuck did we get caught slippin'?"

KoKo picked up her hot tea with a shot of gin. The maid entered the room. "Madam, would you like to see him now?"

"Yes," KoKo answered. The maid walked over to KoKo and handed baby Quran to her. She took him into her arms, smelled his hair, and stared at him. He was beautiful, plenty of thick, curly, and wavy black hair, hazel eyes and a caramel skin tone, with cute little pink lips. Tears ran down KoKo's face as she stared at this beautiful child, a perfect combination of her and Kayson. Now she had to raise this boy into a man without any help from his father. She had given Kayson a son that he would never get to hold or love.

"Your father would have fallen in love with you." She smiled at him as he looked back at her. "Don't worry, mommy will handle it. That nigga won't breathe." As tears ran down her face, she kissed him on both cheeks. "I just have to keep you safe. I'm a go after these muthafuckas and give them some medieval pain." She held him and looked out over the water. KoKo had almost a year to plan and she was just about ready to put her plan into action.

****

Almost a year had passed and KoKo hadn't set foot in New York since Kayson's death. When she walked into the mansion, Kayson's spirit haunted the place. She got chills. As she moved from one room to the next, she thought, *Thank God the maids have been keeping the place in order.*

When she got to the third floor, her stomach sank to her feet. As the last memories of her and Kayson playing around and getting dressed for the party replayed through her mind, she continued to walk through the room headed to the closet. She ran her hands across his clothes and smelled them to see if she could capture a small scent of him. Stepping back, she saw a hoodie he had folded up on his chair; she had instructed them to leave everything as it was. She picked it up, and sank her face deep into it and inhaled. There was still a very slight trace of his cologne. She sat in the chair trying to capture every bit of his essence. Tears fell down her face at a rapid pace. KoKo began to cry so hard and loud she began to lose her breath. She grabbed at her chest and ran to the bathroom. Coughing and gasping for air. Turning on the faucet, she tried to get some water in her mouth with her hands and doused it on her face. With her hands resting on the sink, she took deep breaths and stood there for a minute. She decided that moment that all the love, passion, and admiration she had for Kayson she would turn into revenge.

Once she got herself together. She walked into her room and got out her street gear. It was time for a bitch to go on the hunt. It had been a year and no one was coming up with any info on who killed Kayson. She hopped in the shower and then got dressed. Koko went into Kayson's closet and placed his shirt in a bag to preserve any scent left. Then she hit the button to open the secret compartment, which held the guns. She grabbed midnight, loaded it, and tucked it away.

As KoKo got on the elevator, a strong feeling of anger came over her; she embraced it. She needed no feelings for anyone right now. Even the love for her newborn son had to be disregarded so she could move like she needed to. Everyone was her enemy until she could prove otherwise. When she got to the garage she hopped in Kayson's truck, hit # 3 on the CD changer to his favorite track India Arie, "I am ready for Love."

"Okay baby, let's go get these muthafuckas."

Koko pulled off and grabbed the prepaid out of her pocket and hit Aldeen and Wise. She instructed them to meet her at the spot. Both of them were surprised she was there because they didn't know she was coming and was concerned with where her head was. Since she had only been counseling them over the phone, she would be brief and demanding about what she needed them to do. They were also feeling a bit ashamed that they didn't have any info on who killed their boss and best friend. Baseem, on the other hand, went on a rampage and hit everything moving. If he thought they had anything to do with Kayson's murder, they died, no questions asked. Baseem was now serving a ten-year sentence for possession of a firearm. KoKo was keeping his commissary stacked. He was jailhouse royalty and with his loyalty to Kayson, he had earned her support.

When KoKo arrived, they were already there. She scoped the place out. Her first question was, "Why the fuck these niggas ain't out here to meet me? They slippin'."

Taking tracking monitors out the glove compartment, she then hopped out and pulled her gun just in case. Moving to each of their cars along with the cars next to theirs, she planted one next to the tire. Glimpsing, she saw a black Range Rover approaching her with tinted windows she stood up. It pulled next to her car. The figure emerged from the driver's seat. It was the Black Night, her bodyguard in Dubai. He had been Kayson's trusted confidant for the last fifteen years. Because he did not trust too many people, he always kept his major connections a secret. Because of how Kayson moved, knowing everything and only sharing what was necessary, she was moving the same way. Everybody was suspect until she found out what was going on. The 6'5", 255-pound all-muscle, baldheaded, black as hell with pretty white teeth figure approached her then he hugged her tight.

"You a'ight?"

"I'm good. I'm on the prowl and a nigga getting ready to know that if I ever barked before, the bite this time around will definitely be terror based."

"Let's do this sis," Night said and moved next to her toward the spot.

KoKo did the special knock and the door opened. Troy, the doorman stood guard.

"KoKo. Damn girl, it's good to see you," he said with surprise in his voice.

"Is that right? Well, don't get all celebration on me yet, because a lot of folks are getting ready to wish I was never born." She and Night moved passed him and Night gave Troy the screw face. Troy was uneasy, he didn't know this nigga or why he was here. *What the fuck was KoKo doing?*

KoKo walked in the room with this big black nigga right behind her. Aldeen and Wise tensed up. She walked over to Al and he hugged her, then she moved over to Wise and he gave her the same greeting. "Damn KoKo, you look good. I'm glad to see you."

"Is that right?" KoKo saw that all the men were staring at each other with intensity so she made the introduction. "This

is Night. He was Kayson's personal confidant and has been taking very good care of me for the last year per Kayson's instructions."

Aldeen reluctantly put his fist out in an attempt to give him some dap. Night looked at him like he was dirt.

"I don't shake hands with niggas I don't know unless its business, and right now I'm here on a personal matter and until I find out that your business has nothing to do with my personal endeavor, we ain't shaking no fucking hands."

Aldeen's face was real screwed fast. "Excuse me?" Night didn't blink and neither did Aldeen. In fact, it was getting ready to turn into the Wild Wild West up in there.

"Look. Y'all can measure your dicks later. Night is my right hand man now. Aldeen, we're restructuring. You and Wise are no longer needed for the front line. Several niggas downstairs will be up here in a minute. Debrief them. I'll meet y'all at the mansion later. I want a full report," KoKo said as she turned and walked away.

Night picked up his phone and called down to the squad. "Y'all come up."

Within minutes, seven of the scariest dudes you ever want to see were upstairs, black as hell with bald heads all standing around six feet tall, two hundred pounds with the look of death in their eyes and the heart to match. "This is Aldeen and Wise, is it?" He looked at Aldeen for confirmation but he didn't say shit. "They are going to bring y'all up to speed. KoKo gave y'all the instructions. See y'all later." Night turned and moved out just as KoKo did. All the men were giving each other the stare down. After a few minutes of that, they settled shit, but Aldeen kept a mental note that he and KoKo was having it the fuck out over this shit.

Outside KoKo said to Night, "Something ain't right."

"We getting ready to find out. And if any of them nigga's dirty, KoKo, I'm killing 'em."

"Do what you got to do." She jumped in Kayson's truck and pulled off. Night jumped in his ride and started his headhunt.

KoKo began to move in the streets. She would pull up blocks away and walk in so she could observe. When she rolled up on Lenox, she immediately got heated. Niggas were socializing, being loud, and bitches were posted up laughing and playing. She put on her leather gloves, took the safety off her guns then put on the 'fuck it' attitude and started to walk up the block. When she got close this kid named Kaleef, who ran the block looked down the street and saw KoKo coming. The look on his face was like he saw a ghost. He knew it was KoKo because that walk was unmistakable. He tapped Jerome on the shoulder and his once smile turned into a scared frown immediately. Just then KoKo got close enough to hear him say, "Oh shit."

"What the fuck is going on out here? What y'all niggas selling, dope or pussy?" Niggas were silent. "Don't get quiet now. Shit, I could hear y'all two blocks away a minute ago. Like we running fucking Coney Island out this muthafucka." Her eyes scanned the crowd. All they could see was evil. No one said a word. "Why are all these bitches posted up?" Again, niggas were silent.

The chicks looked at her like: Who the fuck does she think she talking about? One of them got up the courage to say, "Damn, Jerome, a bitch tells y'all what to do? Maybe instead of dutches we should have brought tampons out here." Then they started to giggle. KoKo turned her head and looked at the bitch like she had just slapped her mother. All the dudes backed up because they knew shit was getting ready to get real ugly. KoKo reached for one of her guns, loaded one in the chamber, and then said, "So, Miss Smart ass, I think I want to get fucked up tonight. I know my hearing gets a little off. But for some reason I believe I heard you call me a bitch." The girl took a hard swallow on her spit then looked around at the face of the niggas she came out there to see. All she could read from their expressions was 'bitch you on your own.'

"Oh, so now you all 'cat got my tongue.' A minute ago you thought you were Rambo or some shit. Who brought this silly bitch out here?" KoKo asked, waving her gun through the crowd. This nigga named Cas raised his hand. Wrong move because KoKo shot him right in his palm. He doubled over in pain and yelled, "Ohhhh . . ."

"Pick your bitches better next time. And shut the fuck up. Get his ass outta here, Jerome. I'll deal with you later." He quickly got Cas out of there.

"Now, what was it that you were saying?" She turned her attention back to the chick, who looked as if she just shit herself.

"Look, I don't want no trouble. I thought you was just some girl who was trying to start some shit."

"Bitch, you so dumb you stupid. Bitch, can you read?" KoKo barked at the bitch.

"Yes, I can read," she answered with a tremble in her voice.

"Well, bitch, there were signs. You should have been able to read that this shit was getting ready to get fucked up. But you know why you ignored the signs?"

"No," she answered, scared as hell and shaking.

KoKo looked at her like she was getting ready for an attack then she said, "Pride." KoKo jumped on her and busted her in the head three times with the gun. The last time it went off grazing her forehead. The girl wanted to scream, but didn't want to piss KoKo off any more than she was. Her friends tried to run, but the dudes held them there so they stood there crying.

"Shut them bitches up. I can't hear myself think." KoKo

had her by the throat, gun pointing in her face "You feel that? Bitch, that's called pride. See how it will get you all fucked up? I'm KoKo, muthafucka. Now, I don't want to see you ever again, Dawn Smith." The girl's eyes grew as big as basketballs at the fact that KoKo knew her name.

"Now, you and those two bitches get the fuck off my block and I don't ever want to have this conversation with you again. Do I make myself clear?"

"Yeeeesss!" she said through tears.

As KoKo got up she said, "You're lucky I'm having a good day or instead of patching your head they would be looking for it. Now get the fuck outta here."

The other two chicks scrambled to help her up as they tried to drag her to the corner so they could get a cab. KoKo yelled out, "Don't forget to tell the cops about the two white boys that jumped out and tried to rape her as y'all ran for help. And this good brother helped you." She patted Kaleef on the back. "Go with them and handle this shit. It's your fucking fault she's all fucked up. The rest of y'all niggas go home for the night. I'll get with y'all later."

As KoKo stood there watching everybody do as they were told she mumbled to herself, "Stupid muthafuckas. Good help is hard to find, but you can always find target practice." She headed back down the block disappearing the same way she had come.

New York Trip...

Meanwhile Terrance was sitting in his car having a conversation with one of his boys.

"I'll catch you when we get back." He had been running back and forth trying to get his street credit up for the last year.

"Where the fuck you going?"

"I'm headed to the city of dreams," Terrance responded.

"All I can say is, nigga be careful. Them niggas are slippery as hell."

"Shit, the east ain't ready for the west. That city is sitting there waiting for me to fuck it. I might as well get my dick wet."

"Sheeit. Just don't come home with it in your hand."

They busted out laughing. He and his boy hit fists and he exited the vehicle. "Hit a nigga when y'all get back."

"A'ight." With that, Terrance pulled off with his plan in hand.

Chapter 30
Terrance Meets KoKo

Terrance was sitting in a booth at the club having a few drinks with his boys laughing and talking shit. The music was bumping and everybody was feeling the buzz and enjoying the sights of wall-to-wall big asses in tight jeans and titties spilling out of bras. They were making bets on who was going home with a bitch and who wasn't when Terrance was totally distracted by what he could only describe as a Goddess. KoKo walked out with these tight ass jeans on and a white Chanel tank top and a pair of Gucci clogs. Terrance's eyes were fixed on her ass and was caught in the KoKo trance until his boy hit his arm and yelled, "What the fuck you staring at?"

"Damn, did you see that girl that just went by?" Terrance said to his boy.

"Nah, was she all that?" He started to look around to find what had his boy's dick on high alert.

Then Terrance said, "Hell yeah, she was wife material and she's headed to the VIP section over there." He had caught a visual of her as she headed to her favorite spot where she could watch everything and everyone. KoKo had stopped briefly on the way to say something to one of her informants. If he was on her, she had to make sure someone was on him. Being the hunter she was, she felt his stare and turned and flashed Terrance a sexy smile then turned around to finish her conversation.

"Damn man, did you see the way she looked at you?"

"Yeah, but I ain't tripping. She probably belongs to one of these niggas up in here and I ain't trying to kill no nigga over no pussy." They all busted out laughing. However, Terrance kept his gaze in her area for some reason. She had a certain something that he wanted to get next to. Just then, the waitress was going by and he grabbed her arm and said, "I need to know who sexy is sitting in the VIP section and is she with one of these niggas." Then he slipped her four hundred dollars.

Crystal looked in the direction he was pointing and saw that it was KoKo. At the same time, KoKo looked in his direction and saw him pointing. They made brief eye contact again. Just as the waitress said, "Oh her? That's boss lady." Then she prepared to walk away.

Terrance grabbed her arm again as he asked, "Boss lady? What the fuck does that mean?" Terrance looked perplexed.

Crystal could tell he was not from around there and wasn't trying to give this nigga too much info. "She is a partner in the club," she said, trying to walk off but was stopped by Terrance again.

"Yo. Send her a bottle of La Mondotte for me," he said. La Mondotte went for $600 a bottle. He gave her two hundred dollars to deliver it.

Crystal laughed and then smiled. "Okay," she said, but in the back of her mind, all she could think was KoKo is not going to drink that bullshit. "Is there anything else?" she asked as she turned to walk away.

"Yes, is there a nigga I need to worry about?"

Crystal smiled and said, "Personally, no. But professionally, there are several niggas in here that would kill air over her." She gave him a cold stare then another smile. "I'll be right back." She disappeared into the crowd.

Terrance watched her go to the bar and place the drink

order. She got the bottle of wine and a glass ready to be taken to KoKo.

The bartender started to laugh then he asked, "Who sent that shit?" Crystal pointed to the table where Terrance was sitting. The bartender called over Candy and put her on standby as Crystal headed to the VIP section. She sat the bottle on the table and leaned in to tell KoKo about what happened at Terrance's table.

KoKo gave Crystal a serious look then said, "What's the niggas resume?"

Crystal responded, "I think I heard them call him Terrance. But I don't think he is from around here because he would know who you are."

"Do me a favor. Let me have a pen and a piece of paper." Crystal passed it to her and KoKo started to write him a note.

"Give this note to him along with that bullshit he sent over here. Add three bottles of my shit. I'm bouncing. Watch him and find out who that nigga know and why he's here and then contact me." KoKo got up and walked off. Terrance watched the whole exchange and got a little excited when he saw her writing on the paper.

"Damn, I didn't think it was going to be that easy," he said to his boy.

When Crystal and the other waitress came over to his table with a smile he knew he had hit pay dirt. She handed him the note along with the bottle he sent over. His boys all had puzzled looks wondering what the note said and why she sent back Terrance's bottle of champagne. Terrance opened the note and it read:

Thank you for the gesture, but I don't drink bullshit. Next time do your research. I have sent you what a real woman drinks. Enjoy the rest of the night. It's on me.

One of his boys yelled out, "What the fuck she do? Write you an essay? Because it don't take that long to read

numbers." With that, they all busted out laughing. Terrance had to laugh himself. Then Crystal flagged Candy and three other waitresses who were waiting in the cut and wearing hardly anything. Each girl held one of the three bottles of Mouton Rothschild 1945 standing at $28,000 a bottle, which was KoKo's favorite wine. They brought the bottles over and placed them on the table.

"Boss lady said to take care of y'all. So anything you need is on the house, and I do mean anything."

All his boys were all cheesed up and started reaching for the bottles and rubbing titties and ass like they were prisoners on a conjugal visit. Terrance looked past the chicks and toward the booth for KoKo, but she was gone. All he could do was smile. He had to respect her gangsta.

"Yo, tell your boss I said thanks." Then he poured himself a drink, sat back, and enjoyed the show.

"No problem," Crystal said, sliding off just as smooth and lost herself in the crowd.

When KoKo got to her car, she started it up. She lit her blunt then looked up to see that same chick looking at her as she walked into the bar. She picked up her cell phone and hit Crystal on the waist. "Yes, Boss lady?"

"It's a bitch that just walked in the club wearing dark blue jeans and a yellow tank top. Find out who she is."

"What she look like?"

"Me."

Let the Games Begin

KoKo stepped in the huge walk-in closet. She started picking out her killer outfit, a pair of black Marc Jacobs jeans and a cream colored $1,800 silk Marni tank top with Swarovski crystals and a pair of $1,300 Gucci Sigrid platform sandals with metal embroidery and black zip closure. She had just gotten her hair and nails done, so she just wrapped it around and hopped in the shower. As she washed up she was getting her head right to get herself in a space where she could get close to her husband's killer. She was prepared to sacrifice whatever she had to in order to trap the muthafucka. Now she needed to seek out everything she needed to know to carry out her mission.

It was twelve o'clock and KoKo stepped into the club. Looking good, smelling good, and strapped. She didn't play that. If a nigga got outta line she was going to show them she was that bitch.

She scanned the floor space checking out each VIP room, trying to target her mark. And true to form there he was, sitting in one of the VIP rooms with all the chickens posted up. Getting her mind right, she ordered a double shot of Hennessey Black, downed it, popped a mint in her mouth, and headed his way.

Terrance looked up and saw her coming. She immediately had all his attention. Her hips were swaying to the beat, her breasts were perky and waist small. Her skin was glistening. Lips had a shiny, juicy look that made him want to grab her and suck them for hours. The intensity in her eyes went straight to his soul. KoKo walked right up to him and said, "You feel like fucking with a real bitch or you satisfied with catching fleas from these mutts?" She looked in the eyes of all the chicks in the VIP room. They in turn looked at her and one said, "No the fuck she didn't."

Terrance put his hand up as if to gesture for the girl to shut the fuck up. "Oh, so you ready to fuck with a nigga?" he said, flashing that sexy ass smile.

"I don't know. Let me buy you a drink and we can talk about it," KoKo responded.

"Why can't we drink and talk right here? I'm already comfortable."

"I don't eat and shit in the same place. You sitting with

some gutter bitches and they fucking with my taste buds." KoKo turned her nose up at the chicks. The women at the table were getting upset. They had chilled for a minute, but they were ready to fuck KoKo up.

"Damn ma, you just say whatever you want, huh?"

"I can back up whatever I say. These bitches better know." One of the girl's eyes got big as hell as she thought to herself, *This chick done called us one too many bitches.*

"So playa, you wanted to get close to a sista and the window of opportunity is closing. So what you going to do?" She began backing up. Shit, he wasn't no fool. He stood up slowly. KoKo put her hand out and he took it, leading him off to the VIP section where she always sat. The girls at the table rolled their eyes and sucked their teeth. But it didn't matter to Terrance; he wanted to get the KoKo experience.

Responsibility

KoKo sat in a restaurant in Virginia closing a deal with Mike, Kayson's Virginia connect when her phone kept vibrating. "Shit. Let me see who the fuck this is." She got up from the table and went outside. "Hello."

"Ah. Yes, is this Mrs. Wells?"

"Yes, it is. How may I help you?"

"This is the nurse at Mount Sinai. You are the next of kin on this form so I called you."

"Look Miss, you are going to have to state your business because I'm in the middle of something."

"Your mother in law is very sick and asked us to call you. She needs some medical treatment and wants someone here to help her make deci—"

KoKo cut her off. "I'm on my way; tell her I'll be right

there. I'll be there in the next two hours give or take."

"Thank you, she is very afraid and alone."

"Tell her I said hang in there. I'm on my way." KoKo disconnected the call then went inside and finished the deal. She put in a call to the pilot to have that shit running when she got there.

KoKo got to the hospital and was crushed by what she had seen. Kayson's mother was thin and frail. Tears immediately ran from her eyes. KoKo had been so caught up in her own grief, she had not checked on her like she should have. "Miss Monique."

Monique turned her head and smiled the biggest smile she had smiled in over a year. "I've been waiting for you, KoKo."

KoKo came to her side, grabbed her hand, and brought it to her face. "I'm sorry; I haven't been on point in regards to you. Please forgive me," KoKo pleaded as tears continued to fall down her face. Monique rubbed her hair.

"Baby, I know it's been hard for you. No apology necessary."

Just as KoKo raised her head, the nurse was coming in the room. "Glad to see you made it so fast." The nurse sat down and told her everything that was going on, including all the options. The cancer had come back and was eating away at her system. She had stopped taking her medicine and the depression wasn't helping either. After KoKo listened to everything, she immediately knew what to do. She called all her connections and hired a doctor, nurse, chef, and physical therapist around the clock. She ordered everything needed for her care and had it shipped to Dubai. Then she came back into the room and sat on the bed.

"We are going to fight this. I need you to trust me and do exactly what I say," she told Monique.

"I don't want to live, KoKo. I don't have anything to live

for."

"Don't talk like that."

"It's true. I want to just die." Tears ran down her face. KoKo could see all the pain in her eyes and the surrender she had given to death as she just lay there waiting for its cold hand.

"Look. You do have a reason to live and I'm going to show you. But you have to trust me and come with me. I'm going to pack up your place and put everything in storage. Is there anything you need?"

Monique paused then she said, "Yes. All my pictures of Kayson, and there are three boxes under my bed with things he had given me over the years. They are very special to me."

"Okay, I will get them. It will take another day or two for all the paperwork to get transferred then we are out of here."

"Where are we going?"

"To Kayson's paradise." She smiled.

Two days later, they landed in Dubai. They got the same greeting as usual. "Hello, Mrs. Wells." The chauffeur held his hand out to KoKo.

KoKo took his hand then headed to the limo. They got Monique from the plane and helped her into the limo. They were taken to a small yacht; KoKo didn't think it would be good to put her in the helicopter. When they got to the house, they were greeted by the staff that KoKo had hired along with the staff that they already had in place. Monique was taken to her room, assessed by the doctor, bathed, and dressed. She was fed and given the medication she needed for the night. Once they were done, KoKo came into her room and sat on the bed.

"How do you feel?"

"Much better. Thank you."

KoKo smiled. "Remember I told you that you had one reason left to live for?"

"Yes."

KoKo turned to the door and called the nanny. In she walked holding KoKo's six-month-old son. She took him in her arms and kissed his little lips then handed him to Monique. "This is your grandson."

Monique started to cry as she held him close to her. "What? How? I don't understand."

"I was three months pregnant when Kayson got killed. He was lucky to make it through my surgery from the gunshot, but he did. I came out here, had him, and kept him safe. I couldn't tell anyone because I didn't know who was after us. I fly back and forth and see him when I'm not taking care of business."

"Thank you, KoKo. Thank you," Monique said, raining kisses all over his face and hands. Her strength was not too firm, but she was determined to use it to hold that baby for as long as she could.

"What's his name?"

"Quran."

Monique shook her head in approval. "A name befitting of a king."

KoKo stared at them with such pride and love. "I will make sure that he is in here with you as much as possible."

"Yes. I have two reasons now. A daughter. And. A grandson."

KoKo called the nanny and asked her to sit in there with them until Monique was ready to turn him over. Then she left the room. For a couple days, KoKo stayed out there making sure everything was right and the security was heightened, but she had to continue her mission. She left happy because in just those few days Monique's health had improved and she appeared to be on the road to recovery. But before she left, she told her she could never go back and never under any circumstance tell anybody about Quran. They still had

enemies and until KoKo found them and killed them, they all were targets.

When KoKo got back, she turned many of her accounts over to Monique. If shit happened to her, she needed to make sure they would be all right.

Head Game

For the last couple of weeks, KoKo had been giving Terrance the chase of his life. She would go to dinner with him dressed to kill and sit across from him and talk real nasty then get a call to leave. One night they were in the restaurant and KoKo was sitting real close to him smelling good. He was rubbing her back and whispering in her ear, putting his best moves on. But true to form, she would come up with some excuse to leave. This night he had to say something.

"Why you teasing a brother? You know I'm feeling you."

KoKo had just found out all the info she needed to know about his NY connect and had put a plan in motion. So she decided she had to get him distracted so they could move in.

"I'm feeling you, too. I'm just a busy woman; it's all about my paper. But I think I can pencil you in for tomorrow night. How does ten sound?" she responded.

Terrance jumped all over that. "Ten is good." Her phone went off just as he was getting ready to lean in for a kiss. She answered it then gave him her famous line. "I got to run. I'll see you tomorrow." She got up, hit the table with two yards, and stepped off.

When KoKo got outside, she called Crystal back. "What's up?"

"That girl's name is Imani."

"Find out who she run with. I need to know why this bitch keeps staring at me. Sheeit, I'll fuck around and have those eyes on a chain around my neck."

"Yes ma'am. I'm on it like the stink on shit." They hung up. KoKo figured she had better do some digging of her own. She didn't want to take any chances.

Chapter 31

The next night, Terrance had been waiting for KoKo all night. She said she would meet him around ten o'clock and it was now two in the morning and she was knocking at his hotel door. He walked to the door in his jeans and a t-shirt and opened it. There she stood looking delicious as usual. She had on a pair of black Dolce and Gabbana jeans and a sheer Vera Wang shirt, exposing a sexy black lace bra. And of course, she rocked those red bottom heels.

"Can a sista come in?" she asked in her mischievous voice

"I don't know. You tell me."

"I brought you all this sexy and you acting all salty," she said.

"You treating me like I'm on your payroll," he shot back.

"A'ight. Well, let's rain check-it then, 'cause it is late." she said, looking at him with that 'I was getting ready to fuck the shit out of you' look.

Terrance looked at the big purse she was carrying and realized it was not her usual. *Damn, she came to give a nigga some pussy.* He quickly reassessed the situation.

"Nah, you brought me some sexy, and I want it."

"I thought so," she said, brushing her ass against his dick as she passed him.

"Can I have a kiss?" She turned her cheek to him. He looked puzzled.

"I don't kiss in the mouth." Terrance started laughing.

"You act like I been licking my balls or something. You talk a lot of shit."

KoKo started smiling. "Because I got it like that."

"Yeah well, I'm going to have a lot of fun making you apologize," Terrance said with confidence.

"Apologize? For what?"

"For not giving me some of this pussy sooner." Terrance pulled her to him, unzipped her jeans, and slid his hand inside her pants. As his hand slid between her legs, he softly began to rub back and forth.

KoKo closed her legs then she grabbed his wrist, but it didn't stop him. Terrance forcefully pulled her jeans down over her ass, locked eyes with her as he zoned in on her clit, and began to circle it, picking up a small current of speed.

"What? You scared?"

"Yeah, I'm scared that I'm going to fuck your head up and send you home to your bitch in a trance."

Terrance smiled. The shit that would come out of KoKo's mouth always tickled him. His dick was hard as hell and she had gotten away from him several times. He wasn't letting her get away tonight.

"Let me worry about my girl, and you worry about him," he said, placing her hand on his dick. KoKo was definitely pleased with his size. Her mouth began to water at the thought of him going in and digging deep.

"He feels like he's wide awake," KoKo said, rubbing up and down his stick.

"Yep, and he just punched in."

"Punched in?"

"Yeah. For work." Terrance leaned in and started to kiss and nibble on her neck.

"Terrance . . . wait."

Ignoring her, he bit into one of her breasts as his fingers pulled at the side of her underwear and found their way inside

her. With his other hand, he went under her shirt, released one of her breasts from her bra, placing his mouth on her nipple, and began to suck lightly. He picked up the pace, sliding his fingers in and out trying to bring on contractions. KoKo was trying to stick to her plan and tease him a little more, but he felt so good and was touching all the right spots. She didn't want to stop him. Then the feelings of guilt came over her as thoughts of Kayson started to run through her mind.

"Terrance wait, I don't think I'm ready for all this." KoKo grabbed his wrist, which only made him go faster, and then he hit the spot!

"Ssss . . . Wait . . . Ahhhh." KoKo let her inhibitions down and allowed herself to enjoy his every touch.

Terrance kept going, bringing on a powerful orgasm. He removed his hand, full of her juices then opened his pants. Reaching in his pocket, he pulled out a magnum and put it on. Pulling his pants and boxers all the way down, he stepped out of them. Next, he pulled his shirt over his head revealing his whole self to her. KoKo was impressed by everything she saw. Terrance wasn't taking no for an answer. He pushed KoKo onto the couch, grabbed her by the ankles, and pulled her to the edge of the couch and snatched her jeans off with one pull. KoKo was still slightly resisting, trying not to make it too easy for him. Also, intensifying his craving for her. Terrance got into position, but every time Terrance would try to get his dick close to her, she would move and try to close her legs. This act increased his desire.

"Terrance wait, I don't think we should." At that moment, Terrance pried her legs open and found his way to her opening.

"Let me have it, KoKo," he asked, going deep inside her.

KoKo let out a loud moan. She had not had sex since the night she and Kayson were last together, which was over a year ago. The want was so intense she started to ride him from the bottom. Terrance was so turned on by her tightness and wetness that he was about to be out the game before it got started. He had to get control and quick because she definitely felt like she wasn't fucking anybody. The idea of that alone had him ready to bust. The passion he was sharing with her was like she was truly being fucked for the first time. Every time he would hit the bottom, KoKo would moan out so sweetly, causing Terrance to go into a trance-like state just like she predicted. At that moment in time, nothing else mattered. He had blocked out Star totally. KoKo had him locked in her trap.

Terrance had KoKo in a full buck, handling all the walls until he again found her G-spot. "Uh huh . . . right there," KoKo yelled out.

Terrance picked up the pace to bring it on. KoKo bit his neck and began to suck.

Terrance moaned as the contractions from her orgasm squeezed his dick tight. "Oh shit . . . Damn, baby," Terrance whispered in KoKo's ear.

"I know. Now let me fuck you." KoKo wrapped her legs around his back, flipped him over, and got on top. She glided up and down the length of his dick. Terrance leaned his head back and closed his eyes. He bit his bottom lip and moaned, "Mmmmm . . ."

KoKo watched his facial expressions as she continued to work his dick like a part time job. She'd go fast then slow, rising all the way to the top of his dick then moving down fast, squeezing and tightening around him. Terrance was in heaven. He had only been having sex with Star for the last couple of months and was missing a woman just throwing him down and fucking his brains out. And KoKo was definitely handling his dick like a pro. Terrance placed his finger on her clit and began to vibrate back and forth. KoKo

threw her head back then grabbed his ankles while continuing to ride him, moving faster and harder. This caused him to go deep inside her as she enjoyed the contractions being brought on by his magic fingers. As KoKo began to cum, her legs started to shake uncontrollably.

"Uhhhhhhh . . . sssss," KoKo moaned.

Terrance sat up, placed his lips on her nipples, and then tickled them with the tip of his tongue, still not turning that clit loose. "Do it to me, baby. Ssss . . . Damn," he said, moaning.

After KoKo finished that one, she went in for another. "Lean back," she commanded. He did just that. KoKo began winding her waist and slowly turning on his dick. She was now side straddled and bouncing easy up and down. She did this until she had her back to him, a deadly move Kayson had taught her. Once she heard him breathing heavy, she really went to work, bouncing faster and faster. Terrance gripped her hips, but she didn't slow down. She moved faster causing him to go deeper.

"Sssss . . . Oh shit . . ." Terrance groaned.

KoKo zoned out totally, focused on fucking his head up. She massaged her clit until she skeeted and her juices ran down between his balls. Using her juices, she maneuvered her fingers up and down the line between his balls, sending chills up his spine and heat from his toes to his head. She could tell he was on the brink of cumming.

Wanting him to cum and cum hard; she increased her speed. Just at his breaking point, she placed one foot on each side of his head and grabbed his ankles. KoKo began gliding back and forth in a push up like position. She totally fucked his head up with that move because his dick was leaning all the way forward and moving in and out of her pussy, giving him a full view from the back. He began rubbing her ass and then across the lips of her pussy. Riding slow and easy and winding her waist in circles, she heard him moan again and picked up speed. Terrance could no longer hold back and KoKo wasn't going to let him. Terrance matched her every pump until he busted hard and long.

KoKo brought her legs back into a squatting position and rode him until he released the last drop. Looking over her shoulder at him with a sexy grin she asked, "Fucked your head up, didn't I?"

Terrance smiled, "Only 'cause I let you."

"Lean up," KoKo instructed, maintaining her squatting position and allowing him to move his legs from under her. Terrance grabbed her by her ankles causing her to fall forward. Then getting her on her back and pinning her legs open with his arm, he then dove in deep.

"Ahhhhh . . . mmmm," KoKo moaned. Terrance began stroking steady and deep, raining kisses up and down her spine. Within minutes, KoKo was cumming again.

"You know you fucking with a nigga's emotions?" Terrance whispered in her ear.

KoKo responded, "Faster." Terrance went in deeper. KoKo called for the gods.

"Oh my god . . . Yesss . . . Right there."

KoKo was throwing that ass back at him; his knees buckled. Pulling a real power move on him, she sexily moaned.

"Is that all you got?" she asked. That caused Terrance to go off. He was hitting it from side to side knocking the walls down and in one heavy breath he said, "Ssss . . . gotdamn!"

Terrance couldn't hold back and KoKo knew it. So she kept tossing that ass until he busted again real hard. He crawled all the way inside and just rocked back and forth as he nibbled and kissed KoKo's shoulders and sucked on the back of her neck.

"You dangerous as hell. This pussy should be illegal," he

said, out of breath.

"Is that right?" KoKo said as a smile came across her face. *Got him.* He made another request. "I still can't kiss your lips?"

"Sure you can. But not the ones on my face." She moved forward breaking their contact. "If you will excuse me I have to shower. You can join me if your knees still work."

Terrance started laughing as he turned over on his back. "Your mouth is going to get you in trouble."

"I hope so," KoKo said, getting up and heading for the bathroom. Stopping to grab a little bag from her purse containing her body wash, lotion, deodorant and a toothbrush and toothpaste, she said to herself, *damn, if that fucked him up, wait until I move to the next level of my plan.*

Terrance lay back on the bed in an attempt to catch a second wind and enjoy that nut he had just got off his back. But before he could catch himself, he passed clean out.

KoKo showered and brushed her teeth, applied lotion to her skin, and headed back to the room.

Terrance was knocked out. She put her little purse back in her big bag and slipped on her underwear, jeans, and shirt. She laid something on the nightstand and left out.

When Terrance woke up he reached for KoKo but she wasn't there. He lifted his head, looking around then glanced at the clock on the nightstand. It read 11 A.M. "Damn, it's almost check out. She knocked a nigga out." Placing his feet on the floor, he rubbed his eyes to fix his focus. He looked at the nightstand again and saw a note sitting on a stack of hundred dollar bills.

"What the fuck?" He grabbed the note and the money.

Hey baby,

Thanks for last night. I needed that. I'll catch up with you. I left you four thousand dollars. Get yourself something nice.

KoKo.

Terrance sat on the bed shaking his head. *Damn, was I just paid for a service? That's a bad bitch.* He reached for his cell and dialed the number she gave him, but a machine picked up. Because he wasn't sure of her situation, he decided not to leave a message and just hung up. He placed the phone, letter, and money back on the nightstand then headed for the shower. He turned the water on, and then went to the sink to brush his teeth. When he looked in the mirror, he saw a small bite mark by his collarbone. "Oh shit!" he said. The thought of him going home to Star all marked up ran through his head. His phone rang. He left the bathroom to get it in hopes of it being KoKo, but it was Star.

"Hello," he said slightly disappointed.

"Hey baby. I miss you," she said, excited that she had caught him.

"I miss you, too," he replied.

"When are you coming home? I need to see my baby," she pouted.

"I'll be home in a couple of days."

"Well, I guess I will have to keep myself busy until then."

"Don't worry, baby. I'll be there soon enough."

"Love you."

"Love you, too. I'll call you later."

"Okay. Bye babe." He hung up and then sat on the end of the bed. "What the fuck am I doing?" He sat for a minute pondering what just happened.

By twelve o'clock, he had showered and was checking out and headed to Yonkers to take care of some business. As he got on the elevator, thoughts of what KoKo did to him last night ran through his mind. He was still fucked up that not only did she pull a pussy prowl on him in the middle of the night; she also pulled the oldest trick in the book and left a nigga some money on the fucking nightstand. Now that's gangsta. *That's a bad bitch,* he thought. He hopped in a cab and headed up town.

A *week later...*

KoKo was sitting in the office at Kayson's mansion when she received a phone call from Night. "Hello. What's up, ma? You stationary?"

"Yeah, what's up?"

"I need to talk to you."

"A'ight, come to the mansion."

"Let me ask you something right quick. What you know about them outta town niggas, KoK?" Midnight asked in a suspicious voice. He was leery of the fact that KoKo was hanging out with some nigga that just showed up out of fucking nowhere.

"You know I'm on it, Night. This nigga is fucking with Bo'dee on the Southside. I'm still gathering shit. I know he got paper, but not too sure how long it is. But I'm about to find out."

"I'm in route," Night said then hung up.

With that, KoKo hung up, rolled a blunt, and sat back in Kayson's big chair and inhaled deeply.

When Night arrived, he was let in and came right to the second floor. "You think your ass is grown, huh? Smoking on Kayson's second floor," he said as he entered the room then smirked.

"Whatever! Shit, a sista is stressed the fuck out right about now. What's up?"

"I found out who was involved in that hit on Kayson," Night revealed.

"Don't play with my emotions." KoKo sat forward in her chair and put her head slightly to the side.

"Would I play with something so serious?"

"What's his name?"

"That nigga named Terrance. I think he has something to do with that shit. I still have to get some more information."

"From Cali?" KoKo said with great shock in her voice. She wanted to elude his perception.

"Yeah. But how you know he's from Cali?"

"Nah, that nigga Terrance was at the club and I was wondering who he was, so I put a few bitches on him. Then I ran into him a few times and he tried to holla at me, but I'm on it." She quickly tried to sell Night a story.

"Well, we need to put somebody on him."

"Nah, I got this," KoKo insisted.

"KoKo, we ain't trying to get you in no bullshit."

"I'm already deep in all this shit. And if he is the one responsible for killing Kayson, I need to get up close and personal and find out everything and everyone involved. And then at that point when he least expects it, I'll take that muthafucka's life."

"KoKo, be careful. Kayson would never forgive me if I let something happen to you."

"Don't worry about me. The only one important here is little Quran and I promised him I would seek and destroy anyone involved in his father's death. And my word is bond."

"I'm going to head out and keep the trail on him." Night stood up to leave.

"Yes. Do that. I want to know what he's doing and who he's doing it with. His father, mother, and child, his bitch and the whole fucking nine." KoKo's first plan was to rob this nigga, but that would have to wait until she made him feel some medieval pain.

"What are you getting ready to do?" Night questioned.

"Get dressed. A bitch is about to go on the hunt." KoKo got up and headed upstairs to strap up and hit the streets.

Night didn't know she was already hip to who he was and

what he was doing. She had hit the dude he was doing business with, which caused Terrance to go back to Cali. Within twenty-four hours, she had all the information she needed and was California bound.

Over the next couple of days, Night had confirmed that the nigga was involved and he was trying to find out how deep. KoKo revealed that she was close to Terrance and had found some shit out. She had that nigga in a trance, was getting ready to make a trip, and would settle all this shit.

"You need to be careful, KoK."

"I'm good. I'm getting ready to take a trip out west and do some shit. I got a chick out there who I'm trying to put on my team, so I'm going to pay her a visit. I'll be back in a couple of days."

"You need to take somebody with you."

"I am. My money and my nine."

"Keep being a rebel without a cause."

"I got it. If nothing else, you know Kayson trained me well. I got that nigga by the balls."

Night looked at her and hoped she wasn't slipping and falling in love with some nigga she'd just met.

KoKo went downstairs to give orders to the crew, and when she came back up, Night had left. She sat down, turned around in the chair, and re-lit her blunt. She had the strategy all set dealing with Terrance. She already had Wadoo on it and was making a trip to Cali. Her eyes were on his connections and she was getting ready to see what it was he was really doing in her city. And in order to do that, she would have to move on his turf and see what type of wolves he had howling. She never told Night everything because if she learned anything from Kayson it was this, 'you give a nigga what they need to know and let them find out what they want to know.'

Chapter 32
Shit don't Look Right

KoKo landed at LAX airport and was picked up by Wadoo. He was this cat from Yonkers, who had moved out west and she and Kayson would use him to move guns back and forth from the east coast. Wadoo saw KoKo coming, jumped out the Lexus truck, and gave her a big hug, lifting her off her feet.

"What's up, little sis?"

"Nothing much, just trying to handle some business."

"You got bags?" he asked, looking behind her.

"No, real women just roll with plastic. You know where I want to go."

"Rodeo," he said with a tone of certainty.

"You already know."

"You came out here to go broke?"

"Never that, just going to put a dent in it. You got my info?"

"You know it," he said, proud of the shit he was able to come up with in the short time he had.

"Well, let's take a ride and find somewhere to sit down and talk." KoKo started walking to the car.

"You hungry?" Wadoo asked, headed to the driver's side.

"Yeah, I could eat."

"Let's roll."

They both hopped in the car and shut the door. Before they pulled off, he reached in the glove compartment, pulled out a gun and a blunt, and gave them to KoKo.

"Can you handle this good old Cali bud?"

"I'm about to find out." KoKo pushed in the cigarette lighter as he pulled off."

When they got to the restaurant, they sat down to eat and he told her where Terrance laid his head and where he did business. Also, the place where he was most of the time, which was Star's house. He told her where Star went to school and gave her car make, model, and plate number. By the end of the meal, KoKo was turning the plan over in her head.

The way she saw it, she was going to make some moves that would get in those pockets while she was planning her next move. Wadoo cut into her thoughts.

"Oh yeah, that nigga inherited money from his mother. She set up a trust fund for him and before she got killed, it sat until last year so he just got about two million dollars."

"Is that right?" She was salivating at the thought. "Thanks, big bruh." KoKo slid a small stack of money toward him then put a hundred dollar bill up for the check. Wadoo looked at the stack and then slid it back to her.

"You trying to insult me?" he said with indignation.

"Nah, shit, it's a fucking recession. It ain't easy to pull in information on muthafuckas these days. I just wanted you to know that I appreciate it."

He gave her a real serious look then KoKo grabbed the stack and he put his hand on top of hers and said, "Be careful. Niggas out here are real slippery. I can't function if I know you're out here and some shit happen to you."

"Don't worry, bruh, I got it. Drop a sista off on that strip so I can spend what you won't take." They headed out the restaurant and as they were leaving, a girl came up on them.

"So this is what you do when I can't find your ass?"

He turned around and was shocked as hell. "Oh shit, Michelle, this is KoKo," he said.

269

"What the fuck does that mean to me?" Michelle shot back.

"It better mean that you don't want any problems with me," KoKo said calmly.

"Look, I ain't got time for this shit. I had a long day and then I walk up on you with some bitch."

KoKo looked at Wadoo. He looked back like, please don't. He knew how crazy KoKo was. So he grabbed Michelle, but it was too late.

"You see a bitch, you slap a bitch." KoKo turned into the pit bull she was. Michelle snatched away from Wadoo and went at KoKo. As soon as she got close, KoKo gave her a short jab to the face and knocked her ass down. Michelle's head snapped back as she hit the ground hard. Blood poured from her nose.

"Why you let this bitch hit me?" she yelled while trying to wipe her nose.

Wadoo tried to help her up off the ground, but KoKo grabbed his arm and said, "Nah, hold up. Let me educate this bitch first on who the fuck I am."

Snatching a napkin off one of the outside tables, she pulled out her nine and covered it up. Putting it under her Michelle's chin. The girl looked petrified. Wadoo didn't interfere because he could tell KoKo was only going to give her a warning. Plus, he had been telling Michelle to chill out. So today was lesson number one.

"Look bitch, he told you I was KoKo. This man is like a brother to me so your dick ain't in jeopardy. But if it were, you would never catch us out having a fucking meal. He would be somewhere tasting this luscious nectar then be going coal miner deep in this pussy until I say I don't want no more. Now, the next time you see me, bitch, respect me, because the last muthafucka who called me a bitch is feeling real claustrophobic right now."

Michelle's eyes were glassy and her face pale. She looked like she had just seen a ghost. KoKo threw the napkin in her face, stood up, and looked at her like she was dirt. "You better be glad I'm on vacation or I would blow your gotdamn head off. Now get yourself together and I expect an apology."

Michelle was scared as hell, her eyes got big as saucers, and she kept flinching every time KoKo moved. She took the napkin and began wiping her face. "Let's roll, Wa. I got shit to do. You need to bench that bitch. She is definitely a liability." KoKo went to the truck. Wadoo looked at Michelle and shook his head.

"I tried to tell your ass to calm down. I'll catch you later," he said.

"You're just going to leave me here?" Michelle asked as she started to cry.

"Like she said, we got shit to do." He walked off and didn't look back.

As they approached the car, KoKo said, "That's why Wahida Clark said, 'Every thug needs a lady.'" They hopped in the car and pulled off. Within the hour, he dropped KoKo off on Rodeo Drive. She gave him some dap and then he pulled off. She headed straight for the pay phone and called Gwen, who was right in the area. Just as KoKo had instructed, she met her at the Gucci shop in minutes.

"Hey girl, it is good to see you." Gwen came in the door in rare form and went over to where KoKo was trying on a pair of 'fuck me' pumps.

These muthafucka's are definitely shoulder worthy. Her thoughts came to a halt by Gwen's high-pitched voice. "What up, ma?" KoKo gave her a hug then sat back down.

"Is everything straight?" KoKo went straight to business

"Yes and I—"

KoKo cut her off, putting her finger up to her mouth.

"Don't talk business in the street."

Gwen nodded in agreement and then grabbed a pair of shoes. They spent about an hour in that store then moved down the line. By the time they finished, KoKo was spent. They headed to a nearby hotel and checked in. KoKo had a package waiting on the bed. She had it sent so she could handle something.

"All right, thanks for helping a sista to her room. I will call you later. Be ready to pick me up when I call," KoKo said to Gwen, looking at her like, you're dismissed.

Gwen left thinking, *that bitch is the truth; glad I'm friend not foe.* The elevator came and took her to the lobby. She headed to her vehicle with the plan on her mind.

The Set Up

KoKo opened the package and started to smile. *This is just what I ordered.* She laid it out on the bed and headed for the shower. All oiled up, she slid on her outfit, grabbed her props and rolled out. Once downstairs, she jumped in a cab and headed to her next destination.

After putting on her game face while standing in the hallway, KoKo rang the buzzer. After a few minutes, she heard the door.

"Who?"

"Maintenance."

She heard the locks clicking. When the door opened there stood Terrance shocked as hell. In his doorway, KoKo stood in a navy blue jumpsuit with a tag that read Pipe Works. KoKo looked up from her baseball cap and said in a sensual voice, "I heard they were laying good pipe up in here."

A sneaky grin came over his face as he admired all of KoKo's curves. He hadn't seen her in over two weeks. It was

like somebody brought a man on a desert a tall drink of water.

"Well, are you going to let me in or just stare at me?" KoKo asked, swishing past Terrance making sure his dick was greeted by her juicy ass. It worked because immediately his little friend stood up.

"Oh, this is cute." KoKo looked around the small apartment taking note of everything she saw.

"What you doing here, KoKo?"

"Well, I figured since you couldn't bring me that sweet, long stick I figured I would come and get it."

KoKo sat her toolbox on the bar by the window. Then she turned around slowly and put her hands on her hips. "You like what you see?" she asked.

"Yes, I like what I see, but I don't think I can have company."

"Is that right?" KoKo unzipped her jumpsuit, exposing her perky breasts to Terrance. His eyes wandered down her stomach to her panty line, only to find out that she wasn't wearing any. He asked, "You came all the way here to give me some of this good pussy?"

"Yes. Why? You don't want it? 'Cause a sista can find another worthy candidate." She made a gesture to close her jumpsuit.

"Wait! Hold up," Terrance said, placing his hands in the open space of her uniform. First, caressing her breasts, and then letting his hands roam over her voluptuous ass.

"You missed me?" KoKo said with confidence leaking from her lips.

"Hell yeah, but you know you wrong." He sank his teeth into one of her breasts then licked his way to her navel and back up to her breast, taking time to stop and suck gently on her nipples. He came up for air. "What am I going to do with you?" he asked.

"Well, you could drop this jumpsuit and put me on that counter and fuck me until I cum."

Terrance wasted no time. He knew he didn't have much time before Star would be home. With that thought, he went full force at getting KoKo out of that jumpsuit. Once he got it past her shoulders, he went back to kissing and sucking her breasts and nipples while walking her backward to the counter. The jumpsuit dropped to the floor and he placed KoKo on the counter. Pulling at his sweat pants, eager to release his pipe from its enclosure she started to squeeze and stroke up and down his thickness.

"Ssssss . . ." Terrance allowed the sound of pleasure to escape his lips.

"Fuck me, Terrance," KoKo said, wrapping her legs around his waist as he slid deep inside her. Terrance went to work searching for that spot. He was pumping deep, hard and fast, lifting her off the counter with every thrust. KoKo held on tight to his neck, and threw her head back as she could feel the contractions coming on.

"Right there, Terrance . . . Ahhhhh."

"Right here, baby," Terrance moaned.

"Yessss. Yesss . . . I'm cumming."

Terrance held her hips firmly in place and pumped faster and faster. KoKo started to cum and squeezed him tighter. Terrace was caught between the thought of how good KoKo felt and the fact that here he was pleasing his sidepiece at his girl's house and she was only minutes away from walking in the door. The adrenaline of all these emotions mixed with KoKo fucking the shit out of him and the idea of getting caught caused a rush in his body unlike anything he'd ever felt before. KoKo was calling his name, asking for more, and causing him to give it to her full force.

"Terrance . . . Ahhh . . . don't stop."

"Sssss . . . mmmm." Terrance closed his eyes and held

KoKo tight, preparing for the gut-wrenching orgasm coming. KoKo continued to hop up and down faster and faster and chanting, "Fuck me . . . fuck me." With her last attempt to take all he had, she crossed her legs at the ankle. Pulling him in deep, she placed her palms on the counter lifting herself up in the air and began winding her waist fast and hard. Terrance bit into KoKo's breast and seconds later, he came so hard that he just fell forward onto KoKo.

Terrance panted like a dog out of breath. "Damn, that shit was good as hell."

"Like I always say, I aim to please."

Just then, his cell phone rang. He grabbed it off the counter and looked at the display, which showed that Star was calling. Looking at KoKo, he answered the call, putting his finger up to his lips. "Hello."

"Hey baby. Triple A just changed the tire and I'm going to run by the restaurant and pick up the food I ordered then I'll be right there."

"A'ight."

"What you doing? Why you sound like that?"

"I just woke up. I dozed off after you called about the tire."

KoKo started to ride him, squeezing her muscles around him every time she came up. Terrance closed his eyes and enjoyed KoKo's every move.

"Well, I hope you are up when I get there, because I miss my baby and I want to spend some time with you."

"Okay. I'll be waiting. I miss you, too."

"I love you," Star said, heartfelt.

Terrance looked into KoKo's eyes and said, "I love you."

KoKo whispered in his ear, "Make me cum again." Running her tongue over his earlobe, she then gave him light nibbles under his chin. Terrance pulled her down on him with his free hand. "Bye baby. See you in a minute." He disconnected the call.

"You know your ass is dead wrong, right?" he said.

"Well, make me pay for it," KoKo said in a sinister tone with a smile on her face.

Terrance reached around his back and removed her legs then pulled out of her slowly. Turning and grabbing a chair, he placed it right in front of the counter. KoKo was sitting there with her chocolate legs spread open, pussy glistening. Terrance wasted no time going right to work on that clit, flicking his tongue back and forth and tickling it. He placed his mouth over it and started to suck hard. KoKo placed her foot on his shoulder, shoe, and all. In no time, she was feeling those oh so familiar contractions. Gripping the back of his head, she began circling her hips to the intensity of the orgasm, cumming in his mouth. Terrance sucked lightly to increase the pleasure. KoKo's body jerked and her legs shook. He stood and lifted her exhausted body off the counter then walked over to the sink and washed his face and hands.

"Can I have a wash cloth so I can clean up Miss Kitty?"

"Sheeit, that ain't no kitty. That's a full-grown lioness. The wash cloths are in the bathroom," Terrance said, trying to get his mind right.

KoKo walked away butt ass naked. Terrance shook his head. *What the fuck am I doing?* He went in the closet, grabbed the vacuum and the carpet fresh, and sprinkled it around the room. He was moving fast as hell. Quickly, he went to the counter, put the chair back, and grabbed the Pine Sol from under the sink and wiped the counter down. He was immediately thrown into panic mode when he heard the shower running. "What the fuck?" he mumbled, moving toward the bathroom. Snatching open the shower curtain he said, "What the fuck are you doing, KoKo?"

"What the fuck do you mean, 'what am I doing?'"

"Come on, baby. You know my girl is on the way."

"Look. I don't take no fucking ho bath at no gotdamn sink. You better learn how to keep your bitch in check. The way I see it . . . Your bitch. Your problem." She turned to wash the soap off her body.

Terrance looked at her like she had lost her fucking mind. She turned the water off and put her hands on her hips, placing one of her feet on the side of the tub, exposing her neatly shaved pussy to him. "What? Can you dry a sista off?" KoKo asked nonchalantly.

Terrance grabbed a towel and began to dry KoKo off, taking a minute to rub the towel slowly between her legs.

"Oh, I thought we were worrying about your girl," she said, sarcasm dripping from her lips.

KoKo stepped out the shower brushing past his semi hard on. Even though she wanted to fuck with his head, she wasn't trying to get him busted. That would defeat the purpose. She moved to the living room, snatched up her jumpsuit, and put it on the barstool. Opening her toolbox, she grabbed the trial size of David Yarman lotion and put it all over her body. After putting on her black lace thong and matching bra, she slipped her legs in the jumpsuit then shimmied it past her butt. KoKo placed her shoes back on and combed her hair into a neat ponytail. She then put the hat back on and applied her lip-gloss.

Terrance stood there watching and wanting her, wishing they were not at Star's place. Then he became dumbfounded at the fact that not only did KoKo find out where he lived, but she had just gotten him to fuck and suck her right on Star's kitchen counter. What the fuck was it about her that caused him to have a distorted reality? Whatever it was, he was enjoying the rush and was not planning to let KoKo go. He walked over to her, stood behind her, and wrapped his arms around her placing his dick on her ass. Kissing her neck he said, "When am I going to see you again?" Terrance asked with the sound of desperation in his voice.

KoKo smiled from ear-to-ear. *Another one bites the dust,* she thought. "I don't know. You know my schedule is tight."

"Why don't you come spend the night at my house?"

Checkmate, KoKo thought. She turned and looked him in his eyes. "I have something to do then I'll call you."

"Yeah, you better call me because I hope you don't think that little drive by was enough." Terrance snapped out of KoKo's trance when he heard Star's car pull into the parking lot blasting her favorite song.

"Oh shit!" he said, reaching for his cell phone. He damn sure didn't want them to run into each other. He called to try to delay her while he got KoKo out, but she wasn't picking up. The music was too loud. He was looking out the window watching her get out the car and gathering the bags. Terrance kept hitting redial and he was getting ready to panic, but then she picked up.

"Hello." She fumbled around with everything she had in her hands.

"I need you to get something out my trunk."

"Terrance, are you serious? I have a lot of stuff in my hands."

"I know that. I can see you. I got something for you and I want you to bring it upstairs."

"Terrance, I don't have your key. Why don't you come down here and help me?"

"I'm not dressed. I'm about to hit the remote. Grab that little bag and come on."

"Oh boy. All right, hit the button."

He watched her head toward his truck. All he could think was, thank god he picked up that necklace for KoKo last night. He would have to get her another one. That little diversion would cost him another twenty thousand dollars.

KoKo slipped away from him and headed to the door, grabbing the knob and opening the door. Terrance was right on her ass, worried that she would run into Star.

"KoKo, be good," he said with a sincere look in his eyes.

"Damn nigga, if you scared, get a dog."

Terrance was enjoying his little escapade with KoKo, but he didn't want to hurt Star. She was loyal and loved him with everything she was. He made one last plea, "KoKo."

"Terrance, remember this if nothing else. When I hit a muthafucka I'm in and out and they never see me coming."

With that, she walked out headed to the staircase.

Terrance closed the door and locked it and said to himself, "Fuck it, it is what it is." Then he headed to the shower.

KoKo got to the bottom of the steps. She looked up and saw Star coming her way smiling from ear-to-ear. When she got about three-feet from KoKo, she dropped her keys. KoKo said, "Oh, I'll get that for you."

KoKo bent down to get them and when she rose up their eyes met. KoKo smiled at Star. "Here you go, sweetie," she said. "I see you have your hands full."

"Oh, thank you. My fathead boyfriend could have come down to help me. But you know how they do."

"No, really I don't. I have pussy power. Niggas do what I tell them. Have a good day." KoKo walked off.

Star looked puzzled. "I heard that," she said then proceeded to the elevator. When she got to the apartment, she opened the door and her nose was assaulted by pine and carpet fresh.

"Awww, he tried to clean up. He is so sweet." She started to call him but heard the shower so she placed the food on the counter and headed to the bathroom. But not before she did a quick scope of the room for any evidence. She lifted the comforter. The sheets were intact and so was the rest of the room. Star kept on going and when she reached the bathroom, she opened the shower curtain holding out the bag and swinging it back and forth on her two fingers. "So what did you get me?" she asked playfully.

"Oh, Daddy has a lot of things for you." He turned toward her with a rock hard dick ready to finish what KoKo started but could not. Star had no idea, but Terrance was getting ready to put her out of commission. He pulled her into the shower causing her to drop the little bag to the floor. Her clothes were getting soaking wet. Terrance started to tear off her clothes piece by piece. His lips met hers with such passion and aggression. Everything he felt for KoKo was getting ready to be taken out on Star and she was going to get it KoKo style.

When Star woke up, she stared at the back of Terrance's head. He had just did it to her in ways that she had never experienced before. All she could do was wonder who it was that he had been practicing on. Why would he think that she would enjoy all that rough sex? To Star it was confirmation that her bed was not the only one he was sleeping in. Just as she started to feel down a false reality kicked in. Whatever it was that he did never came home, and if there were any other bitches he lived with her and she definitely knew he loved her. Then she remembered that he had got her a gift. She got up, went right to the bathroom, and retrieved the little bag. Excited, she came back into the room and jumped on the bed waking Terrance up so she could open the gift. She was acting like a kid trying to open the bow and box. What she saw next had her totally blown her away, a platinum and black diamond necklace.

"Awww, this is beautiful."

"Just like you," Terrance said in his sleepy voice. She dove on him and began raining kisses all over his face. Terrance spent the rest of the day with Star then prepared for

his sweet chocolate, KoKo.

Meanwhile, KoKo was on the prowl, setting her plan into motion to get at Terrance's stash and that invite to his place was the welcome mat she needed. That night KoKo obliged Terrance and came to spend the night at his house. She had slipped half of a sleeping pill in his drink so once she got finished riding it until he couldn't take any more he would pass clean out. And lo and behold, it worked like a charm. That gave KoKo the opportunity she needed to take a small snoop around. She found what she needed in a drawer in the kitchen. It was a bank statement. She took a picture of it with her cell phone then went into his wallet and pulled out his license and took a picture of that as well. As she went through it, she saw his social security card in there as well. *Dumb ass! Who the fuck walks around with their SS card? Wow, he needs to get out the game. And I think I'm the one to help him with that.* Once she was done, she sent all the stuff to her bogus e-mail account. Then she got back in the bed. Just as she was about to doze off, Terrance woke up and put his arm around her.

"Thank you, baby," he said in a groggy voice.

"Thank me for what?"

"For just being you. A nigga needs a strong woman who he can depend on by his side."

Koko thought for a minute, *No this nigga cannot possibly think that we are an item. When I get done with him he's going to wish he never met me.* Then she managed to say. "No problem. You stole a piece of my heart. Now go back to sleep. We have to get up early. I have a flight to catch. Plus, you have some shopping to do."

"Shopping? Shopping for what?

"My gift," she said matter-of-factly.

"Why do I have to go get you a gift? Is it because you saw me give Star one? You feeling a little jealous?" he said playfully.

"Why the fuck should I be feeling jealous when you gave her something you were planning on giving me?" Terrance looked at her like: How the fuck did she know that? Then he spoke his thoughts. "How the fuck did you come up with that idea?"

"First of all, you're sleeping with one of the baddest bitches on the planet, who just happens to have you eating pussy on your girl's counter. You're on the road all the time. You woke up with her. If that were for her, you would have given it to her last night when you first saw her. Sheeit, guilt alone would have had you passing shit out like Santa Claus. But it's okay; it's a small price for the games that we play. Just make my shit another color. See you in the morning."

She picked up his arm and kissed his wrist. "Sleep tight," she said. Terrance didn't know whether to go to sleep or look to find a rabbit in the pot. Then he dozed off right behind her.

****

Two days after KoKo left, Terrance received a call in the middle of the night from his partner's wife. She needed him at the hospital right away. Someone had critically wounded four of his top workers. Not bad enough to kill them, but definitely enough to make them suffer and put a big ass dent in his manpower. When he arrived at the hospital, all their wives and girlfriends were standing around accompanied by several of his friends. He and Star walked over to where everyone else was standing.

"Why Terrance? Why did they do this to us?" his boy's wife asked as she put her head on his chest and cried. She was nine months pregnant and closing on their first house. Terrance walked her over to the chairs outside her husband's room. He wanted to be strong for her, but his emotions were riding high and his eyes also filled up with tears.

"Don't worry, sis. I'll find out who's behind this and believe me, they will pay." He tried to comfort her. Star looked on in confusion and wondered what kind of life she had gotten herself into. Was this man who she loved with everything worth it? Terrance saw how much of a toll it was having on Star, so he got two of his boys to take her home. Terrance and his boys spent another two hours at the hospital giving support to the families of his fallen soldiers. Then they broke out to start putting the dogs to the street. He knew he had to put his boys on this shit hard. Hasan was one of his most loyal friends. As Terrance passed out orders, his mind was torn between what had just happened in LA and what he had pending in NY. In fact, this weekend he had a meeting with the Columbians and the Russian dudes to close some shit he had hanging for four months. Terrance was getting ready to go over the next thing when his phone rang.

"Hey baby, I got to the house safe."

"Good. Make sure you're locked in. I got a few boys that are going to keep an eye on you until I get back. I have to leave town for a couple days."

"Well, maybe I can stay by Monica's until you get back, and if she needs to stay with us she can."

"Yeah, that's a good idea. Thank you, baby. I need you to hold shit together for me."

"No problem. I have a few meetings and some personal stuff to wrap up, but I have your back. Will I see you before you leave?"

"I'll try."

"All right. If I don't see you, travel safe, and bring you back to me. Love you."

"Love you, too."

Back in New York ....

"Yo, my nigga, you need to get back here. These niggas said they ain't doing shit without you being here," A man said to Terrance with desperation in his voice.

"Yeah a'ight, I'll be there tomorrow. I got a lot of shit going on."

"Well, hurry up because every day we are losing money."

"Let me handle some shit here. Then I will get on the first flight I can," Terrance assured his partner. Then he hung up.

Star looked at him like are you serious? Terrance had stopped by the house on his way to NY to get him some of those sweet peaches, and then he had to spring the news on her that he was leaving.

"Baby, please don't look at me like that. I got shit to handle. Didn't we go over this already?" Then he got off the bed.

"You got shit here to handle." As she looked at him she didn't know who the fuck he had turned into. Every time he got one of those phone calls, his whole demeanor changed.

"Watch your mouth," Terrance said sternly and disappointed because Star wasn't the cursing type. Terrance put on his pants and shirt. He looked back at Star. "Look, it's something going on and I need my number one to have my back."

"I got your back. But lately, I don't know who you are. All this back and forth and mood swings. You running into something I don't think you're going to be able to get out of." She got off the bed and headed to the bathroom. Terrance sat on the bed and put his head in his hands, running all the shit that was going on through his mind. Then he got up and went to the bathroom behind Star.

"Look, you're right. I'm going to wrap this shit up and then I will make all this up to you. I promise." Then he took her in his arms and hugged her tight.

"I don't want to lose you," she said, inhaling his scent.

"You won't. Just hang in here with me. Everything will be fine."

"I hope you're right," Star said, wanting to convince herself that what he was saying was true, but deep inside she felt him slowly slipping away from her. They stood there for a few minutes more, then he was gone.

Meanwhile ....
Ring . . . Ring . . .
"What's up?"
"I'm on my way over there."
"A'ight."

Thirty minutes later, Night walked into her office. He sat down and lit one of the blunts she had in the ashtray.

"You know that info you were looking for?" Night asked.

"Yeah, what's the verdict?"

"That nigga, Terrance. He sent them niggas after Kayson and is now in a deal with the Russians and our Columbian connects. That nigga is going for your spot. He has been running with my man's brother and he gave him up for a nice penny. The good thing is, he doesn't know you're in charge. He thinks Aldeen is. And it's a bounty on Aldeen's head."

"Is that right?" KoKo said.

"Yeah. Terrance is coming back in town tomorrow. What do you want to do?"

KoKo sat there for a minute. "Tell the Russians to get that money and then wipe out his crew and I'll take care of him. Find out who has the contract on Aldeen, and tell him to lay low until we figure this shit out."

"KoKo. Why don't you just let me take care of that nigga?"

KoKo smiled then said, "Nah, I got it. I want to pay his

bitch a visit first so he can feel what I feel. Then I'll hit that muthafucka with a painful chastisement."

Night stood, walked over to KoKo, and kissed her forehead. "KoKo, please baby girl, don't be no rebel. I can handle this nigga for you."

"I got it, Night. That nigga got to suffer by my hand," she said as she looked up at him. "I got this. Go do what I asked you."

Night nodded in approval then moved out.

KoKo quickly called the pilot and headed to the airport. Star was getting ready to get the KoKo experience.

Chapter 33

KoKo arrived in Cali in full killah mode. She quickly called Gwen to meet her at the hotel. She got the outfit she had for the mission then headed to Star's place. KoKo grabbed the keys she had stolen and copied from Terrance's key chain. Then she headed in the building with her fitted cap pulled down. Reaching the third floor, she tried each key then walked in. Moving slowly through the apartment, careful not to touch anything she went into the closet and squatted down then closed the door. She knew she was going to have a wait because she had her followed to the hospital.

Visiting hours were just about over and KoKo got the call that Star and the others were leaving the hospital. She first had some shit jump off at one of Terrance's spots causing everyone to panic and get off guard.

"Shit. Look, we got to roll out," one of Terrance's boys yelled out.

Star and Monica looked at them like what's wrong? Then watched as they all hurried into the cars. "Look, I'll drop y'all off," Rodney said.

"No, drop off Monica. I'll just drive home and call you when I get there." He hesitated and then said, "A'ight." Escorted Star to her car then drove off.

KoKo's informant called her to let her know that she'd seen Star get in the car. "Thanks, now go into the room and hit that nigga's veins with that shit and move out."

"Got you." Gwen hung up and headed down the hall with her nurses uniform on and a needle of battery acid in her hand. She hit that nigga so quick and then moved out the exit door as she heard him coding. She smiled and was gone.

KoKo was patient and it paid off because she heard keys in the door then heard it close. Then came the sound of her victim's voice. "Hey Rod. I'm in. Yes, I locked the door. I'll see you later." She hung up then KoKo heard the familiar sound of mail being opened. "Yes, it came," Star said, obviously very excited about what she had in her hands. She quickly pulled out her cell then called Terrance.

"Hey baby."

"What's good, sexy?"

"I got the mail I was looking for," Star said with excitement.

"Awww. Baby, that's good," he said, trying not to seem distracted.

"Are you getting any rest?"

"When I can. You know I don't sleep well when you're not in my arms." Terrance shot back.

"You always talk mess when you're thousands of miles away."

"Well, I'll be there soon. Then I'm going to sit down for a little while. And you can sit on my lap."

"I can't wait. Love you."

"Love you more. I'll call you later." He disconnected the call.

Star reached in the envelope and pulled something out then threw the rest on the bed. She headed to the closet to pick out an outfit for tomorrow. She was planning on showering and going straight to bed. She had a big day ahead of her. Picking up the remote, she turned on Floetry's "Feelings," put it down and walked over to the closet. When she opened it, she was met by KoKo and her six-inch blade.

She stuck it right into Star's stomach right under her rib cage.

KoKo stuck her several times then stepped out the closet. Star fell back into the dresser holding her stomach. "Ce'Asia . . . Why?" she mumbled.

KoKo was shocked as hell. "What did you call me?" she asked with anger in her voice.

Star coughed up blood and tears were coming out her eyes. KoKo looked at her with her evil eye. Star cried as she again yelled out, "Why!"

"Ask your punk ass boyfriend why he killed my husband," KoKo said, leaning in to her.

"Ce'Asia I was looking for you."

"Why the fuck was you looking for me? And how do you know my name?"

Star lifted her arm and passed her what she had been holding in her hand. KoKo took the balled up item and opened it. KoKo's heart started to race as the words left Star's mouth. "He wanted us to be close. He wanted us to be close," Star said with the last energy she had left in her little body.

KoKo fell back as she saw the two little girls sitting on the man's lap. One was definitely her and it appeared that the other girl was Star. She looked on the back. Written in black ink: 'Daddies Girls.'

KoKo grabbed her chest as she thought. *Oh shit! Did I just kill my sister?* Her adrenaline started to rush. She got hot and sweat beads dotted her forehead. Quickly, she pulled herself together and looked for the mail she heard her going through and stuffed it in the bag she had with her. She made sure she didn't leave anything behind. Then she left the apartment leaving Star to die alone.

When KoKo got to the car, she was sick. She drove a while then got out the car and leaned up against it and tried to take some deep breaths. It didn't help because she started to throw up. She bent over, put her hands to her face, and cried, "Oh God, please not now." Getting up, she got back in the car then drove to the airport. The pilot was waiting when she arrived. With the plan already started, she got on and sat down.

"Bring me a bottle of Patron," she said to the stewardess. The woman hurried and brought her the bottle and a glass and set it down. KoKo pushed it aside, opened the bottle, and took it to the head. Tears cascaded down her face. She reached in her back pocket and opened the envelope, which read Roberson's Private Detective Firm. It appeared that Star was tracking down her family. Inside the envelope were all kinds of documents. From original adoption papers and the names of each of their parents and right in the father section on both of their birth certificates was Malik Briggs. KoKo's stomach started turning.

Taking the bottle to the head again, before KoKo knew it, she had drank it almost to the bottom. She stared at the picture of her and Star and their dad. Then the various photos of her from her junior high school yearbook. "Damn!" KoKo yelled as she hugged the bottle and cried. She had never felt bad after killing anyone, but this shit right here was definitely going to haunt her for the rest of her life.

Daddy's Home

Terrance stepped off the plane and grabbed his cell phone, which was his practice as soon as he got in town. He kept calling Star, but her phone kept going to voice mail. He was getting worried, and instead of heading to Monica's to pay his respects, he grabbed a cab and went straight home.

When he got to the apartment complex, he saw her car parked outside and was hoping that she was sleep. He parked the car and headed into the building bypassing the elevator. Taking the steps three at a time, he reached her place and put his key in the door and opened it yelling, "Star, baby, Daddy's home." Everything seemed to be in order until he reached the bedroom door. Her feet were visible. Immediately, he started breathing heavy.

"Oh God . . . No! No! No!" he yelled and fell to his knees crawling up to where her head was. Terrance cried like a baby as he cradled her in his arms. "Who did this to you? Baby, you can't be dead!" he yelled as he held her tight, hoping for just a small sign of life. He looked at the dried up blood on her shirt and hands and knew that his prayer to see her speak or smile would never come to pass. He called 9-1-1. When the ambulance arrived, he was in a daze. Thoughts of his mom and now the reality of what misfortune had taken Star's life accompanied by the feeling that this was all his fault had him all fucked up. The cops were trying to ask him questions, but he couldn't hear or think. He watched as they put her lifeless body on the gurney and covered her up. Then he broke down and fell to his knees crying and saying her name. Two cops and the EMS worker tried to console him, but it only made it worst.

It was about two in the morning and Mrs. Pearl was waking up and heading to the kitchen to take her medicine. When she got to the refrigerator, she could hear what sounded like crying. Looking into the living room, she saw Terrance sitting on the floor in front of the couch in the dark. She got close to him and could see he was sitting there with a bottle of Vodka in his hand with tears running down his face. She turned on the dim light.

"What's wrong, chile?"

He could barely get it out. "They took my heart."

"What you talking 'bout, son?"

"They killed her." Tears streamed down his face like a leaking faucet.

"Killed who, baby?" She sat down, put her hand on his

head, and began to rub it.

"Somebody killed Star." Saying it only fucked with him more.

"Oh no. Not that sweet baby." She placed her hand over her mouth as she said the words.

Terrance put his head down on her leg as she continued to rub it. Mrs. Pearl now had tears in her eyes.

"I'm cursed. They should have killed me when they killed mommy."

"Don't you talk like that, chile. You were a blessing to me. The son I never had. Things are rough right now, but we will get through it." She tried to comfort him.

"I want to believe that," he said, but the darkness was far more powerful than the light she was trying to shine into the hole in his heart.

"Don't worry, son. We will get through this. Look at it this way, your mom gets to meet her after all. She'll look after her," she said then smiled.

Terrance looked up and tried to muster up a smile. Mrs. Pearl was always looking at the glass as half full.

"You are all I have left."

"Baby, you have a whole life ahead of you. Take that love and hold it dear. Don't worry, God will send you someone to give it to."

Just as the words left her mouth, he thought about KoKo. He didn't know if she was the one to give it to, but after he put Star to rest, he was headed in her direction. He and Mrs. Pearl sat up until 4 A.M. She had fallen asleep with her hand on his head. Terrance sat up, pulled the small cashmere throw off the couch, and covered her up. He kissed her forehead then left.

Times Up

"Ring . . . Ring . . ."

"Hello," KoKo answered half asleep.

"Hey baby. Did I wake you?" Terrance asked in a very desperate voice.

"Nah. I was just laying here. Are you all right?" KoKo tried to sound concerned.

There was a brief pause. The silence was eerie. Terrance said, "I need to see you. I think if I could get into your arms shit might be a'ight for a minute."

"Awwww. Well, bring KoKo that chocolate and I'll see if I can heat it up."

"A'ight. I'll see you in about thirty minutes," Terrance shot back.

"Nah, give me an hour. I want to give you a night to remember," KoKo said, trying to stall. She knew it would take her at least an hour to get from Kayson's to the apartment she had set up for when Terrance was in town.

"I'll see you then," Terrance said before hanging up.

"I can't wait," KoKo said. She hung up, jumped in the shower, and threw on a pair of jeans and a T-shirt plus her boots and a cap. Then she grabbed the bag she had been waiting to use. Full of the things she was going to use to make Terrance regret ever walking into her and Kayson's life.

As KoKo pulled up to the house, she quickly ran a check list through her mind to make sure she had everything she needed to successfully pull off her mission. She got herself together, exiting the vehicle and making sure to look around for anything out of order. Once she was inside the house, she locked the door and set up her traps. When everything was ready, she jumped back in the shower, oiled her skin, and put on a hot pink lace bra and matching thong then covered herself with a short, silk robe. After brushing her hair into a neat ponytail, she scented her skin, brushed her teeth, and then waited.

Terrance pulled up fifteen minutes later. He walked up the stairs and rang the bell. KoKo took a deep breath in an effort to calm down because at this point her blood was boiling. Tonight would be the first time she saw him since she had gotten final confirmation that he was responsible for Kayson's death. The thought of the night she lost Kayson accompanied with the reality that she had taken her sister's life because of the very muthafucka on the other side of the door had KoKo's hands sweating. Her heart raced and her body slightly trembled with each step. The bell rang again. She was stuck between the thought of making him suffer or just opening up the door and blowing his head off.

Calm down, KoKo. Stay focused. Stay focused. Kayson's voice sounded in her ears. "Create the illusion, baby. And at the moment of comfort, take that nigga's life." She took another deep breath, reached for the doorknob, and then cracked the door. Terrance stood with his head down and his hands at his side. He slowly looked up as she opened the door and tried to muster up a half smile.

"Damn, you're a sight for sore eyes," Terrance said, moving toward KoKo and looking good as usual. The only thing different was he had lost a little weight. A pain was in his eyes that he could not hide and KoKo damn sure couldn't miss it. She put her arms out and he walked right into them and held her tight.

"Awwww. Baby, let KoKo take away the pain."

Little did he know she was going to take more than just his pain. "I need you," Terrance said as he squeezed tighter. The emotions inside him began to run high and he could no longer hold back. Tears ran down his cheeks.

KoKo noticed the change in his breathing and she pulled back and looked into his eyes. Taking both his hands, she

placed them on each side of her face.

"Baby, what's wrong?" she asked, trying to sound sincere.

Terrance looked down and then back up at KoKo. "They killed her," he said as a couple tears rolled down his face.

"Killed who, Terrance? What are you talking about?" KoKo managed to say as a sinking feeling developed in the bottom of her stomach.

"Star," Terrance said, bringing up his hand to wipe his face.

"Oh my god," KoKo said, covering her mouth.

"I know this shit is way out of line to come to the arms of the woman I side with for comfort, but I needed to be somewhere that didn't hurt."

"No, baby, it's all good. Come on in and sit down. Let's talk about it." She shut the door and locked it, took his hand, and led him to the couch. "Do you want a drink?"

"Yeah, I'll take one," Terrance said as he sat down.

"So what happened?" KoKo asked, standing at the bar pouring him a double shot of Grand Marnier.

"I still don't know. I came home and she was dead in our apartment."

"Oh shit! Get the fuck outta here!" KoKo passed him the drink and took a seat next to him. Terrance quickly downed the shot. It was actually child's play in comparison to what he had been drinking over the last couple of weeks.

"I ain't got nobody, KoKo. My family is gone. My wife to be is dead. Our future and plans, all dead." He paused and chuckled. "And here I am sitting on your couch crying like a bitch."

KoKo sat there thinking, *Wife? Plans? You killed my husband and you are the reason I killed my sister. Not to mention, I have to raise my son by myself.* It took everything in her not to stab his ass, but she remained cool.

"It's okay. This type of shit would break the hardest

nigga. Plus, I have feelings for you, Tee, and if you hurt, I hurt." She looked at him with tear-filled eyes. She needed to create a moment so she could get his mind off his pain and onto his dick. Shit, she wasn't trying to sit here all night listening to him bitch and moan. "Maybe I can do something to help you feel better."

KoKo rubbed his thigh and looked into his eyes. He looked at her pretty face and smiled then placed his hand on top of hers. Terrance took the bait. He placed his hand behind KoKo's head and planted a soft kiss on her lips. He slid his tongue in her mouth while moving his hand up her thigh. She felt so soft and tasted so good he immediately got a throbbing erection. The fact that she was so comforting and understanding made him want her more than he ever did.

Meanwhile, KoKo's skin was crawling; she wanted to throw up, but if she made one wrong move, it would spring her pussy trap.

Terrance got between her legs and started to kiss and suck on her neck and breasts. KoKo placed her hands on his chest and said, "Wait."

"What's wrong?" Terrance asked, pausing to attend to her resistance.

"Let's go upstairs. I have something special planned. I want to make you feel real good tonight."

Terrance stood up, took KoKo by the hand, and pulled her toward him. She rubbed his dick and said, "I'm getting ready to make him feel real good."

"Need all the feel good I can get my hands on," he said, following her upstairs.

When they got to the bedroom, KoKo pushed him on the bed. Terrance bounced back. KoKo climbed on top of him, unzipped his pants, and pulled his dick free. Terrance was breathing heavy and watching KoKo stroke his already hard dick. "Sssss . . . KoKo," he called out.

296

"Don't worry, I'm going to take real good care of him tonight," she whispered as she ran her hand up and down the length of his dick playing in his pre-cum. She had to block out her thoughts so she could handle her business.

"Let me grab something so I can make this an experience you will never forget." She climbed off the bed taking his pants and boxers with her. He lifted up and let it all happen. Pulling his shirt over his head, he lay there butt naked.

KoKo grabbed the silk scarves from the bag and returned to the bed. "Let me put you under arrest so I can talk into the mic uninterrupted. All Terrance could think was, *Oh shit, she getting ready to suck my dick?* Then he said it. "I thought you didn't suck dick?"

"I don't. But he looks like he needs some counseling. As she tightened the scarves on his wrist, he was filled with anticipation. KoKo started to kiss his neck and down his chest. Terrance was on fire. She grabbed his dick and began to stroke it to full capacity. "I think I want to ride this first."

"It's your show, ma. I'm just a happy participant," Terrance moaned in pleasure.

KoKo put on a Magnum then slowly slid down on him releasing a soft moan from her lips. She figured it would definitely be a while before she would get some more dick. Why not get her shit off in the mix? KoKo rode him like a wild woman until he was in her spot. Terrance gripped the scarves and held on tight. He was in his joy. She was wet and tight as hell and all her muscles were strangling him.

"Sssss . . . Gotdamn baby . . . Ride that shit," he bellowed, trying to pump up as she came down.

KoKo rode him until she came then she slowed down. Reaching behind her back as if she were going to open her bra she grabbed two razor blades hidden in the straps. Throwing her head back, she rode effortless situating the razors. Terrance looked at her perfect body gliding up and down on his dick and wanted to cum but couldn't. KoKo had slipped him half a Viagra pill and his shit was on swoll. She wanted to make sure he didn't cum right away and fuck up her getting her shit off.

Terrance closed his eyes enjoying her every move. When KoKo saw that he was totally distracted, she whipped out the blades and slit both his wrists from his palm to his elbow. Terrance jumped, trying to free himself, which only made him bleed more. Then she began to talk shit while still riding his dick.

"Remember Kayson?"

Terrance's eyes got big as hell. Everything that had happened in his life over the last couple of weeks became clear. His boys. Star.

"Yeah him. Well, you forgot one, muthafucka." She rode faster as she felt another one coming on.

Terrance continued to struggle as he felt himself getting dizzy followed by the urge to cum. KoKo rode faster and faster. Blood squirted everywhere. KoKo rubbed it all over her breasts as she climaxed. Terrance began cumming right after her. Just as she released the last drop, she slit his throat. His head fell back, neck open. She got up and placed the call. Within minutes, the cleanup crew was there. Everyone was shocked as hell once they got upstairs.

Aldeen asked her, "What the fuck happened in here?"

Night looked at her in confusion. She was moving like nothing happened while getting dressed. "KoKo, you all right? Why is he tied up and naked?"

KoKo looked at them nonchalantly and then said, "Live by the pussy, die by the pussy." She buttoned her jeans. "He came and went at the same time. That muthafucka got caught in a 'pussy trap.'" Turning and grabbing her guns, she put them in place.

"Y'all ready? Get that scumbag then torch the place. I'll

298

call y'all later. I have to go celebrate." She smiled then walked to the door.

"KoKo, how the fuck could you kill a muthafucka, and then go celebrate?" Night asked.

"I'm a natural born killah."

It's Over

A few weeks had passed and KoKo was in the closet getting dressed. She had planned on going out and having some fun. After putting on her underwear and bra, she began putting on her chain and necklace that Kayson got her for a wedding present. Grabbing her diamond earrings out the jewelry box, she put one on. As she went to put the other one on, she dropped it and it rolled under the dresser. "Shit!" KoKo got on her knees and then reached her hand there in an attempt to retrieve it.

The next thing she knew a drawer flew open. "What the fuck?" She looked inside and in it were a few stacks of crisp one hundred dollar bills and a few big yellow envelopes. One envelope had her name written on it in what looked like Kayson's mothers handwriting.

She sat back on her knees, reached for the envelope, and tore it open. Inside were a necklace and a note. Pulling the necklace out, she saw a large gold medallion engraved with the same image on the picture she took from Star's hands. Across the bottom in diamonds read 'Daddies Girls.' KoKo dropped it to the floor, then slowly opened the letter and read it.

Son. Don't let secrets ruin your life like they did mine. When the time is right, give this to KoKo and tell her everything.

Love you always,

Mom

KoKo started to breath heavy as she tried to search her mind for answers. "Why did he have this? What does his mother have to do with me and my father?" she said under her breath. She got up and called Night.

"Hello."

"Hey. We need to make a trip."

"Where the fuck we going? I thought we were partying tonight?"

"Dubai."

****

KoKo stood over Monique's bed holding out the chain with one hand while holding her gun behind her back in the other. Monique opened her eyes and saw KoKo standing there in the dark. Then she saw the chain, she told Kayson to give to her. She sat up and turned on the light.

"I see you found the chain."

KoKo pulled out her gun from her back and let her arm rest at her side, then looked at Monique and said, "Yes, and you betta say something I like to hear or you and Kayson are going to be able to have a long ass conversation. More like eternal."

Monique looked at her with pain in her eyes as a single tear fell. She took a deep breath and started to explain.

- End -

The Pussy Trap Reading Group Discussion Questions

1. Was Kayson justified in killing Raul?

2. Do you think Kayson's boys had anything to do with his death?

3. What connection do you think Kayson's mother had to KoKo?

4. Should KoKo have tried to save her sister?

5. Do you think Terraces' boys will come for KoKo and her crew?

6. Should Aldeen and Wise have been the next in line to take over?

7. Is pussy really that powerful?

8. What should KoKo do to Kayson's mother?

WAHIDA CLARK
PRESENTS
BEST SELLING TITLES

Trust No Man

Trust No Man II

Thirsty

Cheetah

Karma With A Vengeance

The Ultimate Sacrifice

The Game of Deception

Karma 2: For The Love of Money

Thirsty *2*

Lickin' License

Feenin'

Bonded by Blood

Uncle Yah Yah: 21st Century Man of Wisdom

The Ultimate Sacrifice II

Under Pressure (YA)

The Boy Is Mines! (YA)

A Life For A Life

The Pussy Trap

99 Problems (YA)

Country Boys

NUDE
Awakening
A NOVEL

VICTOR L. MARTIN

WAHIDA CLARK PRESENTS

COMING
SOON!

STILL
FEENIN

A NOVEL BY
SERENITI HALL

UNCLE YAH YAH

21ST. Century Man of Wisdom

VOL 2

COMING SOON!

AL DICKENS

WAHIDA CLARK PRESENTS
COMING SOON!
LICKIN' LICENSE II
A NOVEL BY
INTELLIGENT ALLAH

CASH MONEY CONTENT
PRESENTS

Justify
my
THUG

New York Times Bestselling Author of *Payback With Ya Life*
WAHIDA CLARK

WWW.WCLARKPUBLISHING.COM